Alex Bell was born in 1986 in Hampshire. She studied Law on and off for six long years before the boredom became so overwhelming that she had to throw down the textbooks and run madly from the building. Since then she has never looked back. She has travelled widely, is a ferociously strict vegetarian and generally prefers cats to people.

By Alex Bell

The Ninth Circle
Jasmyn
Lex Trent Versus the Gods

LEX TRENT
VERSUS
THE GODS

ALEX BELL

headline

First published in Great Britain in 2010 by
HEADLINE PUBLISHING GROUP

2

Cataloguing in Publication Data is available from the British Library

ISBN 978 0 7553 5518 1

Typeset in Aldine401 by Ellipsis Books Limited, Glasgow

Printed and bound by CPI Group
(UK) Ltd, Croydon, CR0 4YY

HEADLINE PUBLISHING GROUP
An Hachette UK Company
338 Euston Road
London NW1 3BH

www.headline.co.uk
www.hachette.co.uk

For my grandparents, Ali and Joy Bell,
and John and Joan Willrich

ACKNOWLEDGEMENTS

I would like to thank my agent, Carolyn Whitaker, and everyone at Headline for all their work on this book. Special thanks must also go to my editor, Hannah Sheppard, who was the first person to really *get* Lex, and whose suggestions and advice made it a much better book. It has been a real pleasure working with her from start to finish.

My family, as always, have offered support and encouragement from the beginning. And my cats – Cindy, Chloe and Suki – have kept me company and prevented me from going bonkers.

Last of all, I should acknowledge EU law and how dreadfully – *dreadfully* – dull it is. If I hadn't been so bored out of my mind late one Friday afternoon whilst sitting in an EU law lecture, then Lex might never have walked into my head and I wouldn't have pencilled his name into the margin of my lecture notes to write about him once I finally got the hell out of there.

PROLOGUE

No one knew the precise date when the Globe had split in half. For many hundreds of years the Lands Above and the Lands Beneath had been nothing more than a metaphorical, symbolical divide. But then, one day, the Gods decided that they had had enough – more than enough, in fact – of their subjects complaining and pestering and whining at them day and night. Being the focus of so much worship can be a tiring business. The Gods needed somewhere that would be quiet – a place they could call their own. And thus, one fateful day, the earth shook and trembled and a great split appeared right across the centre and then the two halves cracked apart like a giant, cosmic, galactic Easter egg. No one alive today could remember the Great Divide, of course, for it had happened many millennia ago now. One might think the planet had never split in half at all had it not been for the ladders . . .

Physicists had happily debated for hours on end how

the split was even possible, for the general consensus seemed to be that the planet had been spherical once but now . . . now it was more like a . . . well, like a dumbbell – those weights that impressive-looking men use to make themselves look even more impressive. A dumbbell that had been stood up vertically. The top weight was the Lands Above, the bottom weight was the Lands Beneath and the bar in the middle was the ladders stretching between the two discs.

If you travelled to a certain place in the centre of the Lands Above, you could look down over the edge and see them – thousands and thousands of ladders stretching away through space, linking the top of the planet to its bottom half – the province of the Gods. It was a breathtaking, awe-inspiring sight. Some of the ladders were solid, built of wood and metal and attached to platforms below. Others were no more than rope ladders, waving lightly in the breeze and dusted with space frost.

Just as physicists had debated the mechanics of the Split itself, philosophers had argued heatedly about the theological significance of *ladders* being used to join the two halves of the planet together. After all, it seemed a most curious choice when the Gods had *forbidden* people to ever attempt the journey down to the Lands Beneath. If they truly didn't want people climbing them then why not use poles or wires or anything other than ladders? It was like giving a fat child a gigantic chocolate lolly and sternly telling him he must never lick it . . .

Some said the Gods had used ladders as a test or a temptation or a trick or some other grandly significant theological, symbolical, philosophical form of gesture. Others said it was just because Ladderworld went into liquidation around that time as a consequence of being supremely dull and so there was a surplus of raw materials readily available.

But – at any rate – no one had ever attempted the forbidden journey. For one thing, it would take hundreds of years to travel from one end to the other and so only with magical help would the person actually reach their destination before they perished from old age. But, in addition, people were afraid, for no one could remember what creatures had gone with the Lands Beneath and what might be waiting down there. It was well known that a griffin guarded the ladders near the top and as for what else there might be . . . the mind filled with horrible visions of sharp-toothed, many-tentacled carnivorous things. Besides which, the Gods lived down there. The people of the Lands Above agreed that there was no point whatsoever in attempting the treacherous journey down the Space Ladders to the Lands Beneath when the only things down there were teeth, tentacles and wrathful Gods waiting for them with lightning bolts. There had to be better things to risk your life for.

But . . . but . . . there were also tales of treasure, because there always are. The most beautiful, breathtaking, golden treasures they had down there. And it is a well-known and universal rule that there will always be – has always been – one stupid sod whose strength of greed outweighs their common sense and suppresses that all-important instinct of self-preservation.

CHAPTER ONE

LADY LUCK'S THIEF

The thief, the infamous cat burglar – dubbed the Shadowman by the press – buckled on his safety harness and slowly lowered himself through the hole he had just cut into the glass ceiling of the museum . . .

There are some people who are born lucky. They seem to float through life on little golden wings whilst misfortune, hardship and calamity hurry to get out of their hallowed way. One might say that Lex Trent was such a person.

Last year he had started his apprenticeship with a prestigious law firm in the Wither City. The idea was that he studied the law whilst also working in a firm although, as a seventeen year old, the work Lex was able to do had been disappointingly limited. The novelty of filing and fetching coffee and doughnuts for the real lawyers had been practically nonexistent even to begin with. But the lawyers certainly liked Lex for he had a pleasant manner and an open, honest face. He was always ready to help with a smile and there was no denying that he was a clever, hard-working kid.

Everyone knew that Lex was committed to becoming a real lawyer. He was said to spend every evening of every night cooped up in his accommodation, poring over old law books, soaking up the knowledge they contained, memorising legal rules and precedents. He was going places. The lawyers liked him, the clients liked him and he'd been lucky enough to win the most sought-after apprenticeship in the legal capital of the Globe. The Gods themselves were smiling on him.

But it is a universal law that eventually . . . sooner or later . . . one way or another . . . everyone's luck runs out . . .

The Shadowman was halfway down the rope, suspended from the cavernous glass ceiling, with the floor of the great hall stretching out twenty feet beneath him, when he felt something on his safety harness break with a horrible, nauseating little *snap*. He tried to compensate for it, but within seconds one of the ropes had broken free, falling in a long coil to the ground below. Then another ring stretched and broke under the additional pressure. And then the thing buckled altogether and the thief, despite his mad flailing at the ropes, was unable to stop himself from freefalling the rest of the way.

Lex Trent landed with a crash and a shattering of glass, right on top of one of the large display cabinets. Sparkling glass shards skittered across the vast tiled floor like broken diamonds and alarm bells started to wail loudly.

Lex groaned as he struggled off the broken cabinet, relieved to see that he miraculously didn't seem to have suffered any broken bones or hideous loss of limb, although there were several small pieces of glass sticking into his back, making him rather uncomfortable. As soon as he was on his feet, five guards with dogs all rushed into the room, surrounding him. Lex glanced round at the broken glass at his feet, the remains of the cabinet behind him and his own completely black outfit and realised he probably wasn't going to be able to talk his way out of this. But, because habit is an inbred thing, he looked up at the guards, pointed towards the door on the left and said, 'Um. He went that way.'

Mr Joseph Lucas was the senior partner at the law firm of Lucas, Jones and Schmidt. He was a kindly man and he had come to feel genuine fondness for Lex. He knew that Lex was quite small for his age – not very tall and quite thin – so he'd been alarmed and worried when he received a message from the city guards saying they thought they had Lex Trent in one of their cells and that the circumstances were . . . unusual. It would be altogether best if Mr Lucas came down to the station as soon as he could. So half an hour later, the old lawyer was standing in the foyer, shaking the rain from his coat and being apologised to uncertainly by the inspector on duty.

'I'm sorry to have to call you out at this time of night, sir, but I understand that Lex Trent has no family in the city and—'

'Yes, that's right. Where is he? Is he badly hurt? What happened – was he attacked?'

'Er . . . he . . . '

'Well? Come on, out with it!' the lawyer barked impatiently.

'The boy we have in the cell is claiming to be Lex Trent,' the inspector said carefully. 'But I . . . ' He shook his head and handed the lawyer a sheaf of paper. 'You'd better have a look at the report, Mr Lucas.'

Lex sat on the hard, lumpy bed and tried not to twiddle his thumbs. The guards glaring in at him were making him a little nervous. A cell. So it had come to this, at last.

'I suppose a couple of aspirin would be out of the question?' he tried, without much hope. 'I've got a splitting headache.'

'You *should* be dead falling from that height,' one of the inspectors said, slightly sullenly.

'I've always been a lucky guy,' Lex said, managing a pained grin.

'Ha! That luck's run out now, if I'm any judge!'

Lex glanced round the cell. He could see his bag of equipment on the table outside along with his black balaclava and a stack of the Shadowman calling cards that had been in his pocket. More than enough to convict him. More than enough to send him straight to the hangman's gallows. More than enough to get him a one-way ticket straight to an unmarked grave in the Criminals' Quarter. But giving up, caving in, quitting . . . these were not reactions that Lex was at all familiar with. Something would turn up because it always did. Lex was, after all, one of the lucky people. Because he had a deal with her. A bargain he was sure she would make good on. Mostly.

'There will no doubt be scratches and bruises,' she had said. 'Quite possibly the odd broken bone, if you're careless. But you won't die. I promise you won't die, Lex.'

And it was nice to have that assurance, although Lex had certainly never been fool enough to trust her word completely. But he was sure it would be all right and that he'd get out of this present mess. After all, the Gods were on his side. Or, more accurately, *a* God was on his side . . . the Goddess of Fortune, to be exact.

It had been just over a year ago, right before he came to the Wither City, when he was on the run from an angry mob . . . well, perhaps not a *mob* as such, but a couple of coppers who were really quite irate, anyway. He'd been carrying out a scam that had backfired rather unpleasantly. He'd been caught out and forced to flee. This rarely happened to Lex by that point, for he had worked on the scams during the twelve months since he'd run away from home, refining them and improving them until they were almost perfect. It wasn't his fault – he was a penniless farm boy – he had to do something to survive. If he hadn't learnt how to cheat and lie and swindle then he would most likely have been dead in a ditch before the first month was out.

But then he had discovered that not only could he cheat, but that he was *good* at it. A born natural, in fact.

And it was fun, too – much more fun than sweating away on a farm, getting straw in your hair and blisters on your palms. Lex was born to be a crook and had taken to it like a duck to water.

But the day the jewellers came after him was not a good day, for they wouldn't accept his apologies for trying to sell them a fake ruby brooch. Instead, they were adamant that he was to pay for his crime and so had set the police on him to arrest him for criminal fraud. Prison cells and courtrooms did not sound like a lot of fun to Lex and so he ran – out of the city with the two policemen close behind him. He didn't have enough of a head start to outrun them and so he ducked into the church on the edge of town. It was big and looked like it had once been grand but was now rundown and derelict, obviously belonging to a God who had lost favour with the people and become unpopular. When Lex slipped inside, pulling the door closed behind him, he saw that it was dark and dank and the amount of dust covering the pews and altar made him sneeze loudly.

This startled the woman who had been sobbing on one of the pews near the front. At once she jumped to her feet and whirled round to face him. Lex cursed his bad luck for he had been sure the manky old place would be deserted.

'I'm so sorry to disturb you, ma'am . . . ' Lex began but then trailed off, staring at her. For this was no woman at all but the Goddess of Luck herself. He recognised her from one of the Games he had recently made a lot of money on. She'd been there in the Box of the Gods, watching the rounds. Standing before him now, she was the spitting image of her statues with her long, white toga, trimmed with gold braid and her fair hair piled rather precariously on top of her head. The only difference was that she seemed to have been using her sleeve in lieu of a tissue and a few strands of blond hair had escaped to hang loosely around her face.

'My Lady,' Lex said, trying to disguise his shock at finding the Goddess in such a state. 'Please forgive me. I had no idea that you were here.'

The Goddess gave a loud, pathetic sniff. 'Doesn't matter,' she said. 'They're going to close the church today anyway.'

Lex glanced round the abandoned place and noticed the life-sized chess pieces for the first time – one knight and one bishop. They were covered in dust like every-thing else but Lex knew what they really were, or at least, *had* been – people who had refused to participate in the Games and so had been turned into chess pieces as punish-ment.

'Is this *your* church, my Lady?'

'It was,' she sniffled. 'Before I lost all my followers. They've all taken off to worship the Gods of Wealth or Fame or Beauty instead. I lost my last official worshipper last night . . . ' She trailed off, the faintest glimmer of hope coming into her eyes as her gaze rested on Lex. 'Whose church are *you* in, young man?' she asked.

'Jezra's,' Lex replied proudly. The God of Wit and

Daring was everything Lex had ever wanted to be and he was proud to pledge his special allegiance to him.

The Goddess pulled a face. 'Jezra!' She practically spat the name. 'What can he do for you that I can't? It's not a rhetorical question, boy – give me an answer this instant!'

Lex hesitated then said, 'Well . . . forgive me . . . but he's a little more consistent than . . . you . . . are.'

Everyone knew that Lady Luck was dreadfully flighty and unreliable and most people would sooner try and build a house of cards on a trampoline than put any faith in her. It didn't come as any great shock to Lex that she'd lost all her followers.

'Lex Trent!' came the sudden bellow from outside. 'We know you're in there! Come out this instant – you're only making it worse for yourself!'

'Damn it!' Lex muttered with a scowl.

But the Goddess was already rushing down the aisle towards him, a radiant smile on her face as she grasped his arms and said, 'My dear boy, why didn't you tell me your name was Lex Trent? I've been looking everywhere for you!'

'Er . . . what?' Lex replied, trying to work out why the Goddess of Fortune herself would be looking for a petty crook like him whilst at the same time trying to work out how he was ever going to get out of the church without the two burly policemen outside spotting him.

'Yes, I want to recruit you to my church; I want you as one of my followers! You're a natural, my dear. I heard a few months ago about a little boy who was travelling across the provinces, swindling, cheating, lying and getting away with it and I knew with luck like that I just had to have you in my church.'

'I am *not* a little boy!' Lex said, shaking her off irritably. 'I'm small for my age, that's all! Anyway, I wouldn't want to join your church even if I wasn't already in Jezra's. You said it yourself – I'm already lucky – so how can you possibly help me?'

'You can never have too much luck, Lex Trent. Especially doing what you do. As your current situation aptly demonstrates.'

As if on cue, one of the policemen outside shouted, 'You've got ten seconds to come out before we come in and drag you out ourselves!'

Lex started walking away from the door towards the back of the church but Lady Luck called after him, 'You can look until you're blue in the face but you won't find it.'

'Won't find what?' Lex said, turning back suspiciously.

'The secret back door,' the Goddess replied with a smirk. 'The only way in or out of this place is through the front entrance. They've got you trapped, Lex. It's a dreary prison cell for you and no mistake. I must say it seems a shame – like putting a beautiful songbird in a tiny little cage. But you don't want to join my church so I guess that's that.'

And then, to Lex's horror, she opened one of the front doors, stuck her head out and called, 'He's in here, officers. Please come and take him away at once.'

'All right, all right!' Lex said, panic stricken. 'I'll join your church as long as you help me out of this mess!'

'You swear to be one of my official followers?' Lady Luck said, eyebrow arched. 'And thereby prevent my church from being closed down?'

'Yes, yes, I swear it!' Lex exclaimed breathlessly, his eyes glued to the door handle that was suddenly moving downwards beneath the policeman's hand on the other side.

'Then that's settled!' she exclaimed, beaming. 'Your new oath overrides the old one you made to Jezra and you are now a member of my church. Well done.'

'What about the policemen—?' Lex began.

But, no sooner had the large wooden door started to open than there was a horrible, tearing sound from the metal hinges. The whole thing came loose and fell forwards onto the two officers outside with a crunch, crushing them to the ground with its weight so that, although they squirmed and struggled, they were trapped like pinned butterflies.

'Well, go on then,' Lady Luck said. 'I'm sure they'll get out eventually. You don't want to still be standing there with your mouth open like that when they do.'

Lex didn't need telling twice. He raced out of the church, quite unable to resist the temptation of jumping onto the fallen door on his way out and running along it, hearing the muffled grunt from beneath with a tremendous sense of smug satisfaction. And from that day on, he and the Goddess of Fortune were a team. Eventually she got a handful of followers back, but the point was that Lex had saved her church. And in return she gave him a little extra help with his more disreputable activities . . . Or, at least, she *usually* did. But she hadn't come through for him this time and now it seemed that Lex really was in a huge amount of trouble.

The door outside the cell opened and shut and Lex scrambled respectfully to his feet when he saw his employer approaching with the inspector.

'Mr Lucas,' he began, in his best tone of 'sincere reasonableness'. 'I can explain everything.'

'Having just heard the evidence from this officer, Lex, I doubt that very much.'

'It wasn't me, sir.'

'I beg your pardon?'

Lex knew he wouldn't be able to bluster and bluff his way out of this one. But a bit of defensive anger usually went down quite well and it might help to take them off guard. He certainly wasn't going to sit there and *confess* to being the Shadowman if that was what they were expecting.

'I would like to file an official complaint, Mr Lucas,' Lex said, 'for wrongful arrest and detention. Plus the service here has been dreadful. I haven't even been given any aspirin or anything—'

'Lex, are you maintaining that you are *innocent?*' Mr Lucas asked.

Lex allowed his mouth to fall open in stunned surprise for a moment. 'Well, of *course* I . . . Mr Lucas, with respect, how could you even *think* that I would . . . that I would commit such a heinous act?'

'We found the Shadowman cards *on* him!' the inspector snapped. 'He cut a hole in the ceiling and lowered himself through it on a harness and he—'

'Thank you, Inspector,' Mr Lucas said sharply. 'I should like to speak with my client alone now, if you don't mind. And please be so good as to have someone bring in some aspirin.'

There had been a momentary flicker of doubt there, it was true, but after over an hour, Lex was sure he had Mr Lucas believing him. Because he *wanted* to believe him – for both professional and personal reasons, the lawyer wanted to believe that Lex Trent was in fact an honest, upstanding citizen rather than an infamous cat burglar, a manipulative scoundrel and an opportunistic crook. There was also the fact that Lex didn't look the part. The Shadowman was notorious and daring and thrilling and people probably expected some dashingly handsome thirty year old behind the mask – a gypsy, possibly, with olive skin and dark eyes. They certainly wouldn't be expecting some skinny kid from a city law firm.

'It's true that the black disguise is mine. I was using it to track him,' Lex said again. He had decided to go for the 'plucky-but-incredibly-dim teenager tries to single-handedly capture criminal' routine. 'But then the Shadowman saw me and shoved those calling cards in my pocket before *pushing* me through that hole in the ceiling! He tried to frame me! It's just . . . Mr Lucas, it's just insane for anyone to say I'm the Shadowman! I mean, I'm *seventeen* – I wouldn't know the first thing about stealing from such a well-guarded museum!'

'All right, Lex,' Mr Lucas said soothingly. 'I'm confident we will be able to sort this whole unfortunate business out. There are no witnesses, there is no motive and there is certainly room for reasonable doubt. We must only be thankful that you were not hurt. I hope you'll remember that criminal apprehension is something much better left to the authorities, my boy.'

'Yes, sir.'

And it might have all been all right then if Mr Montgomery Schmidt hadn't suddenly burst into the room, his eyes shining like a madman's.

'Ah *ha*!' he cried rapturously, pointing a shaking finger at Lex. 'You have him! You have him! You've got him at last! I always knew that boy was no good, right from the very minute I set eyes on him!'

'Montgomery, pray compose yourself,' Mr Lucas said, removing his reading spectacles and dropping them on the papers spread before him on the table. 'What in the name of the Gods is the matter?'

The two lawyers were old friends, as Lex understood it, and had started the law firm together some thirty years ago. And whilst Lex had come to feel something of a mild liking for Mr Lucas, he felt nothing but irritation and frustration towards his partner, Mr Schmidt. For Montgomery Schmidt could *see through* Lex. There weren't many who could see him for what he was. But Mr Schmidt was one of them.

When Lex first joined the firm, he had intended to skim a little off the top of the extortionate fees the lawyers were paid. It only seemed fair. The firm wouldn't miss it. Although it was true that Lex didn't need it. But money wasn't the point. He had plenty of money as a result of two years spent betting shrewdly on Games, picking pockets and devising and carrying out mastermind scams. He therefore had more than enough money to survive comfortably in the Wither City, even without the wage the law firm paid him. He didn't steal and thieve in the interests of survival. He did it because he could. And it gave him a thrill.

It wasn't like he'd ever genuinely wanted to be a lawyer, anyway. In fact, just the very idea of anyone actually *wanting* to be a lawyer made him shudder all over. It was something he struggled to believe. Such a desire went against the natural order of things. But a knowledge of the law was useful – very useful – to a crook like Lex. So when, shortly after making a bargain with Lady Luck, he had strolled into a tavern in a new town and just happened to meet a boy his own age travelling alone on his way to the Wither City – the legal capital of the Globe – having obtained a letter of introduction to secure him a most feted apprenticeship at Lucas, Jones and Schmidt, Lex had lost no time in pinching it from him while he slept and making his way to the Wither City where he then presented himself as the new intern. As luck would have it, Lex had studied law for a brief time before he had left home so he had a grasp on the basics. And it hadn't been a very difficult thing to doctor the letter of introduction so that the name read Lex Trent rather than Harold Gibbons. Poor Harold – really, with such a name, how could he be anything *but* one of life's losers? When he trailed into the city a week later, he was brusquely turned away by the doormen because they knew full well that only genuine law students with introductions from genuine law schools could become interns and this boy had nothing – nothing but a pathetic and entirely unoriginal sob story about how he *had* had one, but it had been stolen from him.

It was a mixture of greed and ambition on Lex's part. He wanted to better himself even if he wanted to better himself as a criminal rather than as a human being. And what could possibly be more invincible than a crook with a full working knowledge of the law? Besides which, the firm was in itself a good place to practise scams. When paying for consultations, clients often paid Lex at the front desk in Withian dollars. It had been an easy enough thing for him to overcharge them a little and pocket the difference. But for some ungodly reason, Schmidt had taken it upon himself to *check* what Lex was doing at the desk. He had realised after questioning his own clients that Lex had overcharged some of them. When he challenged Lex about it, Lex had of course vigorously denied that it had been anything other than purely accidental. But he had had to act pretty fast to replace the money in the safe so that the extra was accounted for when Schmidt doggedly started counting it.

Even then, despite finding that the figures added up, Mr Schmidt had been all eager to press the matter, but Mr Lucas had pulled rank as the senior partner and proclaimed that of course it had been an easily-made, innocent mistake; the money would be returned to the clients and there was to be no more said about it. No, it was not Mr Lucas who was the problem, it was his overly zealous friend who had been watching Lex like a hawk ever since, eagerly waiting for a chance to catch him out, to trip him up, to bring ruin crashing down about his head. Now was undoubtedly the time for some serious damage control.

'Mr Schmidt, I assure you I am entirely blameless,' Lex began. 'I was only trying to help but—'

'Oh, save it for the jury!' the lawyer snapped.

'Montgomery!' Mr Lucas exclaimed, standing up. 'A word with you outside, please.'

Feeling a little apprehensive, Lex remained behind in his cell whilst the two lawyers stepped out of the room. He could see them arguing heatedly through the tiny window in the cell door and could just catch snatches of what they were saying. The two men were very close and it was a rare thing for them to quarrel. Lex distinctly heard Mr Lucas, the silly old twit, saying patiently, 'Just an over-enthusiastic boy, Monty . . . ' and, 'certainly not capable of such criminal mastery . . . '

Lex grinned, although the grin faded somewhat at Mr

Schmidt's outraged response: 'clear sign of a disturbed mind . . . ' and, 'told you before, Joseph, that boy is no good . . . ' and, '*prison* sentence like he deserves . . . '

Lex silently cursed him and his bitter tongue. After the overcharging affair, Lex had looked grave and apologised to Mr Schmidt himself with an earnest expression of humble sincerity. The sharp-eyed lawyer hadn't bought it then and he wasn't buying it now, blast him. But, luckily for Lex, Mr Lucas was buying it. And, as the senior partner, it was his opinion that would ultimately count.

After a while, Mr Schmidt stormed off and Mr Lucas returned to tell Lex that he was free to go. 'I've persuaded the guards to allow you to leave. The trial's next week. I'm sure I don't have to remind you, Lex, of the gravity of the situation. I'm taking full responsibility for your not being kept in here. Do I make myself clear?'

'Perfectly, sir. And thank you. I won't let you down.'

CHAPTER TWO

THE MIDNIGHT MARKETS

Lex examined his face carefully in the mirror when he got home. To his relief, the cuts were not deep. He could not have scarring on his face. That would not do at all. It would quite ruin his honest, respectable appearance. He turned when he saw her behind him in the mirror. She was dressed in her usual white toga-like dress with her blond hair piled up high on her head.

'Well?' he snapped. 'What do you have to say to me?'

He gestured to his impressive collection of cuts and bruises.

'Well, you're not dead, are you, Lex? You've just been careless,' the Goddess of Fortune said with a disapproving click of her tongue as she eyed him up and down. 'You should *check* your equipment each time. Luck can only take you so far, you know. Really, I turn my back for one minute and you go crashing through ceilings and getting yourself arrested.'

'You are supposed to be watching out for me! You're

supposed to be making sure this kind of thing doesn't happen! You're so unreliable!'

'Well of course, darling. I'm the Goddess of *Luck*, what do you expect? Anyway, Lex, I just came to give you the heads up. That odious little man, Schmidt, is on his way over.'

'What the heck for—?'

'With the guards.'

'But why? I've been released on bail.'

'A witness has come forward, I'm afraid. Most bothersome thing, but someone saw you go down through the roof of the museum. Anyway, they can testify that there was only one person there.'

She had not finished speaking before Lex had grabbed a bag and was stuffing things into it. He had been betting on Mr Lucas's support and the sympathy of the jury to get him a not guilty verdict, but a witness would surely be enough to tip the scales against him. He wasn't prepared to risk it. He would have to leave the Wither City. He had known it would come to this sooner or later, and it had certainly never been his intention to remain in the city for ever. It had offered him an escape route when he'd needed one before but he had never seriously intended to become a lawyer. He'd known that one day he would be found out. And then he would have to run because they would try to catch him. But they wouldn't succeed because Lex knew how to run and he knew how to hide. And he was quite capable of doing both without any hint of guilt.

'What are you doing?' the Goddess asked, gazing at Lex in surprise.

'I'm running away, you stupid woman!' Lex replied as he dragged the carefully concealed money belt out from under his bed and fastened it round his waist beneath his shirt.

'Whatever for? Can't you just talk your way out of it?'

'Believe it or not, my Lady, I cannot talk my way out of *everything*. Some things cannot be talked out of. This is one of those things. They can prove I'm the Shadowman if they've got a witness. They'll lock me up for a very long time if they catch me. Do you understand that?'

No one could deny that the Goddess of Fortune was a useful ally to have but Lex sometimes couldn't help wishing that his benefactress were a little less dim-witted.

'Oh dear,' she said, fluttering her hands in dismay. 'You'd better be off then, hadn't you, Lex?'

'Yes,' Lex replied, giving the deity a mocking bow. 'Your servant, my Lady, until next time. Perhaps you could see your way clear to giving me a little help getting out of the city?'

It was a mutually beneficial arrangement. The Goddess had her church – and therefore her pride – and Lex had that greatest of gifts to a thief, fraudster and all-round good-for-nothing – luck. Mr Montgomery Schmidt could have torn his hair out at the way fate seemed to conspire against him that evening.

The Wither City was the centre of all trade and

commerce in the Lands Above and as such, the city never slept. There were midnight markets set up all round the docks – the hub of all activity in the city. Stalls were randomly set up all over the place, selling crafts, spices, talismans, amulets and black enchantments from across the Azure Sea. Enterprising local Withians had set up their own stalls to supply the foreigners with Withian delicacies such as mini-sea-squids-on-sticks and candied insects although really the main export of the Wither City was its books. Great leather-bound tomes tied up with string and musty with the smell of ancient, valuable old pages. Books like those made in the Wither City could not be found anywhere else on the Globe. Smoke hung over the place from various cooking fires and the air was filled with the aroma of roasting squid and the sound of hundreds of voices jabbering away in as many different languages.

Lex dodged through crowds that seemed to magically part for him whilst Mr Schmidt and the guards at his heels had to fight their way through the throngs of seamen and merchants. Carts that did not in any way hinder Lex seemed to get right in the way of Schmidt and his henchmen. At one point, an entire market stall went over and, glancing over his shoulder, Lex distinctly saw his employer slipping about on the ground covered in slimy squid tentacles. He did not look very happy about it.

Lex grinned, kept his head down and pushed on through the midnight markets to the docks. Her Ladyship was living up to her side of the bargain tonight. Luck was on his side. The trouble was that luck could only take a person so far and Lex was sometimes in danger of forgetting that in the heady thrill of having everything going his way. 'Good luck' did not equal 'invincibility'. Nor did it equal 'unbeatable' or 'unconquerable' or any other of those impressively God-like sounding words. Luck was what it was – a helping hand and nothing more. For the most part, it was all still up to Lex and his own native wits to escape from any situation that he had willingly launched himself headlong into.

He would buy his passage aboard one of the ships setting sail tonight. Once he was out of Withian territory, the law of the Wither City would have no jurisdiction over him anyway and Mr Schmidt would never be able to find him once he'd escaped to the Eastern Provinces. He would start again somewhere else. He had done it before. With his almost photographic memory and ability to adapt and pick up new skills, Lex was sure he would excel at pretty much anything he put his hand to. It wasn't arrogance. It would only be arrogance if you didn't know you were a multi-talented genius. But there was no one else like Lex – he was the best at everything. Everything. And he knew it too.

But it would be the rash actions of an inexperienced amateur to hop onto the nearest ship and set sail for who-knew-where without first *providing* for the journey and *planning* for the destination. Money was not a problem for Lex. Quite apart from the money belt and the stash of stolen goods he was carrying in his bag, he was an accomplished enough thief to be sure of surviving wherever he ended up. But there was more to travelling on the Globe than mere money and Lex had learnt long ago that it did not pay to be ill prepared, especially when travelling across provinces. There were things he would have to purchase before leaving the Wither City, the place that had been his home for just under a year.

Although it certainly hadn't been Lex's *plan* to leave the city that night, in some ways he was almost glad that fate had forced his hand. There was nothing like the excitement of running. And there was most definitely nothing like the excitement of being *chased*! And he had stayed here too long anyway – law and the Wither City had only ever been a means to an end. But before he left, he needed to make his purchases and whilst the midnight markets were the place to buy everything and anything, it would be a tedious bother to have to conduct his shopping in a hasty rush with Mr Schmidt yapping at his heels. Much as Lex was enjoying the chase, he was therefore forced to cut it off short.

He stripped off the distinctive bright red jacket he had donned just for that purpose and paid a cabin boy to put it on and scamper aboard his ship just as it was setting sail. Then he lurked about at the docks, coiling up the ropes with the other dockworkers, as Mr Schmidt burst out onto the wooden planks and gave a visual demonstration of just what exactly the word 'apoplectic' means. Although he was keeping his head down, Lex could easily understand the cause of his employer's rage for Lex had paid the boy with instructions to take off the red coat once he boarded the ship and wave it energetically from the prow until the harbour was out of sight. Mr Schmidt could not fail to see it and, from that distance, he would be unable to tell that the boy was not in fact the iniquitous Lex Trent but a mere cabin boy instead.

The lawyer could have been no more than a dozen paces away but as Lex was wearing the cabin boy's grubby old cap and jacket, Mr Schmidt would have had no reason to pay him any heed. Lex could have just sidled away into the shadows without any risk of discovery. But then a piece of paper fell from the lawyer's hand and, because Lex was Lex, he picked it up as Mr Schmidt turned away and hurried after him to tug at his sleeve, raising the tone of his voice and being careful to keep his face hidden beneath the cap.

'Lost sumfing, guv?'

Mr Schmidt glanced down at the abandoned, useless warrant and snatched it from Lex's hand with a bad-natured word of thanks. Although, to his credit, he rummaged in his pocket for the customary coin and tossed it to Lex, even if it was with the same lack of grace.

'Thanks, guv'nor!' Lex called after him as the lawyer strode off into the throng.

It really was too easy. It was on the tip of his tongue to call out some other parting comment that would give away his identity – just for the pure deliciousness of seeing the look on Schmidt's already anger-flushed face. But it would be reckless to start the chase off again and

Lex forced himself to accept that this one at least would have to remain a private victory.

Lex had always loved the midnight markets. They were a way of life on the Globe and could be found in most western towns and cities in the Lands Above. But, as the centre of all trade, the markets in the Wither City were the largest and the most impressive, with the widest array of goods and services on offer.

Lex had often wandered down late at night to talk to the merchants, partly to keep abreast of all the goings on across the Azure Sea and partly because it never hurt to be on friendly terms with the local salesmen – they were much less likely to rip you off if they knew you to be a local and not simply one of the many travellers that passed through the Wither City each year.

'Hello Cara,' Lex said, stepping up to one of the sea-gypsy stalls.

'Hi, Lex,' the girl behind the wooden stall said.

She was about Lex's age and had the typical black hair, dark eyes and olive skin of the sea-gypsies she sailed with. And she was sweet on Lex. Which helped him enormously whenever he wanted to get any information out of her. Not that he was a ladies' man in general – in an era where teenage girls all seemed to be for the 'treat 'em mean to keep 'em keen' school of male wooing, Lex's honest face (even if it was as false as he was) did not earn him many points where the fairer sex were concerned.

'What happened to you?' Cara asked, eyeing the bruises

and cuts on Lex's face and arms in the flickering light from the torches and fires. 'And why are you wearing those old sailor clothes?'

'Because I'm going sailing,' Lex replied, glancing at the black outline of the ships in the harbour. 'I'm leaving the Wither City.'

'Why?' Cara asked. 'How long for?'

'Did you hear about the Shadowman? He struck again today.'

Cara nodded. 'Yes, I've heard people talking about it in the market. They said they arrested some kid . . . ' She trailed off, staring at Lex, who nodded sadly. 'But . . . surely . . . surely they can't really think that *you* are the Shadowman?'

The way she said it was like she couldn't think of a more absurd suggestion, and Lex had to bite his tongue to keep himself from asking defensively: *why not?*

'I was framed,' he said, making his eyes go all big and scared. 'I never stole whatever it was. I tried to tell them, but they won't listen.'

'You must come with us,' Cara said at once.

Sea-gypsies had been badly stigmatised over the years for thieving, double-crossing and casting spells over people – a reputation the facts suggested they did not deserve. But Lex had known that mention of an unwarranted accusation would strike a chord with Cara and might get him passage on board her family's ship.

'When do you leave?' Lex asked. 'They're looking for me. I must get out of the Wither City as soon as I can.'

'In the morning,' Cara said. 'But you can stay in one of the wagons until then if you want. They'll be empty now because everyone else is out on the stalls.'

She took a key from one of the pockets on her dress and handed it to him.

'Are you sure it's all right?' Lex asked. 'Your family won't mind me coming along? I can pay my way.'

'You're more than welcome, Lex.' She shook her head and added, 'You, the Shadowman! Honestly, I don't think I've ever heard of anything more ridiculous in my life! Everyone knows what a hard-working, upstanding citizen you are. I mean you don't even drink or smoke or anything.'

Lex nodded and looked pathetic. 'I'll go back to the wagon later. I have some things I need to get in the market first.'

CHAPTER THREE

THE WISHING SWANNS OF DESARETH

It was straight to the seedy, less respectable area of the markets that Lex went, away from all the gimmicky, tourist stalls. This was for several reasons, one of which being that the more dangerous and unique goods could be found at that end. But mostly it was for pragmatic purposes because Lex needed buyers who were not going to ask any inconvenient questions about where exactly his goods had come from. He had plenty of money tucked away in his money belt with which he could have made his purchases but he didn't want to tap into that if he could help it. The belt was his nest egg, his backup – light, easy to carry, easy to grab in a hurry and easy to run with if necessary. The *goods* he carried, on the other hand, were heavy, bulky and likely to slow him down. Besides which, a bulging bag would make him a target for thieves. He needed to lighten the load a little whilst he still could and the markets were the perfect place in which to do it.

There is always a dark area of any town and it was the same with the midnight markets all over the Globe. There was the bright, bustling part next to the docks, filled with merchants and sailors and tourists and honest men. And then there was the dark area on the outskirts frequented by enchanters and criminals. Decent people stayed away from these stalls, not wanting to know what things were being traded in the squalid dimness or what whispered words were pouring poison into ears and minds.

Lex was not afraid to move among such company. In the clothes of a mere cabin boy, no one was likely to pay him much attention anyway. From the look of him he certainly had nothing to steal. He always had his mouth, which had never let him down yet. And of course, Lady Luck was on his side. She always had been, really, even before he joined her church. It was just that, as an honest farm boy, Lex had not had the opportunity to discover his talents for fast-talking, quick-dealing and pick–pocketing before he left home two years ago. He had always had the capacity for it – always been ambitious with a strong craving for adventure and a disgruntled discontentment with his mediocre life on the farm. He'd known that he was destined for something more.

It had all started when, one fateful day just a week after running away, he had gone to one of the Games to bet his last penny out of sheer desperation. He'd never been to a Game before because his grandfather did not think they were suitable for children – what with the fact that at least one player usually came to a sticky end or lost a hand or a foot or some other limb before the Game was over. After all, it was a Game of the Gods so it was bound to be dangerous. But Lex found it all thoroughly exhilarating. He loved the huge circular stadium with the bustling noise and the activity of hundreds of spectators placing bets before taking their seats to watch the next round being broadcast in the gigantic crystal ball in the centre. The Box of the Gods, suspended high above it all and commanding the best view, was where deities could lounge about eating grapes and watching the Game.

There were always three Gods who each had one human player who would be put through three dangerous, exciting rounds. The winning God would experience an increase in popularity – oftentimes gaining a few more followers from other churches. For, once you made an oath of allegiance to a God, that oath was not for life and you were free to pick another God whenever you liked. The Gods were flexible and realistic about such things. As for the winning human . . . they got glory, fame, adoration . . . everything they'd ever wanted in fact. The only problem was that this only tended to last for a few minutes before everything more or less went back to normal. They'd sign a few autographs, pose for a few pictures. And then everyone would forget them. For the Games simply occurred too frequently for *everyone* who played in them to be some sort of superstar.

Lex handed over his penultimate penny to get admittance to the stadium – although it was standing room only by that time, which was just as well for Lex could not have afforded a seat anyway. The Game that day was between Haarii, God of Abundance, Jessope, Goddess of Fertility, and Manneron, God of Hunting. Each Game consisted of three rounds that each lasted for an hour or two, spread across a period of about three weeks. This Game was only just beginning and people had gathered that day to watch the first round. As Lex walked through he stopped to look at the souvenir carts selling t-shirts, lollies and lunch boxes, each emblazoned with the face of one of the competing Gods. There were flags for the kids too, Lex noticed, for – despite his grandfather's feelings on the matter – there were quite a lot of children in the audience.

Lex bet his last penny on Haarii. As it happened, Jessope won that round and Lex lost the bet, but he strolled out of the stadium with three fat wallets in his pocket. He hadn't meant to do it. He'd turned up fully expecting just to stand there and watch the Game with everyone else. But then he'd noticed a wallet sticking out of the pocket of the man in the top hat in front of him. Really it would have been stupid *not* to take it. It slid out as though it had been greased and soon it was buried away in Lex's coat. And that was when he first discovered that he had light fingers.

With the money he stole on that first occasion he went straight out and purchased a set of fine clothes for himself. He had noticed a few people shoot him suspicious looks that first time in the stadium because he looked exactly like what he was – a farm boy and a poor, dirty, hungry, desperate one at that. So he bought himself a ridiculous-looking waistcoat and top hat and gloves and a shiny black stick with a golden knob at the end. Dressed like that no one would imagine for a moment that he was really a pickpocket in disguise. They wouldn't be on guard around him and – if someone were to discover that their wallet had gone and raise the alarm (as, in fact, happened on more than one occasion) – then Lex could simply stroll out of the stadium, twirling his stick between his gloved fingers without any worry that the guards would try to stop him.

But, of course, there was more to it than clothes. There was another week to go before the second round so Lex bought himself a mirror and then rented a small, basic room in a local inn where he spent hours practising various different facial expressions ranging from haughty to superior to smug to self-righteous – basically any expression that a young toff might wear depending on how he was feeling. After only a few days he had it down pat. He was quite delighted to discover that he was a born natural at this sort of thing and he didn't even have a mentor telling him what to do and showing him the ropes. Lex did not fall in with a bad crowd who were a corrupting influence on him – seducing him to the dark side. Nor did a more experienced criminal take him under his wing and teach him all he knew. Rather it all came from within himself as if the predisposition had been there all along just waiting to come out. He instinctively knew what to do and he was good at it.

Lex also practised the posh accent to go with the clothes, which came in very handy when he went back to the stadium a week later for the second round, and a lah-di-dah lady in a ridiculous hat towering with waxed fruit turned round to catch Lex with his hand practically in her handbag.

'Just *what* do you think you're doing, young man?' she demanded, narrowing her eyes suspiciously. If he'd been scruffily dressed she would have been shrieking accusations of theft at him already but his posh clothes and the way he held his chin so haughtily high threw her temporarily.

'Oh ai say, ai'm most *dreadfully* sorry but ai fear you have just been robbed by some *miscreant*,' Lex said, adapting a nasal drawl as he discreetly slipped her purse into his pocket. He gazed round until he found what he was looking for – a young, scruffy-looking boy with big, helpless eyes and wearing dirty clothes who was apparently there on his own – probably from the local orphanage – looking rather like a lost puppy and just a few aisles away from them. Perfect. Absolutely perfect. 'Yaas, it was him over thereyah.' Lex pointed with his gloved hand. 'Ai just saw him with his hand in your bag and thought ai'd better do mey duty and come and inform you at once, you know—'

The frightening woman with the obscene hat was already storming towards the unfortunate young boy before Lex had even finished his sentence. Deeming it wise not to linger in case her suspicions should return to him once she discovered that the scruffy boy did not have her wallet after all, Lex slipped out of the stadium, sniggering to himself in satisfaction at his effortless escape from what could have been a most unpleasant situation. He was utterly gifted, there was no doubt at all about that. And to think how much time he had wasted embroiled in the toils of honest work . . . Slaving away on his grandfather's farm like a sucker! His older, wiser, more experienced self practically shuddered at the recollection.

The third and final round of the Game was on a week after the second. The gaps between the Games varied but they tended to be at least a week apart for the simple reason that each round took place in a different location and the players needed time to get there. Besides which, the delay gave the spectators time to book days off work, obtain babysitters and so on, so that they could attend the stadiums.

Lex went to every round of that first Game, as well as the Winner's Ceremony where the winning human was given a cup and some prize money before being able to escape gratefully home. By the time it was over, Lex had accumulated quite a respectable amount of cash and fine, leather-lined wallets. Then the stadium was empty during the day but Lex was bored with pickpocketing by that time anyway. It kept him in money well enough but it wasn't exciting. He wanted an element of human interaction. Something to make it fun. Something to make him feel exhilarated and alive. Something to make it dangerous and risky. So he moved on to the next town, found another inn to stay at and started devising scams. They required careful planning and preparation but they were glorious fun and Lex enjoyed himself immensely, even when he was caught out and had to flee with what he had on him. Perhaps even especially then . . .

Lex walked through the midnight market and approached a few stalls until he found people who were looking to buy as well as sell. Over the next hour he purchased all the provisions he would need and sold some of the antiques and works of art he had stolen, insisting on a fair price and payment in mirror-gold rather than Withian dollars. M-gold was a universal currency that could be used anywhere on the Globe and Lex wasn't sure how far he would have to go before he would find a town that would suit him. He was careful never to sell more than one or two pieces at each stall before moving on as he didn't want anyone to see just how much wealth he was carrying in the grubby pack on his back.

Most of the traders in the dark part of the market carefully kept themselves to themselves but there were some who were decidedly pushy. The magical people, for instance, were, by nature, predators, moving among their non-magical prey. Which wasn't to say that the entire magical population on the Globe was evil. But those frequenting this kind of place had to be at least a little unsavoury and Lex would have done well to stay away from them. But the enchanters fascinated him.

They were very tall men and they always seemed to be old. Lex had often wondered where all the young enchanters were. Was there even such a thing? For all the ones Lex had seen had been very tall, silver haired with long silver beards and bushy eyebrows. Most of them had dark blue robes stitched with silver stars and grand pointed hats although Lex was sure that this was just for effect and to make the magical men seem even taller than they really were. As a conman himself, Lex could recognise showmanship when he saw it.

He was bothered by crones a couple of times but when he protested that he had no money they lost interest pretty fast. But there was one old witch who wouldn't be dissuaded. She appeared out of nowhere and gripped Lex's wrist with a gnarled, crooked hand. 'H's waiting f'r us!' she hissed in Lex's ear.

'Pardon?' Lex asked.

The crone gestured over her shoulder to the black velvet tent that stood sullenly behind her. It was so cloaked in shadows that Lex hadn't noticed it.

'He 'as great magics in there. We will sell them to you.'

'No, thank you,' Lex said politely, tugging at his wrist. 'I don't need any magics at the moment.'

It was well known that magical people very rarely allowed anything of real supernatural significance to fall into the hands of laypeople. Giving such powers to the unskilled was the last thing they wanted and was frowned on by the magical community. But it did happen on occasion and Lex was always on the lookout for such an opportunity. Enchanters were dangerous people. What greater thrill could there be than to steal something from one of them? But tonight was not the night for such recklessness. Lex was on the run and there was enough danger already.

Crones served the enchanters and didn't tend to be dangerous in themselves but, if she did become violent, Lex was sure he would be able to knock her over and run for it. In the markets they were sent out to find customers and bring them back to the stall or tent at which their master was waiting. A lot of traders in the dark area had tents rather than stalls in order that business could be conducted more privately. Crones had some magical powers of their own but they tended to be unbalanced or, at the very least, dim-witted, with child-like minds that made them virtually powerless without the protection of an enchanter.

The crone barely came up to Lex's shoulder and walked with the aid of two sticks. Various drably-coloured shawls were draped around her hunched form and the tiniest movement made her jingle softly with the many charms and amulets that hung about her. She was a crooked old woman, from the hunch of her back to the uneven lengths of her knobbly fingers.

'Maybe some other time,' Lex said, making another attempt to free his wrist from her surprisingly tight grip.

At that point, the crone started to get agitated; her voice

rose and took on a cackle-like edge and she dropped her walking sticks to grip Lex's collar and pull his head down closer to her level.

'He knows! He watches everyone! You must come with me, little boy—'

'Hey, I'm not a little boy, all right? I'm seventeen! I'm just small for my age, that's all.'

'Come. Come with me,' the old witch insisted, still tugging doggedly at his collar.

'Enough, Jabitha. Release him.'

The old crone let go of Lex with all the instinctive panic as if he had suddenly burnt her and slowly bent to retrieve her sticks, hobbling back to return to the enchanter's side. It was too dark for Lex to see him properly. The glow of light from within the tent silhouetted him where he stood in the entrance.

'What is your name?' the enchanter asked after a moment.

'Harold Gibbons,' Lex lied smoothly.

He would never have been stupid enough to give his true name to one of the enchanters, for then they would hold his soul in the palms of their hands.

They were unusual, even in the Wither City. Lex had been seven the first time he'd seen one. He'd been fascinated then and he was fascinated now. These men had real *power*. They talked to the stars and the stars talked *back*!

'Just what exactly are you selling?' Lex asked, taking a step closer to the tent.

'Nothing you would be able to afford, boy. My apologies for the behaviour of my crone.'

And then, without another word, the enchanter steered Jabitha into the tent, drawing the flap closed behind him. The danger had passed and Lex was free to go on his way. And yet he hesitated. There was a pull, a hunger inside him to know what was inside that tent. It was what he lived for – balancing on the edge. Lex was not, in fact, a stupid person. He knew that tangling with enchanters was dangerous. But there was this thing that sometimes came over him; this urge that silenced reason and filled his mind with shrill shrieks of longing for something that was never meant to be his. And he always gave in to it because he enjoyed it so much.

Making up his mind, Lex strode to the tent entrance, drew back the flap and stepped inside, letting it fall back down behind him. The crone was now huddled in a corner of the tent, a cat curled about her shoulders. Lex had heard stories that the crones favoured animal familiars to aid them in the performance of their magics. The faint, guttering light from the green lamp that stood on the table in the centre reflected from the cat's eyes in eerie flashes that sent shivers down Lex's spine.

Charm strings hung from the ceiling – threaded with beads, feathers and the skulls of small animals. There were masks too, grinning down from the coarse, canvas walls and an altar in one corner to Thaddeus, the God of Illusion and Waking Dreams. Thaddeus was the patron deity of the crones and the enchanters and had been worshipped loyally by them for many hundreds of years. There was a vase on the altar, holding purple sticks of burning incense that filled the tent with twisting ribbons of purple smoke.

The enchanter was seated at the table, gazing down at the lamp. The green light played shadows across his lined face and gave his long silver hair and beard a greenish tint. Lex cleared his throat. 'I am wealthier than my appearance would suggest,' he said. 'Please, what goods are you offering for sale?'

The enchanter gazed up at him through a mist of the purple incense smoke, the tips of his curiously long fingers resting together.

'Very well, Mr Harold Gibbons,' he said at last. 'Be seated.'

Lex took the seat indicated on the other side of the table.

The enchanter put a hand in his pocket and drew out a small velvet pouch. From this he withdrew a small, sculptured swan carved out of black obelisk, no more than an inch tall and the same across, and placed it on the table. Two more of the exact same sculpture followed – one made from pale ivory, the other from dusky bloodstone. Lex could see each intricately-carved feather, the indentation of their slanting eyes, the graceful curve of their long necks.

The three identical swans gleamed in the light of the lamp and a familiar sensation of selfish greed rushed through Lex. They were beautiful, they were perfect, they were his. Of course he knew that they could not be mere sculptures – if there was nothing darker about them then they would be with the other arts and crafts in the main collection of stalls, rather than hidden away in the pocket of an enchanter in this dark corner of the market.

Lex had always had an eye for beauty. Of course, he was unprincipled and without scruples when it came to thieving for he enjoyed the act for the simple thrill of it. But he had always been moved to steal beautiful, precious things from museums and art collections and it would often be some time before he could bring himself to sell them on. He liked owning these masterpieces, even if it was for a short while, for he felt sure that he appreciated them far more than the gawping sightseers that traipsed through the museums. These things *belonged* to him in every sense of the word (excluding the legal sense, of course).

'What *are* they?' Lex breathed.

'They are the Wishing Swanns of Desareth,' the enchanter replied. 'They have touched the lives of many men. Beautiful, aren't they?'

'They certainly are. How much are you asking for them?'

The enchanter smiled. 'One million pieces of m-gold.'

'One *million*?' Lex repeated incredulously. 'There's probably no one left on the Globe with that kind of money any more. Perhaps the Golden Valley where the last kings live but you'll certainly find no buyer in the Wither City.'

'Is that so?' the enchanter drawled, slowly replacing

the exquisite Swanns in their velvet pouch. 'Then I suppose I must keep hold of them a little longer.'

Lex watched helplessly as the enchanter put the beautiful things away. In ordinary circumstances, he would have simply stolen them. But he knew that this would be no easy feat and that only a fool would attempt such a task without extremely careful preparation. If he was going to get the Swanns, he would have to do so honestly.

'I have a few hundred pieces of m-gold,' Lex said. 'But I also have some artefacts, some precious artefacts that I have collected over the years and I would be happy to trade them all. Please, let me show you what I—'

'I am not interested in a trade,' the enchanter replied firmly. 'But there is another way of purchasing them that might make the price more amenable to you.'

'Which is?'

The enchanter reached into his robes once again and placed a bracelet on the table between them. It was a simple piece and looked like two bracelets moulded together – one an ivory white colour and the other an obelisk black. Engravings in ancient runes ran round the edge.

'The bracelet's price is fifty pieces of m-gold,' the enchanter said. 'If you buy the bracelet, you can take the Swanns for free.'

'Excuse me?' Lex asked, staring at him.

'Yes, they're part of a set and I would hate to see them broken up. So, if you buy the bracelet, I would have no choice but to give you the Swanns.'

Lex hesitated, forcing himself to think the thing through and not just snatch the Swanns away greedily. Of course, enchanters were known for their eccentricity and occasionally hazy logic and the Swanns were being offered for a fraction of their value . . .

'On the condition that you promise to wear it until the time comes to take it off,' the enchanter said.

Alarm bells sounded in Lex's head. Few people would be fool enough to wear a piece of quite-possibly-enchanted jewellery they knew nothing about. Suddenly, he regretted his rash action in entering the tent. This wasn't fun any more. He was aware of the old crone muttering to herself in the corner, and the unnaturally loud purring of the cat draped across her shoulders, blocking out the everyday sounds of the market outside. The masks and strings of grinning skulls clicking together softly were beginning to unnerve him and the cloying purple incense smoke was making the tent tiny and hot. He was very aware of the blueness of the enchanter's eyes, the lines on his face and the slightly hypnotic quality of his voice. Lex got to his feet quickly, feeling slightly alarmed.

'No, thank you. I think I'd better be going now.'

'A pity,' the enchanter said, standing up just as abruptly and sticking out his hand. Lex shook it, thanked him for his hospitality and turned to go.

'Aren't you forgetting something, Lex?' the enchanter asked sharply.

Lex turned back to inquire what that might be and instinctively caught the velvet pouch the enchanter threw to him. He could feel the three Swanns clicking lightly together through the fabric.

'But . . . I thought you said . . . one million pieces of—'

'I changed my mind,' the enchanter said brusquely. 'Now please go. My crone requires rest.'

Lex was eager enough to comply with the request. He still had quite a lot of stolen goods in his backpack but he'd had enough of the midnight markets for one night, and had enough cash to be going on with now at any rate, so he decided to head back to the docks. He was almost there before he realised he was wearing the black and white bracelet, which was odd because he distinctly remembered seeing the enchanter replace it in his pocket. And the alarming thing of it was that he didn't seem to be able to take it off.

CHAPTER FOUR

THE BINDING BRACELETS

Lex managed to snatch two hours of sleep in one of the brightly-painted gypsy wagons stationed down by the harbour before Cara was knocking on the door, waking him up and telling him it was time to go. With an effort, Lex forced himself reluctantly from the cosy warmth of the wagon into the cool early-morning mist outside. The stalls of the midnight market had been shuttered up for the day and a temporary peace lay over the harbour, the bright flags from the gypsy ship fluttering softly in the early-morning breeze.

Lex had always loved ships, but for a long while his favourite had been the gypsy ships for they were painted bright colours and were adorned with bright sails and flags and Cara's family's ship – the *Breathless* – was no exception. Painted sea monsters danced across the hull and a sculptured wooden mermaid rose up along the prow.

Lex stood at the hull as they set sail, and gazed back at the roofline of the Wither City, not knowing when he would ever be able to go back. It didn't bother him overly. He had enjoyed the city with its books and its museums and law courts, but in some ways the Wither City had been too civilised for him. Thieving from the museums had been a passing amusement but few things compared to the thrill of travelling.

The one faint pang of regret Lex felt was for Mr Lucas since he knew that his employer would suffer the consequences of Lex's flight. But even this did not overly prey on his mind for it was not in Lex's nature to give much thought to the plight of others. It served the old lawyer right, really, for trusting him. Selfishness was part of human nature. And at least Lex was honest about his dishonesty. He didn't hide behind a screen of pious hypocrisy like the rest of the world.

The gypsies had not said much to him but had merely quietly accepted that he was to be accompanying them on their voyage. Lex had been careful to conceal the bracelet on his arm. The gypsies were a superstitious lot and it would not do for them to discover that an enchanter had put it there. Still, the thing itself seemed to be harmless. It was just a bracelet, after all. It wasn't tight to the point of being uncomfortable, but it followed the curve of Lex's wrist exactly and no matter how he fiddled with the thing it would not come loose.

The enchanter had called Lex by his name before he left. His real name. Lex had been too preoccupied to notice at the time. But it came back to him later with a small thrill of unease . . . But, after all, nothing dreadful had happened and it was a small price to pay for the beautiful Wishing Swanns of Desareth. Lex took them out of his pocket and balanced them in his palm, examining them in the glimmering half-light of the morning. He felt a great pride in owning these utterly priceless things and felt glad now that he had ventured into the enchanter's tent.

'My name is Lex Trent,' Lex muttered smugly to himself. 'And I always get what I want.'

Then he turned from the railings and walked straight into Mr Schmidt.

'You're actually going to have a heart attack if you carry on like that,' Lex said eventually, eyeing the elderly lawyer warily.

As someone who had studied the laws on murder, manslaughter and causation, Lex was feeling distinctly uneasy about the state that the lawyer was winding himself into. It would be just like the spiteful old man to land Lex with a manslaughter conviction. Apparently he had decided to give chase and had paid for his way on the gypsy ship as the only vessel leaving the harbour that morning. Of course, he had believed Lex to be on the ship that had left the harbour some hours earlier, having witnessed the cabin boy scampering aboard wearing Lex's coat.

'How is it possible?' he had spluttered, on running into Lex. 'I *saw* you board that other—'

'Lost sumfing, guv?' Lex asked with a grin, holding up

the coin that the lawyer had given him the previous night, believing him to be a cabin boy.

A look of startled comprehension crossed Mr Schmidt's face and that was when he got really angry and started shouting and a couple of nearby gypsies became aware of the dispute and came to watch. Entertainment was scarce when you were at sea.

'I'm flattered, Mr Schmidt, I never realised you hated me quite that much,' Lex drawled. 'But surely you must realise that you have no jurisdiction over me now that we are outside the province of the Wither City.'

'You contemptible villain!' the lawyer snarled. 'Are you not even going to show any remorse for what you've done?'

'What, the thieving or the lying?'

'Both!'

'No. Why should I? I've done it before and I'll do it again.'

The nearby gypsies laughed. One of them smacked Lex on the back.

'This is not a laughing matter!' Mr Schmidt snapped. 'I am placing this boy under a citizen's arrest. Fetch whoever's in charge at once. I demand to be taken back to the mainland.'

Lex winced involuntarily. Only a very stupid person would attempt to order a sea-gypsy to do anything. Lex knew his employer to be a clever man and could therefore only assume that it was the sheer extent of his anger clouding his judgement that made him do such a foolish thing. The gypsies glared sullenly at Mr Schmidt.

'We take orders from no one, lawyer.'

'Then I will pay for a life-raft and the two of us will *row* back to the shore—' Schmidt began, dropping his hand to grip Lex's wrist.

It felt more like a mild electric shock than anything as the black and white bracelet split, as if the two halves had suddenly become magnets that were repelling each other. The black half pressed into Lex's skin as the white half shot from his hand and straight round the wrist of Mr Schmidt. The lawyer withdrew his hand with a yell and the nearby gypsies shrank back in fear.

Lex glanced at the black bracelet around his wrist, puzzled.

'What have you done?' Mr Schmidt hissed on finding himself unable to remove the bracelet.

'Where did they come from?' one of the gypsies asked sharply.

Lex thought about lying but there seemed little point in attempting to deny that the bracelets were anything other than magical objects.

'Where did you get them?' the gypsy repeated loudly.

Lex sighed. 'From an enchanter.'

Lex couldn't help feeling a little resentful. After all, it wasn't like the sea-gypsies themselves never meddled in the magical arts. They were all up on deck, near the prow of the ship, as it was one of the only places large enough for everyone to gather. Below deck the ship was a cata-comb of tiny rooms, tunnels and hidey-holes and the galley was one of the only places big enough to accommodate everyone inside. Indeed, with his height, Schmidt would probably be forced to keep his head carefully lowered inside the ship if he wanted to avoid getting a concussion.

Gypsy families tended to be large and always travelled together. All twenty-three of the crew were now clustered up on the deck around Lex and his distinctly unhappy employer. The Globe had four suns, each ruled over by a different God. Weather was an arbitrary affair, very much dependent on whose sun happened to be in the sky that day. Unfortunately, it was Heetha's sun that morning. As the God of War and Strife, Heetha's sun was the hottest and the most unrelenting. The wooden boards of the gypsy ship had warmed whilst they had all been gathered there and the steel railings were scalding to the touch.

A lot of the younger people Lex had known in the Wither City had had a preference for Heetha's sun since it brought good sunbathing weather, and tanned brown skin had been desirable for several seasons now. But Lex had always keenly disliked Heetha's sun for the way it turned the air thick and dimmed the mind and brought out insect swarms in hordes. The one saving grace was that there was at least a strong sea breeze on the deck, with the ship slicing swiftly through the broiling waves.

Cara's grandmother – a tiny, wizened woman, with a lot of brightly-coloured scarves tied around her waist – had been brought up on deck to examine the twin bracelets. She reported that she had never seen their like before but that the runes around each of them were of the ancient tongue of Khestrii, although she was unable to translate the precise meaning.

The gypsies had been fidgeting about nervously ever since; discussing what was to be done about their troublesome guests and their bothersome bracelets. Montgomery Schmidt was being predictably vocal in the debate but Lex wasn't paying the proceedings much heed. At one point, one of the gypsies had suggested that tipping the pair of them overboard would be the best way to placate the Gods for any enchanted evil Lex had brought on board, but the suggestion had not been warmly received by the others and Lex had not been overly worried. He knew gypsies and that was not the gypsy way. Hospitality and honour were very important to them as a people – more important than the fear they felt of the nameless enchanters.

Lex had been leaning against the rail until the sun had made it too hot. Then he had switched to idling with his hands in his pockets and had continued his conversation with Cara. Actually, she was doing most of the talking, babbling on agitatedly about what a disaster the bracelets were and what trouble she would be in with her family over this whole affair and so on and so on. Lex thought she was overreacting a bit. After all, she would probably only receive a mild chastisement from her family, so he didn't trouble himself to reassure her.

He liked the gold hoops that hung from her ears. They glimmered in the light from the sun, casting golden freckles onto the bare brown skin of her shoulders. And she had the characteristic strong, dark eyes of the gypsies and a prominent nose. If she wasn't exactly beautiful, she was still something pleasant to look at whilst this tedious altercation was going on.

Lex realised that he had been admiring her too openly when one of Cara's older brothers took her by the arm with a sullen glare at Lex and led her away to the other side of the ship. Lex sighed and, with no other diversion to occupy him, decided he'd better get involved in the main debate that was still raging between the indecisive gypsies and the incensed lawyer.

He cleared his throat loudly. 'Excuse me,' he said, spreading his hands and breaking easily into the group conversation. 'Sorry to interrupt but I'd just like to reiterate my apologies once again. I know you're busy people and you don't have time to be bothering about this kind of thing, but I can assure you that the bracelets are in no way dangerous – you have my personal assurances on that. If you would just be so good as to honour our agreement of passage and set us down on the eastern shores of the Fallows – I believe that's where you're going anyway? – Mr Schmidt and myself will then go about our business and this problem will cease to be yours. And thank you again for agreeing to help us so graciously. We really are both very grateful. But please don't linger up here on our account. I know you must all be busy with the running of the ship to attend to.'

He beamed at the assembled crew and then turned

away as if fully confident that that was the end of the matter. It was undoubtedly something about Lex's manner. It was the *sincerity* there. Lex was a law student. He was also a thief. And a wastrel. But what he really was, deep down inside, was an actor. Lex knew how to play the necessary roles. And he knew how to be utterly convincing. Of course, it certainly helped that he had what was generally considered to be an honest face. It was something about the set of his eyes.

After a moment of hesitation, the gypsies wandered away back to their various tasks, looking slightly bemused and possibly wondering how they had managed to be dismissed in such a manner. Lex and Schmidt were left alone at the prow of the ship, with Heetha's sun beating down in searing pulses and salt spray blowing in every now and then from the white froth of the sea. It never stained the planks of the deck for long since it evaporated in the heat within moments.

'What do you think you're playing at?' Mr Schmidt snapped, rounding on Lex as soon as the gypsies had gone.

'Pardon?' Lex asked.

He wasn't to know the further anger he had just caused the lawyer who had been reasoning and arguing with the gypsies for almost an hour until Lex had troubled himself to tear his eyes from the gypsy girl and intervene. And then, he had managed to do with a few sentences what Mr Schmidt (who had always considered himself quite the eloquent orator) had not been able to do in a whole hour of discussion, and get the gypsies to calm down and disband. It really was most vexing.

'How could you possibly give them your assurance that the bracelets were not dangerous when you know absolutely nothing about them?'

'My dear Mr Schmidt – may I call you Monty? – I hardly think that truthfulness would be a pragmatic virtue at this particular time. Do you wish them to throw us overboard? If we're careful, we should be able to make it to the Farrows.'

'Whence, be assured, I will be taking every available action to have you deported straight back to the Wither City where you will be properly charged with all due—'

'Excuse me for interrupting, Mr Schmidt, but the sun is very strong out here and you have no hat,' Lex said smoothly, slipping straight back into the respectful manner he had been forced to adopt towards his employer at work. 'I have no wish to seem presumptuous, sir, but perhaps it would be better if you sought shade some- where on the ship. I would hate for you to become dehy- drated or suffer heat rash and, as I'm sure you are aware, there is perhaps not quite so much hair on your head as there once was—'

Lex broke off from his arrogant monologue as the lawyer made an angry gesture of impatience, for he had been pushed almost to the limit over the last twenty-four hours.

'Enjoy it, Lex,' Schmidt hissed. 'Just enjoy it whilst you can. I'll find a loophole once we reach the Farrows.

A legal loophole, Lex, you remember them? Believe me, you will be deported back to the Wither City and I'll have you strung up before a jury before you even know what's hit you.'

He turned on his heel and stalked away, leaving Lex alone at the prow. Lex grinned, gave an easy shrug and turned back to the railings, watching the ship skim along the foaming surface of the sea. The truth was he had no intention of sticking around once they reached the Farrows. He had no doubt that Schmidt could achieve his aim, given time. He knew him to be a formidable and determined advocate and there was no doubt that he hated Lex with a vengeance. But another thing Lex was good at was running. The Farrows would be a mere blur to him. It would be an easy enough thing to give the elderly lawyer the slip at the harbour and after that he need only linger in the Farrows long enough to secure transportation. And then it hardly mattered where he went. Lady Luck would be watching over him, as long as she didn't choose this inopportune time to go off on holiday or something, and he would go wherever the wind took him until he found a town of likely-looking suckers waiting to be scammed. That was the wonderful thing for a fraud like Lex – the world seemed to have an endless supply of willing suckers who were practically *begging* him to take their money.

CHAPTER FIVE

MIRROR, MIRROR ON THE WALL

It took the *Breathless* two days to reach the Farrows. It would usually have taken much longer but, after that first day, Heetha's sun fled far from the sky to be replaced with Holli's – Goddess of Tranquillity and Gentleness. Hers was a mild, lukewarm sun at the best of times but, as often happened, she was closely followed by her jealous sister, Gersha. It was said that Gersha had originally been the Goddess of a noble and virtuous province. But in the aftermath of her jealous rage at not being given her own sun along with her sister, Gersha had evolved into the Goddess of Resentment and Bitterness and her savage gales were often twinned with Holli's sun so that what little warmth the gentle Goddess gave was quickly snatched away by her poisonous sister.

But this was so much the better for Lex, who was eager to reach the Farrows quickly. He did not suffer from seasickness and, on the contrary, keenly enjoyed standing at the prow of the ship as it bucked, flew and crashed back down upon the ferocious waves. There had only been one spare cabin on board and Lex had let Mr Schmidt claim this without argument. This wasn't due to any particularly charitable outburst of feeling on Lex's part but rather a certain disinterest, for Lex enjoyed sleeping in the huge storage room. Not only was it much bigger than the tiny, claustrophobic cabins, but it was also closer to the cold sea and so was probably the coolest part of the otherwise stuffy ship. The gypsies gave him some spare blankets and pillows and with these he was able to make himself quite comfortable down below.

But he wasn't accustomed to living on the sea and, although he enjoyed it during the day, at night he had trouble adjusting to the bucking movement of the ship, for Lex was a light sleeper and often found himself jerking awake from dreams of falling. But the storage area was comfortable and it was at least a large area all to himself. There were even a few useful things stored away down there that he took the opportunity of placing, solely for safekeeping, in his own bag.

Lex hadn't seen her Ladyship since the night he was arrested but this did not unduly bother him. Lady Luck was a flighty, fickle being and there had been times when she had taken off and Lex had not seen her for weeks. The protection she gave him helped, but Lex had managed fine before she came along and he would be fine without her again if he needed to be.

For the last few days he had wandered about the ship, making sure to keep out of the gypsies' way apart from at the evening meal when everyone ate together. Mr Schmidt had been confined to his cabin the first day due to seasickness. Lex had felt rather pleased about that. Served the vicious old stick right for chasing after him and causing so many complications.

Lex knocked on his door that first evening and told the lawyer that the gypsies had prepared dinner down in the galley and that he'd better come and eat something or he would be seen as offending their hospitality – and an offended gypsy was an angry gypsy. This was quite untrue. The gypsies couldn't have cared less who came down to eat in the evenings but it was quite fun for Lex to watch Schmidt valiantly try and eat something for a few minutes before rushing upstairs to throw up over the side of the ship.

When he came up on deck the day they docked at the Farrows he still looked slightly green and was glaring daggers at Lex as if he were responsible for all the lawyer's worldly problems. Lex gave him a cheerful grin, sauntered over, and politely inquired as to his health. He was answered with a snarl and a promise that the lawyer would be sticking to him like glue as soon as they landed. Lex shrugged, completely confident in his abilities to give Schmidt the slip.

They docked at the harbour at about midday. The sun was still weak and the gales still stormy when they landed. Lex had been to the Farrows last year on his way to the Wither City. He had an excellent memory and so had a pretty good idea of the layout of the town.

As they made their way down the gangplank, Schmidt had his hand clamped tightly around Lex's upper arm. The old man actually had a stronger grip than Lex had imagined and he had to tug forcefully, finally pushing the lawyer over hard to get away. Schmidt went sprawling into one of the shut-up stalls of the midnight market that was, as usual, set up around the harbour, and by the time he got to his feet again, Lex was several paces away, weaving through the crowd towards Jani's Tavern.

You had to do what they weren't expecting you to do, that was the nub of it. Speed alone was rarely enough. Any unintelligent thug could bolt for it. Schmidt was probably expecting Lex to head for the nearest transportation dealership and get out of the Farrows as fast as he possibly could. He probably wasn't expecting him to go and have a drink in a tavern. Such an action, after all, would have been arrogant beyond words.

The Farrows had sprouted up in a haphazard manner and was a very ancient town. The buildings were crooked, as they had all been added to over the years, and second and third floors often didn't fit properly on the first ones so that layers would jut out over each other. Many of them had dark, thatched roofs and signs above the doors pronouncing the occupier's trade. Of course, most of the Farrow folk were miners as a result of the town's proximity to the great mineral mines.

Jani's Tavern was near to the station that transported workers to the mines and, as such, was a much-favoured haunt for miners as well as sailors. When Lex went in, the tavern was full of miners on their lunch break. He was glad of the smoke-laden air for it would help to hide him if Schmidt did turn out to be bright enough to search for him there.

Not being a huge fan of gypsy food, Lex was glad to order a proper meal and squeeze himself onto the end of one of the tables. The miners paid him no heed since he was still wearing his sailor-boy clothes and it was not unusual for sailors to come and eat at Jani's whilst their ship was in the docks. Lex still wasn't old enough to enjoy any of the real ales that the miners were drinking, but he ordered a pint of Grandy to go with his meal and settled down to enjoy some good Farrian cuisine.

He carefully tore the bread roll in half, dipped it into the bowl of delicious-looking soup and had just put it in his mouth when there was a kind of *shing* noise and a horrible lurching feeling and a man handed him a few copper coins and the reins of a mantha beast.

'You'll be pleased with this one, sir, she's a bargain for the price.'

Lex kept his cool. He didn't scream or shriek or jump back. But the fact was that he was outside, at a mantha stables in the centre of town when moments ago he had been at Jani's Tavern about to eat his lunch. His plan had been to travel to the stables later on in the afternoon once he could be sure that Mr Schmidt would no longer be in the town. For a moment, he feared that he must have had some kind of mental memory gap.

But then he became aware of the strange feeling.

He glanced down at the mantha beast – a sort of shaggy cow thing, with lots of hair – cropping on the scrubby grass at his feet. It seemed to be further away than it should be. He glanced at the seller and was alarmed to find that the man was shorter than him. Lex was not a tall person. He was shorter than most other men. The joints in his wrists ached and so did his feet. And his stomach had that horrible *empty* feeling, as of one who had spent most of their time during the last couple of days with their head down a toilet. A horrible, incredible, disgusting, *revolting* suspicion crept over Lex.

'Are you all right, sir?' the mantha seller asked, suddenly looking concerned. 'Only you've gone all white and sickly-looking, like.'

Lex automatically went to assure the man that he was fine. He had learnt long ago that it did not do to attract unwonted attention to oneself. 'Thank you, but—'

And it was after those three words that his usual self-assurance shattered into so many tiny fragments. For the voice he had spoken in had not been his own. There was no mistaking the cold, hard, slightly nasally tones of his employer, Mr Montgomery Schmidt.

He almost screamed. He almost did. But discipline was an inbuilt thing with Lex and he clapped a hand over his mouth just in time. Misinterpreting the action, the mantha seller took a hasty step back and asked Lex if he'd like him to go and fetch a bucket. Lex knew the sensible thing would be to tell the seller that he had just remembered an important engagement and to ask him to hold the mantha for him. But he found he just couldn't face speaking only to have Mr Schmidt's voice coming out of his mouth. So he shook his head and stumbled away in the general direction of Jani's Tavern, tugging the mantha beast behind him. It took him a while to adjust to the longer legs and the added height.

He was in Mr Schmidt's body. Somehow his consciousness had been transported into the body of his employer . . . urgh, urgh, urgh! But he was remaining calm. He was being *logical*. If he was in Schmidt's body, then it only made sense that the lawyer would be in Lex's body. Lex was at Jani's Tavern, about to eat his lunch. It must have been the bracelets, Lex thought, glancing down at the white one on Schmidt's wrist. The wretched bracelets he had taken from the enchanter. For once, there was no long-term plan in Lex's mind. All he could think to do was to get the both of them together again. Then everything would surely sort itself all out. Spring back together like a released cosmic elastic band.

It was only once he'd arrived at Jani's Tavern and was tying the mantha beast up outside that the thought occurred to him that Mr Schmidt . . . Lex Trent . . . whoever, might not be in there any more. On discovering what had happened, Schmidt had most likely had the same idea as Lex and set straight off for the mantha stables to find his body. The Farrows was a large town; they could end up wandering about for ever without finding each other.

Not feeling at all cheered, Lex went into the tavern anyway on the off chance that Schmidt would still be inside. Luck, as it so happened, was with Lex, for as soon as he walked in he experienced the strange sensation of seeing himself sat where he'd left him, at the end of one of the tables. Schmidt was holding a soup spoon with a trembling hand and gazing at his reflection in the back of it.

It must have been a twenty-minute walk from the mantha stables. Surely Schmidt had not been sat there staring at himself in the spoon for all that time? A few of the miners had gone back to their shifts and the tavern was now a little quieter. As Lex made his way towards the table he saw Jani approach Mr Schmidt.

'Is everything all right, lovey? Is there something wrong with the soup?'

'Yes, it's cold,' Lex said, pulling up a chair and inwardly shuddering at the sound of his employer's voice. 'Take it away and heat it up, please. He ordered it for me but I was unavoidably detained. Bring a crust of bread or something for the boy too, will you?'

Jani gave him a bit of a dirty look but took the soup away without questions. Lex Trent was a grubby, skinny kid wearing old sailor-boy clothes and Mr Schmidt was an elderly, well-groomed lawyer. It was commonplace on the Globe for distinguished professionals to take young male servants who were lower down the social scale, could be paid a pittance and were expected to be grateful for it, too.

Schmidt slowly lowered the soup spoon onto the wooden table where it rocked a little on the uneven boards before settling. He stared at Lex in silence for a while. He still hadn't said a word and Lex guessed that he too was struggling with the alien sensation of speaking with someone else's voice. The situation wasn't at all funny to either of them but, in spite of himself, Lex found he wanted to laugh. Schmidt, despite being a lawyer, was not as accomplished as Lex when it came to hiding his emotions. And right now he looked as he felt: absolutely and completely horrified to the very marrow.

After a few moments of silence, Lex grinned and raised his eyebrows at his old employer in the most insolent manner he could muster. Schmidt scowled, leant forwards across the table and hissed, 'Is that you in there, Trent?'

Lex was unprepared for the strength of the distaste he felt at hearing his voice coming from someone else's mouth like that. Especially as he could almost *hear* Schmidt's voice beneath it – in the manner of his pronunciation, the clipped precision of the words and the particular way he pronounced his vowels. But he recovered well with a broad grin. 'My dear Monty, I hope so, or else we have both gone mad.'

'What do you *mean* by this?' Schmidt hissed.

Lex wasn't sure if the lawyer was talking quietly for fear of being overheard or whether he just hated hearing his words coming out in Lex's voice.

'I suppose having me arrested would be a bit futile

now, wouldn't it?' Lex said, with a nasty smile as the thought occurred to him.

'So that's it!' Schmidt snarled. 'You've done this to escape arrest, you depraved boy!'

Lex was impressed. He hadn't realised that his face could look so vicious. He must practise in front of a mirror as soon as he got his body back. Viciousness could be useful at times. Of course he *was* going to get his body back, of course. Of course. He turned his mind away from those thoughts quickly. They must be kept for a more private place.

'You flatter me,' Lex drawled. Or tried to. Schmidt's cold, rather high voice was not built for drawling. 'But this is no deliberate ploy of mine. The logical conclusion is that it's the enchanter's bracelets.'

'What the *hell* were you doing fraternising with enchanters anyway? Don't you know they're dangerous?'

'That's what makes it fun,' Lex replied, being deliberately flippant in his attempt to irritate. The truth was that he was regretting his recklessness himself at that moment.

'We're going back *anyway*,' the lawyer snarled with sudden vehemence. 'We're going back to the Wither City, *Mister* Trent, where you will be locked up and—'

'Where *you'll* be locked up, you mean,' Lex said. 'I am Montgomery Schmidt, the great litigator. I have captured and returned the notorious criminal, Lex Trent. Aren't I clever?'

'You fool! I'll explain to them what happened. I'll tell them—'

'You know, I've heard that Lex Trent will say anything to get out of punishment,' Lex said pleasantly.

Schmidt gave him an incredulous look. 'Do you honestly think you could pass yourself off as me? You haven't the discipline!'

Discipline! Ah, but that was the one thing Lex did have!

He removed his elbows from the table, sat up straighter, narrowed his eyes just a little to give himself a haughtier look and gazed down his hooked nose at Mr Schmidt.

'I did inform you that that boy was without a stable sense of moral awareness, Inspector, did I not? I believe I did warn you as to the chain of events that would occur should you release him on bail. It is only fortunate that I managed to capture the delinquent before any more atrocities could be committed. Pray, do not lose him again. I did not go to all this tedious bother to watch him slip through your incompetent grasp a second time.'

It was an excellent mimicry. Of course, Lex was helped immensely by not having to alter his voice, but he got the facial expressions just right, the nuances of every sentence, the cold hostility. It was Mr Schmidt down to the very last hair. It threw the lawyer, Lex noted with satisfaction. He suddenly looked much less sure of himself.

'What do you think?' Lex asked. 'I think it could do with being toned down slightly. And there was something a little off about the pronunciation of the rhetorical question. Still, with a mirror and a little practice, your own mother would have believed me to be you.'

'There is more to it than mimicry . . . ' Schmidt began, but there was uncertainty in his voice. 'There are things I know that you don't—'

Lex pounced on the uncertainty instantly. 'I'll improvise,' he said, smiling only with his mouth. 'I'll invent a medical condition if I have to, Mr Schmidt. After all, you're getting on a bit now, aren't you? Who do you think they're going to believe? I mean, who do you *really* think they'll choose to trust? What about your old pal Mr Lucas? He'll be hating me by now, I'm sure. Lots of people will. All those angry victims of all my heinous crimes. We can go back to the Wither City right now if you like but it will only be a temporary detour for me – to put you behind bars. It would be satisfying, I'll admit, but something of a tedious waste of my time. For I will *lie*, Mr Schmidt. And I will lie *convincingly*. I have never been blessed with modesty, so believe me when I say that there is no one who can beat me when it comes to lying, thieving, conniving and *cheating*, Mr Schmidt.' He leant back in his chair with a slight smile. 'I've had a lot of practice. As an honest man, I would advise you not to attempt to beat me in this particular game. You'll never win it, sir.'

Lex would worry about this situation later but, for now, he was unashamedly and immensely enjoying himself.

'You say this is not your own doing,' the lawyer said quietly after a few moments. 'You do *want* your own body back, I presume?'

'You would presume correctly, Monty. I am certainly not so fond of yours that I would wish to—'

'Yes, yes, all right,' Schmidt snapped. 'Could you stop trying to be clever for just two minutes? Do you know how to get the bracelets off?'

'No.'

'Do you know anyone who might be able to help us?'

'No.'

'Do you know *anything* at all?'

'No, not really. Except that the bracelets were made in Khestrii, the gypsy woman said. The Khestrians might know something.'

Mr Schmidt gazed at him coldly. 'I am *not* travelling with you all the way to Khestrii. I am not that eager for your company.'

'Nor I yours,' Lex replied smoothly. 'But I don't need to tell you that it's not a good idea to show the bracelets to anyone around here. We were lucky with the gypsies because of their isolationist ways. But if anyone else discovers this little . . . problem we have—'

'Yes, all right; discretion is obviously paramount,' Schmidt agreed irritably.

'Look, neither of us wants to stay this way,' Lex said reasonably. 'I've got years of life left in that body, but who knows how much time you've got left before you cop it?'

To his surprise, Schmidt did not go instantly red with anger this time but leant back in his seat with a smile. 'I daresay I would become accustomed to the lice, given time,' the lawyer drawled. Lex's voice was well suited to drawling. 'But even so, it will be really quite blissful to return to my own hygienic self after this—'

'I have no lice!' Lex snapped and then scowled, annoyed with himself for the slight lapse of control.

'Oh dear, have I touched a nerve, my boy?' the lawyer sneered.

Lex cursed inwardly. Hygiene was a thing with Lex. He hated . . . he *loathed* and detested being unclean, but sometimes it was necessary for the role and sailor boys were not known for their cleanliness.

'Khestrii is the province of the enchanters,' Lex said brusquely. 'And any Khestrian will be able to translate the runes for us. The bracelets came from there, we may be able to find someone who can get them off. The mantha beast you purchased is tethered outside. If we can buy a wagon from someone we can travel to the harbour in Gandylow and buy passage aboard one of the enchanters' magical boats. Well? What do you think?'

'I think you're crazy if you think you're going to find an enchanter willing to allow non-magical people on his boat,' Schmidt retorted.

'Well, we can sort the details out later. Don't worry, I'll get us there.'

They stopped talking as Jani arrived with their food. Lex stirred the soup with his spoon, enjoying the smell and watching in immense satisfaction as Schmidt picked angrily at the dry crust of bread he had been given. One spoonful told him that it tasted just as delicious as it smelt and he had been about to make a smug remark to Schmidt when the lawyer put a piece of stale bread in his mouth, there was a *shing* and suddenly it was Lex who was chewing on the dry piece of bread.

It was only then that Lex realised how stupid he'd been to only order a crust of bread for Schmidt, for now that he had his own body back he had nothing to eat. The thick, delicious, nourishing soup was on the table before Montgomery Schmidt and, by the attitude Lex had assumed as the lawyer, he would not now be able to order soup for himself without drawing attention. Very much aware of the suddenly smug expression on his employer's face, Lex tore the bread in half and ate it, trying his best to look like he was enjoying it.

Half an hour later, Lex locked himself in the little shower room where Jani had agreed to let him have a wash.

'Are you there?' he said softly.

'Yes, darling, indeed I am,' the Goddess of Luck said, appearing in the little room beside him.

Lex scowled at her. 'Well you've made a right cock up of this, haven't you?' he snapped. 'I thought you were going to help me get out of the city. Why didn't you stop that crone from dragging me into that tent?'

'She hardly dragged you, dear. You went in willingly. Anyway, I was the one who sent her to you in the first place.'

'You *what*? Why? Look where it's got me!'

He held up his wrist where the black obelisk bracelet gleamed in the light from the small window.

'It's exciting, isn't it? The Game has begun!'

'G-Game?' Lex repeated, his mouth dropping open as he gaped at her in delight. 'You don't mean . . . ?'

'Yes, Lex. One of *the* Games.'

Lex was so thrilled – so beside himself with excitement – that he actually hugged the Goddess. He just couldn't help himself. A Game! A Game at last! He had made a lot of money on them in the past but betting on them was hardly the same thing as actually *playing* in one! And he had longed to take part for such a long time.

'I can't believe it!' he beamed. 'When does it start, my Lady? When can we begin?'

The Goddess smiled. 'Well, I can see that I'm not going to have to threaten to turn *you* into a chessman.'

Playing in the Games held by the Gods brought fortune, fame and glory – if you were the winner. But it could also bring . . . well . . . danger, death and loss of limb. It could bring suffering, misery, discomfort and hardship. In short, if you were not a natural winner then the Games could be very unpleasant indeed. Many players were motivated by vanity and greed but others didn't think the chance of glory was worth the risk of painful death. More and more people had started refusing to play, which hadn't been much fun for the Gods at all. They couldn't force them because all players had to be willing. So they came up with the idea that potential players would have a choice – either they could agree to play the Game or they could choose instead to be turned into life-sized chessmen, which the Gods would then put on display in their own churches. No one could quite tell whether these chessmen had any degree of sentient awareness but the general consensus seemed to be that it was better to take your chances with the Game than to resign yourself to being turned into an inanimate lump of wood. So not many people got turned into chessmen nowadays, but most Gods had one or two pieces in their churches from the olden days when people had half thought the whole thing was a bluff. One thing it's always worth bearing in mind is that Gods very rarely bluff.

'How do the Swanns come into this?' Lex asked.

'What Swanns?'

'The Wishing Swanns of Desareth,' Lex replied, pulling the velvet pouch from his pocket. 'The enchanter gave them to me with the bracelet.'

'Oh, I don't know anything about any Swanns,' Lady Luck said with a touch of impatience. 'Perhaps the enchanter wanted to get rid of them for some reason, the silly man. I just sent you to him because I knew he had a Binding Bracelet for sale and we need one to secure you a companion for the Game.'

'Companion?' Lex repeated, pulling a face. 'I've never heard of that before.'

'Yes, it's new. From now on, all players must have companions.'

'But why?'

'It was felt that companionship and camaraderie would

add a little something for the spectators, dear. And . . . they'll also act as a backup in case the first player should become . . . indisposed. Not that you need to worry about that, Lex. I'm sure you'll do just fine. I fully expect you to win.'

'I *will* win,' Lex replied vehemently. 'But I don't want a companion. I don't need one.'

'It's compulsory, I'm afraid. You must have one. The two of you must eat every meal together, until the Game is over, otherwise you'll switch bodies. It's a companionship thing.'

'All right, but why Schmidt? If I must have a companion, why can't it be one of the raven-haired, doe-eyed variety—'

'Yes, I did think Schmidt was an odd choice. I rather thought you might go for that little gypsy girl but the lawyer was the first person you had direct skin to skin contact with and that's how the Binding Bracelets work so—'

'But nobody *told* me!' Lex wailed, thinking of Cara and mentally comparing her to Mr Schmidt.

'I am sorry, dear. I meant to let you know but it must have slipped my mind.'

Lex could have shaken her. Instead, he gritted his teeth and said, 'What do the runes say?'

'*So Begins The Game*,' she said, dropping her voice dramatically. 'Of course. It starts at Khestrii the day after tomorrow. Make sure you are there at the Black Tower by sunset. When you get there, everything will be explained and it will be announced to the stadiums. It will be glorious, Lex. You and I are going to win this by a long shot.'

CHAPTER SIX

THE SOULLESS WAKE

Lex decided not to say anything to Schmidt about the Game or anything else the Goddess had told him. After all, he didn't owe the lawyer anything. He hadn't *asked* him to come chasing after him across the sea to try and arrest him and drag him back to the Wither City.

Lex had talked Jani into letting them purchase a wagon she had stored in the courtyard. The mantha beast was tethered to it and was plodding along a country road out of the Farrows with the slow, consistent gait peculiar to its kind, seemingly oblivious to Gersha's cold winds whipping about them. Lex and Schmidt were sitting on the narrow wooden seat at the front, with some food and their bags stored in the back. It was not a particularly comfortable way of travelling, but it was certainly preferable to travelling on the mantha's back.

It was an odd thing because, in Lex's experience, no one was usually that upset in the aftermath of his crimes. After all, most of his thieving in the Wither City had been limited to large museums that would be insured anyway. He'd never managed to successfully steal anything from Schmidt himself or the partners of his precious firm, so why all the fuss? It surely couldn't stem only from dislike, for Lex was likeable. People *liked* him. He had an honest, open face, he could be charming and he was accomplished in the vital art of showmanship.

'What was it?' he asked, suddenly eager to know, raising his voice to be heard over the gales that whipped about them.

'What was what?' the lawyer snapped.

'What gave me away?' Lex asked. 'How did you know that I was a conniving thief rather than a hard-working sucker-of-a-student?'

When he was playing a part, Lex was always very, very careful not to give away just how clever he really was. He wanted to appear industrious and hardworking at the law firm, certainly, but not clever. Clever people were watched and accused and suspected and Lex had to be careful not to draw unwanted attention to himself. He had to appear incapable of hatching devious plots, let alone carrying them out. He had learnt, right at the start, that one of the most important things a fraudster should aim for was to be underestimated. If they were scorned and ridiculed as well then so much the better.

Before coming to the Wither City, when he'd still been travelling across the Globe, moving from place to place and scamming people blind, he had almost always chosen to play the part of a young man who was fabulously wealthy but at the same time extraordinarily dim, with a dash of rakishness thrown in as well. The trick was to make the merchant or the jeweller or the pawnbroker or whoever think that *they* were the ones scamming *him*.

One scam he often used was to buy a brooch – the cheapest he could find – and then dirty it up with some grime, put it in a velvet box and cover the whole thing with dust. Then he would put on his poshest clothes, his sulkiest, most superior expression and saunter into a jeweller's with the most arrogant manner he could summon up – which was not such a very difficult thing for Lex. And then came the fun part.

'Ai say!' he would whine as soon as he was in the door. 'Is someone going to attend to mey or am ai just to be left standing hereyah all day? Ai am not accustomed to being treated in such a mannah!'

'I beg your pardon, sir. How can I help?' the jeweller would ask, hackles raised already.

Lex would give him a haughty stare. 'Ai am Trent Lexington IV of the Galswick Lexingtons.' Of course, there was no such family but the jeweller would nod anyway and look suitably impressed. 'Ai've come to talk about a brooch that was recently discovahed in the attic at the country home, you know.'

'Very good, sir. Do you have the brooch with you today?'

'Yaas, naturally. Ai made the discovery maiself and ai would like to sell . . . ah, that is . . . ai have come to get it valued at the bequest of mey parents.'

The jeweller would smile knowingly, for most of them

had seen this sort of thing before – young Lords dissatisfied with their allowances coming in to try and fob off some of the family jewels, no doubt pinched straight from dear Mama's jewellery box itself – the sort of women who had so very many little trinkets that they wouldn't miss one here and there. But attic jewellery was the very best kind for no one was going to miss that and, being older, it was usually more valuable, too.

It was all in how the thing was presented. Of course, if Lex had walked in wearing second-hand clothes and talking like the country boy that he was then he would never in a million years have been able to pass some cheap bit of costume jewellery off as the real deal. But – between his own immaculate outfit and sneeringly aristocratic manner and the dust and grime of hundreds of years with which the brooch was covered – the jewellers believed him every time. To begin with. Of course, later on, under a more careful inspection, they would instantly discover the piece to be a fake. But at the time they would be so preoccupied with their greedy eagerness to scam the arrogant young toff that they would see in the velvet box only what they fully expected to see.

After a very, *very* great deal of practice, Lex was even able to blush on command. This turned out to be exceedingly useful as he had taken to carrying a pack of cards into the jewellers with him. At some point, he would reach into his pocket for something, and the cards would come tumbling out – apparently quite by accident – and one of the jewellers would hurry to help him pick them up and Lex would blush crimson and mutter a bad-natured word of thanks before snatching the incriminating cards back – the clear implication being that he was indulging in gambling, very probably without his parents' knowledge, that he was in over his head and that that was why he needed to sell the brooch in a hurry.

It was very important to make it as easy for the jewellers to believe the scam as possible and Lex had learnt that the little details were very important – and added a certain authenticity to the proceedings. He had therefore taken to spending as much time as possible in smoky bars or taverns whilst he was wearing the posh clothes so that they would smell of smoke when he went to the jewellers as if he had spent all night in a gamblers' den. Sometimes he even rubbed a tiny amount of alcohol around the collar for good measure. He found that jewellers would fall over themselves to short-change a gambling, smoking, drinking, arrogant young aristocrat – there appeared to be a sort of special satisfaction for them in it and the nastier Lex was, the more eager they would be to get him. They would offer a sum that was far less than the brooch would be worth if it were genuine, but actually far more than it was really worth seeing as the item was, in fact, quite as fake as Lex himself.

But the day he had made his deal with Lady Luck it had all gone a bit wrong because there happened to be a ruby expert in that morning who was promptly called over in order that Lex could be given a more accurate estimation of the brooch's worth. And, of course, it was immediately apparent that, wherever the brooch had come from, it had not come from any attic – stately home or otherwise.

'It's a fake,' the jeweller said flatly, looking accusingly at Lex.

'A fake?' Lex repeated shrilly, looking genuinely horrified. 'A fake, you say? Mey good man, that is quaite, quaite impossible. This brooch came from the attic at mey country house – ai found it thereyah meyself. Mey mother believes that it may once have belonged to her own great-great-grandmother Ethel, you know . . . ' But he could see that there was to be no bluffing and blustering his way out of this one. He could insist that it wasn't a fake until he was blue in the face but that seemed quite pointless considering the jeweller knew full well that it was not a genuine antique.

'I shall call for the police,' the man said, 'and report you for trying to defraud me.'

'Ah, come on now,' Lex said pleadingly, switching back to his ordinary voice. 'It's a fair cop – you haven't given me any money so there's no harm done. I promise I won't ever do it again; cross my heart.'

But all of Lex's feigned sincerity and reasonableness did nothing and soon he was racing from the town as fast as his legs would carry him – his top hat falling abandoned in the dust and the tails of his ridiculous frock coat flapping out behind him as he ran towards the church where he was to have his most fateful meeting with Lady Luck herself.

Aah – those were simpler days before Lex became so ambitious. Fobbing off fake brooches couldn't possibly compare to the skills he had trained himself in since coming to the Wither City. Everyone knew that he spent hours and hours at a time in his rooms studying and this was true – in a manner of speaking. But he had not been studying the law. With his practically photographic memory, he only needed to flick through the textbooks to get a grasp of the basics anyway. The majority of the time spent in his room had been practising on the ropes.

No one ever came into Lex's room for he insisted on doing all the cleaning himself, much to the landlady's pleased surprise. But, if anyone *had* gone in, they would have seen a most strange arrangement of ropes hanging from the ceiling. They were of different thicknesses and different materials and had several different types of safety harness attached to them. Lex spent hours and hours and hours practising on what he called the *Climbing Frame*. If you're going to fall, better to do so when you're only hanging four feet above the floor over a carefully-positioned mattress. For whilst it was true that Lex may have been lucky, he was also careful, and he certainly had no intention of lowering himself through any holes in great, cavernous ceilings before he'd practised climbing, spinning, lowering and twisting on his own precisely-constructed spider web. He wasn't doing anything for real until he could climb those ropes like a monkey. That sort of preparation was – he felt – what truly separated the men from the boys in this game. But he was vigilant that no one should ever suspect what really went on in his bedroom, to which end he had put about the story that he was a sap who studied all the time.

There had been one occasion, though, when he had been dangling from the middle of the ceiling in one of his safety harnesses when the landlady had started hammering on his door saying that she absolutely must speak to him about some triviality or other.

'Can't it wait, Mrs Humphrey?' Lex called, praying that she wouldn't notice that his voice was coming from nearer the ceiling than the floor.

'I'm afraid not, dear. I've got to talk to you about the new locks.'

Lex sighed. There was no use arguing with her. She wouldn't go away until he opened the door. He made to lower himself down to the ground on the rope. And that was when he found out that it wouldn't move an inch and, no matter how he tugged, he didn't seem to be able to go up or down. He was stuck – dangling there ridiculously like a fly caught in a web.

'Are you all right in there, dear?' the landlady called after a moment, pushing down on the door handle, which thankfully was securely locked.

'Yes! Just a minute!' Lex called, desperately unbuckling himself from the harness before doing a sort of half-leap through the air to catch the nearby rope and slither down to the floor by hand, landing lightly on the mattress.

He was a little out of breath by the time he opened

the door, which instantly made Mrs Humphrey suspicious.

'What have you been doing in there?' she said, trying to see over his shoulder.

But Lex stepped out into the corridor and closed the door behind him. 'I was . . . ' He quickly racked his brain for an excuse, then, once he'd found it, willed the colour to rush to his cheeks in a blush. 'Exercising,' he said. 'Weight lifting, actually. There's . . . this girl . . . and . . . ' He trailed off pathetically and looked morose.

Mrs Humphrey eyed his scrawny frame and instantly looked understanding and sympathetic, fully believing that Lex had been in there bodybuilding to impress some girl.

'There're more important things than muscles, dear,' she said kindly.

Of course, the truth of it was that Lex didn't actually have any interest whatsoever in having a neck that was thicker than his head. He may have been slender, but all that time going up and down the ropes like a monkey had given him a wiry strength as well as a certain agility. But he didn't mind Mrs Humphrey's comments. In fact he liked it when people underestimated him. It was only ever a help and never a hindrance to have people think that he was less than what he truly was.

In actual fact, Lex had very few of the vices that most teenage boys had. He stayed well away from drink and drugs and, indeed, was rather horrified just at the very thought of using them. For Lex liked to be sharp and quick – sharper and quicker than everyone else where possible – and intentionally dimming his mind and his wits was not something he was ever likely to do. Nor had he ever had much time for girls. They were something nice to look at when Heetha's sun was out and they were sunbathing, not wearing an awful lot; but he certainly didn't want to date. Growing up without a mother and no women in the house, the fairer sex was a bit of an enigma to Lex. He had the feeling that a girlfriend would probably spend most of her time complaining at him, whining at him, demanding that he spend all his free time with *her*, asking if she looked good in *this* dress or *that* dress when the truth was that he simply didn't *care* . . . But Mrs Humphrey wasn't to know all that, so when Lex told her he was working out to impress some girl, she believed him completely.

Lex's past experiences had taught him very well about playing a part and playing it faultlessly, even when no one was looking. He knew he hadn't faltered the whole time he'd been working at Lucas, Jones and Schmidt. He had kept up the charade, he had worn the mask and played the role, so what had Mr Montgomery Schmidt seen in his performance that had given him away? What hairline crack in the otherwise perfect jewel had his gimlet eyes picked up that no one else had been bright enough to spot?

'What was it?' Lex said again.

'Perhaps it was that time I caught you scamming the clients that tipped me off,' the lawyer said. 'Honest students do not skim a little off the top for their own usage, Mr Trent. So tell me, have you always been this way or did you fall in with a bad crowd, or have you just been consumed with greed all your life? What is it? What made you this way?'

Lex looked him right in the eye and said, 'My parents died when I was five.'

This was, in fact, perfectly true, but it was not what had made Lex the way he was. He had been born like this. Born for adventure and excitement and misbehaving, and he would probably have been exactly the same even if he hadn't been orphaned at a young age. Still, no sense in admitting that to the old lawyer. Lex could tell from the expression on Schmidt's face that he was struggling with himself, trying to work out whether Lex was even telling the truth, and if he was, whether dead parents constituted a valid excuse for theft, lies and fraud.

'You disliked me before that thing with the clients or you wouldn't have bothered checking on me to begin with,' Lex went on. 'Tell me, Mr Schmidt, what did I ever do to deserve such hostility?'

'Did you know about Mr Lucas's wife?' the lawyer said with sudden sharpness. 'You who knows everything about everything; did you know about her, Lex?'

'Of course. She's ill,' Lex replied promptly.

As an actor, he knew the value of playing to an audience. And he understood the importance of *knowing* that audience. It was crucial. So he always took in any information that any of his audience unwittingly gave out about themselves. Mr Lucas rarely said anything about his personal life, but Lex knew from what he'd heard other people saying that Mr Lucas's wife was in a bad way and that he was increasingly withdrawing from the time-consuming responsibilities of the law firm to care for her himself.

'Do you know what illness? Do you care?' Mr Schmidt asked, in that same unnaturally calm voice.

Lex shrugged. What did it matter? All old people became ill, sooner or later. It was the natural way of things—

'She has the soulless wake.'

The caustic remark that Lex had been preparing died in his throat. The soulless wake. Old people became ill and died. It was nature; it was inevitable; it was something that everyone accepted. Sooner or later, everyone died. No arguments there. But to die before death . . . that was surely cheating, wasn't it? The soulless wake was no illness. It was a curse from the Gods of the very worst kind. It could not be fought or beaten. It could only be endured.

The soulless wake caused people to forget their loved ones, forget life, forget *themselves*. It stripped them of everything they were inside. It was said to be the result of the Gods prematurely taking away a person's soul whilst they were still living, leaving nothing but an empty, wandering shell-of-a-person. This wasn't true, Lex knew. If it were, then you wouldn't be able to catch those occasional glimpses, those tiny little moments, of the person they had been before. But it was certainly true that the disease carried a stigma. For the condition was a rare one and it was said that the Gods would surely not curse anyone in such a way unless that person was immensely vile and despicable.

'You wouldn't think it to look at him, would you?' Schmidt said softly. 'The kind manner he has with the clients and . . . the interns.' He gave Lex an evil look. 'The way he left her to rush out of his home in the middle of the night to assist you and vouch for your character. You would never have guessed, Lex, would you?'

'Of course I knew about her condition,' Lex lied. 'As you rightly pointed out, I know everything about everything. A conman has to, you know. I didn't see how the issue could benefit me personally but I consigned it to the back of my mind, just in case.'

He almost *wanted* the lawyer to strike him. Mr Schmidt didn't raise a finger, although, if looks could kill, someone would have had to use a bucket and shovel to scrape Lex off the floor.

'You know, Lex, I think I'm going to go have a lie down in the wagon,' Schmidt said, with exaggerated courtesy. 'I'm not as young as I once was, after all, and you seem to be handling the mantha so expertly.'

Lex frowned as the lawyer swung his long legs round, pulled back the curtain and clambered into the warmth of the wagon. Lex caught a glimpse of the interior before the curtain fell back. There were blankets back there, piled up on flat wooden beds. Gods, it looked tempting! Lex hadn't slept properly since fleeing the Wither City. The gypsy ship had been moving too much on the restless waves and he had kept jerking awake.

Now that the lawyer had gone, Lex realised that he had been left outside to drive the mantha alone through Gertha's savage gales. It hadn't seemed so bad when they were plodding through the winding streets with tall, crooked buildings piled up on top of one another on each side of them to block the wind. But out here in the open, the gales were painfully chafing.

Lex pulled back the curtain of the wagon slightly and turned his head to yell inside, 'Pass me a blanket would you, Monty? It's a little chilly out here.'

'Here,' Mr Schmidt said, throwing out the thinnest, most moth-eaten blanket there was.

Really it was more a bit of rag than a blanket. Lex stared at the thing in disgust but let the curtain drop. He wasn't going to beg, if that was what the lawyer wanted. He would rather die before asking any favours of the man. Well . . . okay, perhaps not actually *die* but . . . well, he would rather be really quite uncomfortable, anyway.

Lex was a hoarder when it came to money, so he had quite happily stood by and let Schmidt purchase the wagon and the blankets. Now it didn't seem like such a good idea. He had no *right* to the blankets now and the lawyer had made it quite clear that he was not in a sharing mood.

'Selfish sod,' Lex muttered.

As is a common characteristic with the selfish, Lex simply couldn't stand selfishness in others. The mantha beast plodded solidly on as the sky began to dim to twilight and Lex tried not to think about the soulless wake. When they at last arrived on the outskirts of Gandylow, the boats were all moored in the docks for the night, so they took a couple of rooms at a boarding house with the idea of seeking passage on a ship in the morning.

They ignored each other over dinner and went to their separate rooms afterwards. As he fell asleep, Lex vowed not to think about the soulless wake any more, or the person he had left behind at the farm back home, and promised himself that all his energy would be put into playing the Game.

CHAPTER SEVEN

THE ENCHANTERS' BOATS

Lex's definition of a boat was something that travelled on water. The magical boats of the enchanters then, strictly speaking, were not in fact boats, for they hovered above the sea rather than floating on its surface. They were quite different from the gypsy ships. Being propelled by magic instead of wind they could sail against the currents. They could glide above the treacherous coral reefs. And they could keep right on travelling once they hit dry land if they wanted to.

When they reached the docks that morning Schmidt again voiced concerns as to whether they would be able to find an enchanter willing to take them. They rarely took passengers since they had no need for paying customers and it was unheard of for an enchanter to allow non-magical people on board his boat.

'You'd be amazed at the endless supply of luck I seem to have,' Lex had said with his most insolent smile.

Schmidt had simply shrugged his bony shoulders. 'Then

I will leave you to it, Mr Trent. You'll find out it's hopeless quickly enough.'

There were always enchanted boats at Gandylow as it was the nearest port to the Island of Algathon – the native land of the enchanters and their crones. Khestrii was situated on the western shore of the island and, although there were some humans living there, on the whole people preferred not to live so close to enchanters. There were five enchanted boats in the harbour that day – great, silver monstrosities with black runes painted across their metallic exteriors. Even the sails were thin sheets of metal, being there solely for decoration since the wind certainly didn't dictate the places these ships went.

Lex stood looking at the five great ships, wondering how best to go about stealing one. For Schmidt was quite right in saying that buying passage would be hopeless. There was no way an enchanter was simply going to *allow* them to come aboard his precious ship. It was strictly forbidden for any non-magical person to board the boats. Lex had always wanted to steal something from an enchanter. Some little trinket, just for the dangerous thrill of brushing so close to something so powerful. But this wasn't some little trinket. It was a huge, hulking monster of a ship and stealing it would not be so easy.

Lex eyed the staff of a nearby enchanter warily. It was as tall as the wizard himself, made out of twisted metal and set with a blue star-crystal at the top. The staffs were the centre of all the enchanters' powers and it was said that they could turn a man inside out if they

95

wanted to, just by pointing at him with their horrible sticks. Lex grinned as Schmidt caught sight of the enchanter and hurriedly turned away, pretending to inspect a shut-up stall to avoid having to look directly at the magician.

But Lex wasn't afraid and remained where he was. As divine luck would have it, his dilemma was solved for him, for whilst he stood musing over the problem of the boats, he happened to overhear the conversation that took place between the nearby enchanter and his crone.

'It will be your responsibility to guard the ship until I return,' the enchanter said.

Lex's ears pricked up at that. He eyed the old crone with dubious glee. She hardly looked capable of guarding anything. She was hunched over the usual pair of sticks, her gnarled old hands shaking on them slightly, and she was bent almost double under the weight of the slim grey cat that was draped languidly about her shoulders.

'I will be gone for seven days and nights. You will stay on the ship. Do not leave it for anything. Not for anything, you understand?' he snapped, leaning a little closer to the old woman. 'Do not fail me again, Bessa. If anyone inquires as to the ship's prolonged presence here, you may tell them that I will return shortly and that the boat is not to be touched by anybody until then, not even the maritime authorities. I won't have any non-magical people on board my ship.'

The crone nodded and grovelled to the wizard, assuring him all the while of her eternal and undying devotion.

Lex chuckled with glee. It really was too easy. The old woman would go over like a house of cards.

'What are you sniggering at?' Schmidt said sharply, without looking away from the stall.

Lex ignored him. Of course, the crones were often left behind to look after the ships. It wasn't as if anyone was actually going to try and *steal* them. Such an action would have been reckless beyond words. Lex watched the old crone hobble painfully up the gangplank back on board the huge, gleaming silver ship. It was not touching the water, even here in the harbour. It hovered unnaturally, just above the sea, secured by ropes to the docks, drifting ever so slightly in the force of the wind from the ocean.

'Voilà!' Lex exclaimed as soon as the enchanter had left for the town. 'And here we have our transportation, Mr Schmidt.'

'Where?' the lawyer asked, gazing round stupidly.

Lex pointed at the ship. 'There.'

'Don't be ridiculous. Didn't you hear that enchanter say he was going away for a week? I won't wait here for a week; I want to be off today so we can get this whole sorry mess over and done with. You'll have to go and bargain with one of the other enchanters.'

'Bargain? My dear Monty, who ever said anything about *bargaining*?'

Schmidt frowned at him. 'But you said you were going to get us passage on board one of the enchanters'—'

'They'll never take us!'

'Then how are you going to—?'

'I'm going to *pinch* it!' Lex declared gleefully.

He allowed himself a moment to take in the expression of utter horror on his employer's face and then ducked smoothly under his arm as the old lawyer made a grab for him. In another moment, he had fled lightly up the gangplank and was staring down over the side of the ship, grinning at Mr Schmidt.

'Get back down here,' the lawyer hissed.

Or something of that sort. He was too far away for Lex to be able to hear him but the body language was quite plain.

'Make me,' Lex laughed and then disappeared into the ship in search of the defenceless old crone.

The thrill at finally being on an enchanter's ship was immense. It was dangerous. Of course it was dangerous. The enchanter would be furious, *incensed* when he found out. But it was irresistible at times – that urge to plummet recklessly into something that all sane men would shrink from. And after a year of stealing nothing more thrilling than trinkets from museums, an enchanter's ship would be a fine prize indeed. What better way to begin the Game against the Gods?

Lex walked over to a door on the deck, trying to find a way into the ship. Schmidt would follow him. After all, he had no choice. If they didn't eat together then he would only find himself stranded in Lex's body anyway.

Lex opened the door and stopped dead. He was standing at the foot of an immensely long corridor. But he was not alone. There were hundreds and hundreds of other Lex's on either side of him, above him and below him, each looking as disoriented as he was. The hallway was entirely mirrored. The walls, the floor and the ceiling, reflected back at each other into infinity. Lex shuddered.

He was only allowed a moment of discomfort however, since the sounds of labouring coming from outside told him that his employer was making his way up the long gangplank and it was important that they got under way before the old lawyer tried to bodily drag him from the ship. Lex started to walk carefully down the corridor, both arms stretched out so that his fingers brushed against each wall in an attempt to keep himself oriented.

It reminded him of the fayre his grandfather, Alistair Trent, had taken him to when he'd been little. It had all been fun and games until he had scared himself by getting lost in the Maze of Mirrors. When he had at last caught sight of his grandfather, he had made a grateful dash towards him, not realising it was only his reflection he was chasing, and had crashed straight into a mirror, smacking his head and splitting his lip. He had started bawling then and his grandfather had had to buy him a big stick of blue candyfloss to shut him up. You don't run in mirror mazes, although many children, it seemed, were destined to find that out the hard way.

The mirrored walls were so flawless that it was only the feel of a hinge beneath his fingers that alerted Lex to the fact that there was a door. There was no doorknob or handle but when he pushed the mirrored glass, it swung open easily and silently into a room that, he noted with relief, was not lined with mirrors.

It was a tiny little white box-of-a-room because the walls, floors and ceiling were made entirely out of white marble. It was completely bare but for one basket in the corner, in which the old crone was hunched, her sticks leaning against the wall, the grey cat about her shoulders, staring into space.

'It's Bessa, isn't it?' Lex asked pleasantly.

At the sound of his voice, the crone flinched as if she had been struck and was on her feet at a speed that was remarkable for a woman so obviously crippled.

'Get *out!*' she shrieked, grabbing her sticks and hobbling out of the basket. '*Out!*'

'Don't be like that, Bessa,' Lex drawled. 'Wherever are your manners—?'

He broke off rather suddenly as she whacked him across the chest with one of her sticks. For such an infirm old lady, there was certainly a lot of force behind that stick. He grunted in surprise and staggered back into the mirrored hallway, wincing because she had struck the tender bruises he had acquired just three nights ago falling from the roof of the museum. He ducked sharply, barely missing the stick that whipped past his head, and then jumped back with equal speed to avoid a vicious blow from the second stick.

'I just want to talk!' he exclaimed, holding up his hands in what he hoped was a pacifying manner.

He had expected her to be upset, to shout even, but

this kind of viciousness was ridiculous. Who would have thought the old woman would be *armed*?

'Get off! Get off! Get off my master's ship you vile scourge!' She was virtually sobbing. Lex was forced to back away from her as she kept coming at him, both sticks flailing.

'Steady on,' he tried. 'You'll dislocate a hip or something if you're not careful.'

But she wasn't listening. She wasn't even speaking now, just shrieking at an earsplitting pitch. Lex turned and ran down the corridor back towards the door that led onto the deck. The dreadful wailing didn't stop and when Lex risked a glance back over his shoulder he saw that the old crone was coming after him at a high-speed hobble, her long skirts flapping around her crooked legs, her many amulets getting tangled up together and the grey cat still draped over her shoulders. Her face was contorted into an expression of pure anguish as she pursued him as fast as her crippled body would allow.

Lex had always had rather a cruel sense of humour and the sight of the old woman trying to run after him made him burst out into helpless laughter so that by the time he neared the end of the corridor he was bent almost double with it. What on earth did she think she'd be able to do if she caught him? Whatever made her think that giving chase would be a good idea when he was probably at least ten times stronger than her? The image so amused Lex that he found he could manage no more than a stagger himself even though he was aware that the horrible old witch was catching up with him.

He almost crashed into Schmidt as he appeared in the doorway. 'Get out of the way!' he shrieked through his laughter. 'She's going to *get* me!'

The lawyer backed away from the doorway in obvious alarm. Lex was blocking his view of the old woman but her insane wailing made it sound like some awful, banshee-like monster was giving chase.

Lex broke out into the fresh air of the silver deck and tried to stop laughing. When the wild old crone appeared in the doorway, Lex treated her to a mocking bow. 'I've had some high-speed chases in my time, Bessa, but yours was by far the most thrilling. I don't know when I've ever been more scared for my life.'

The crone glared at him, angry tears rolling down her withered cheeks. Schmidt stared at the old woman and then back at Lex. 'What in God's name did you do to her?' he snapped before turning back to the crone. 'I am sorry, ma'am, if this boy said anything to offend you. Please allow me to— urgh!'

The lawyer, who had been walking towards the old lady, broke off abruptly as one of her sticks clipped him across the side of the head.

'*Get off my master's ship!*' she screamed.

Lex dissolved into laughter once again at the delightful sight of his employer reeling back in alarm from the old lady with the decidedly deadly walking sticks. His laughter was short lived however, when she scuttled up to him and managed a well-aimed blow directly to the stomach. Lex bent over double, momentarily robbed of air, gasping for breath, his eyes watering. He was only saved from a second skull-shattering blow by Schmidt's fortuitously timely recovery as he succeeded in wrestling the sticks from the mad old woman, whereupon she promptly lost her balance and fell over onto the gleaming silver deck.

'Calm yourself, madam,' the lawyer exclaimed. 'No one is going to harm you. Are you all right, Lex?'

'What do you think?' Lex wheezed.

'Serves you right!' the old lawyer retorted.

Lex straightened up with an effort and took a step towards the sprawled crone. 'All we want is the boat, you mad old bat!' he snarled.

That last strike had evaporated Lex's previous good humour. Who would have thought one old woman could have given Lex Trent so much trouble? His temper flared angrily at the thought. 'How does the ship run?' he asked.

'Horrible boy! I'll never tell you! Never!' the crone wept. 'Bessa is a loyal servant to her master!'

Lex looked down as something brushed against his legs. It was the crone's grey cat. It must have fallen from her shoulders when she lost her balance. A thought occurred to Lex and a nasty smile tugged at his mouth. He picked up the animal and in a few strides he was at the edge of the ship, his arm outstretched over the side with the terrified cat dangling in his hand, so many feet above the ocean below.

The crone screamed in horror.

'How does it run?' Lex asked with an uncharacteristic maliciousness.

'Piewacket!' the old woman sobbed. 'Don't hurt him! Don't drop him! He fears the water! He cannot swim!'

'I won't be able to help it in a minute, the way he's thrashing around,' Lex said, struggling to maintain his grip on the frantic animal. 'For God's sake, just tell me how to get the ship moving!'

'That's enough, Lex!' Schmidt snapped. 'Put the cat down!'

'How does the ship work?' Lex asked again, staring at the crone.

'I will tell you. Only give Piewacket back to me and I will tell you!'

Lex slowly retracted his arm, bringing the cat back over the side of the boat. He had meant to maintain his grip on the animal but disgruntled cats are not so easy to keep hold of without being scratched to pieces and he dropped the creature instinctively as it succeeded in sinking its claws into his arm.

Lex cursed as it scampered back to the crone, jumping onto her humped back and draping itself round her shoulders once again, staring evilly at Lex with its ears flat against its ugly head.

'It's a magical key, down below,' the crone said. 'For all the good the knowledge will do you, nasty boy; my master has taken the key with him!'

'Show me.'

Mr Schmidt protested most vigorously as Lex forced the old crone before them, down the maze of mirrored hallways within the great ship. Lex had given her one of her sticks back but the other he had snatched from Schmidt and thrown into the sea. She was unable to attack them with just the one stick for she needed it to keep her balance. Schmidt had protested about that, too, but Lex had cut him off short with a bit of timely truth: 'We have to be in Khestrii by sunset tomorrow or else we'll be too late to reach the Black Tower. There's no way of getting there that fast without using magical means.'

'Black Tower? What's that got to do with anything? What are you babbling about?' the lawyer asked, staring at him suspiciously. 'I will not be made an accomplice in such reprehensible criminal activity!'

'If you don't come with me to Khestrii then you won't ever be free of the bracelets,' Lex said. 'You'll be stuck with me, Mr Schmidt, until the end of your days. However long that might be. Don't worry about stealing the ship,' he winked at him. 'I won't tell anybody you helped.'

He pushed the crone on down the corridor as she led them to the 'Bone Room', as she called it. It had been an enjoyable thing, watching Schmidt wrestle with himself over the problem. For Lex was right. Unless they stole this ship, right now, then they would not get to Khestrii for a very long time. It could take weeks – months, even. Mr Schmidt was a moral man. He was against crime. But he didn't want to be stuck with a body that was not his own, joined to a person that he loathed, saddled with the company of a selfish, contemptible fool for the rest of his life. And they had come this far already . . .

'We're not stealing it,' he said at last. 'We're just borrowing it.'

'It starts with all of us like that,' Lex said, grinning.

It was not long before they were both completely disoriented because of the cursed mirrors that were everywhere. Eventually the crone stopped and pushed open a mirrored door and they stepped into a cream-coloured room, made entirely of ivory. They must have ended up at the top of the ship for panoramic windows ran all the way round the circular room, showing the view of the sea stretching out before them to one side, the sprawling docks to the other.

The walls, the floor and the window seat running around the panoramic windows were all made from the same polished ivory. The large floor was bare but for an ivory basin stood on a pedestal in the centre of the room. When Lex walked over to it he saw that it held salt water.

'The master's key goes in there,' Bessa crowed. 'His magic bone is the key for the Bone Room that makes the ship fly. It is a magic bone, shaped like a fish. He took it with him. You cannot work the ship without it,' she finished triumphantly.

'Magic bone,' Lex muttered, fingering the Wishing Swanns through their pouch in his pocket and taking in the ivory room.

He turned with a smile to the crone. 'Tell me, Bessa, does it have to be a particular magic bone or will any one do?'

The crone stared at him suspiciously. 'You have no

magic bone, horrible boy. Only great enchanters have them, horrible liar!'

Lex laughed softly as he drew the velvet pouch out of his pocket and tipped the three beautiful Swanns out onto the palm of his hand. There was the black obelisk one and the one carved from deep red bloodstone. But it was the pale cream Swann made from ivory that he selected. He glanced at the trembling crone. 'As luck would have it,' he said with a grin, 'I happen to have a little magic bone of my own right here.'

He ignored the crone's little screech of alarm . . .

. . . and dropped the ivory Swann into the basin.

Dockhands and sailors ducked for cover as great wooden shards splintered in all directions. A great chunk of the harbour was ripped away by one of the enchanted boats suddenly soaring out over the sea, easily tearing free of the ropes that anchored it and taking half the harbour with it.

Wooden splinters crashed through the shut-up stalls of the midnight market and embedded themselves in the hulls of the other boats anchored in the harbour. Lex, Schmidt and Bessa were all thrown to the ivory floor with the vicious suddenness of the movement, water sloshing over from the basin in the centre and Bessa's one remaining cane skittering across the well-polished floor.

Lex recovered first, pulling himself up by one of the window seats and staring back at the chaotic harbour as the ship flew ever further away, not even touching the waves beneath them. He took in the damage that had been done by virtue of the great ship's strength and laughed delightedly. 'I hope we didn't impale anybody back there.'

Schmidt staggered to his feet and joined Lex at the window, gasping in horror at the damage that had been done.

'My God, Lex, don't you care anything for the safety of other people?'

Lex waved a hand dismissively. 'I'm sure no one was hurt,' he said, stepping over the sprawled crone to the basin and looking in at the Swann resting on the bottom.

After that sudden shock of movement the boat seemed remarkably calm considering the speed at which it was travelling. There was no rocking on the waves as there had been on the gypsy ship for this magical boat was hardly sailing at all; it was *flying* over the restless ocean, not even touching the water.

'How do you get it to stop?' Lex asked the crone.

But even as he spoke the words, the ship slowed rapidly until it had come to a complete halt, hovering over the waves, the harbour now some way behind them.

'Aha,' Lex said with a slow grin.

'It reads the mind of the key holder,' Bessa said miserably.

'What are you stopping for anyway? I thought you were all eager to be away?' Schmidt asked.

'Yes, but we don't want any unwanted passengers, Monty,' Lex said, smiling horribly at the old crone.

★ ★ ★

Half an hour later, Bessa was sat hunched up in her basket, which was floating on the surface of the ocean next to the great ship. They'd lowered her down over the side with ropes, having been forced to use the basket in the absence of any lifeboats.

'It seems to be floating well enough. What did I tell you?' Lex said to the lawyer.

Schmidt gazed back at him coldly. The old crone was still screaming for her bloody cat, which seemed to have disappeared into the ship somewhere.

'She'll be able to row back to shore all right with that, she's got an oar. And she has her cane. What more does she need?'

'You're the most selfish person I've ever met,' Schmidt said coldly. 'You really don't care about anyone at all, do you? She will be punished by her enchanter.'

'She'll be in more trouble if she stays with us. And, like you said, we are only borrowing the boat.'

'Yes,' Schmidt replied with a horrible smile. 'So I know you won't mind leaving her with a deposit. As you fully intend to bring the ship back.'

'Deposit? What dep—?'

Lex broke off in pure horror as the lawyer suddenly grabbed his bag which had been lying on the deck and threw it overboard where it landed with a splash next to the crone, who promptly pulled it into her basket, crowing with glee at the valuable nature of the things inside.

'How dare you!' Lex hissed, rounding angrily on the lawyer. 'How *dare* you! Do you know how *long* it took me to collect all those beautiful things? Do you know how *hard* I had to work to get them?'

'It hurts, doesn't it, Lex? Losing things that are important to you? Good, I'm glad you're upset.'

Discipline, Lex told himself. *He's baiting you. Don't rise to it . . . Don't rise to it . . .* After all, he still had his money belt – not that Schmidt needed to know anything about that . . .

'I'm not upset, Mr Schmidt,' Lex said with exaggerated politeness. 'Just a little concerned about how we're going to finance our journey now that you've given away all my valuables. After all, I have no money now and there will be travelling expenses and food expenses and things . . . but that's okay because you still have your wallet, don't you? I must say it's very sportsmanlike of you to agree to pay for all this out of your own pocket, Mr Schimdt,' Lex gloated, noting with relish the distinctly unhappy expression that was now on his employer's face.

'Didn't think it through, did you?' Lex asked, with sudden coldness. 'It takes practice, you know, swindling people. You really shouldn't try it unless you're absolutely sure it won't backfire on you.'

He glanced over the edge of the ship. 'You know, Monty, I have the sneaking suspicion that you might have overpaid her.'

The old crone was paddling for the shore as fast as her oar would take her, one arm still crooked around Lex's bag.

CHAPTER EIGHT

LEX AND LUCIUS TRENT

Mahara was a dead Goddess. She had died, they said, for love. For the love of a mortal man. She had given up her immortality for him. And now her abandoned sun was cold and useless, its light shedding no warmth so that it was unable to prevent the ice storms from sweeping in, blowing snow across the land and freezing the ocean solid. It was a problem for the gypsies and the fishermen, for their boats would become stuck on the frozen sea. But, to an enchanted boat, Mahara's sun was no obstacle. The ship flew over the solidifying ocean and sliced through the gales, the shards of ice shattering harmlessly against the steel prow where they would have punched straight through a wooden gypsy boat.

Lex and Schmidt had taken to using lengths of rope to guide themselves round the mirrored boat. They feared that, without something to guide them back to the bridge, they might become permanently lost within the vast, winding, reflecting corridors. Schmidt had warned Lex not to go poking around. The bridge seemed harmless enough, as had Bessa's little cabin, but who knew what might be lurking elsewhere within the ship?

Predictably, Lex had scoffed at the words of caution and set out to explore or – more accurately – to *loot the ship*. Who knew what manner of valuable, dangerous, beautiful things he might find on such a vessel? He was disappointed to discover that many of the rooms were similar to Bessa's cabin – nothing more than tiny little marble boxes. He did find a wardrobe, though, and amused himself there for a while, trying on the enchanter's tall, pointed hats. He also took some white fur coats to make the hard-surfaced bridge more comfortable. He found a bathroom too and the kitchen by following the grey cat, which seemed to appear from nowhere, watching Lex warily with narrowed, yellow eyes. The creature gave Lex the creeps and he was sorely tempted to drop the wretched thing overboard. But he had some vague notion that cats on ships were supposed to be good luck or something and it ran off when he tried to approach it, so he shrugged and left Piewacket to himself.

Schmidt had steadfastly refused to eat a thing that Lex had found on board in case the food was enchanted, preferring instead to eat what they had brought with them from Jani's Tavern. But Lex had sampled some of the pantry's supplies and found the food to be very good indeed. He had continued his systematic exploring of the ship until he had some idea of its layout. Any conman knows that it is important to have *escape routes* very firmly fixed in your mind in case the worst should happen.

Lex knew how to get out on deck and he knew how to escape into the bowels of the ship to hide if need be. But he had not been inside all of the rooms. His natural explorer's instinct had been somewhat curbed after opening an innocuous little door to find a rabid rabbit on the other side that almost roasted him with a blast of flame from its foaming mouth before lunging for his feet. The thing had chewed halfway through his boot before he managed to kick it off and slam the door shut. Lex had no idea what it was there for – it might have been a pet, a magical experiment gone wrong or the enchanter's breakfast for all he knew – but he marked the door with a big X to make sure he didn't go in there again and when Schmidt asked him where the scorch marks had come from, Lex told him that he had discovered a small dragon down below. It sounded better than rabid bunny rabbit.

But the incident made him wary of opening any closed door too readily. Furthermore, he had a sneaking suspicion that some of the rooms sometimes changed size. Or moved. He was almost sure that he had been near the bottom of the ship the first time he encountered the ferocious, fire-breathing rabbit and yet, the next day, he saw the same door on the top floor just outside the bridge, the X he had drawn on it still there, undisturbed.

Lex had since drawn X's on several of the doors just on the basis of the strange sounds he had heard coming out of them. There had been a decided *munching, crunching* kind of sound from one and from another Lex was sure he had heard the rustle and tap of some many-legged creature walking about on the mirrored floor. So, in spite of his initial bravado, Lex had decided, after all, that he would sleep on the bridge with the lawyer that night. He wasn't scared of the ship. Not at all. He just liked being able to see the sea going by and the only windows in the whole ship were on the bridge. The wall-to-wall mirrors everywhere else did not allow any portholes and that gave the ship a stifling, claustrophobic air, especially considering the ease with which one could get lost.

Bessa had said that the ship read the mind of the key holder and so Lex had assumed that it was heading for Khestrii. His hope was confirmed when they began to catch sight of other enchanted boats the next day, heading in the same direction as them. The boats never strayed too close to each other and Lex could only assume that they could somehow sense each other and keep on separate courses.

They arrived at the great metal harbour an hour before sunset. Lex had worried about this moment. Khestrii was the home of the enchanters and it would never do for them to see Lex and Schmidt getting off the ship – they would immediately suspect foul play for no enchanter would willingly allow his ship to be used by non-magical people. As it was, the ice storms let in by Mahara's sun had driven the enchanters away from the harbour and, as they had no midnight markets here, the port was deserted. Besides which, the white fur coats that Lex had found effectively shielded them from any suspicious glances and, with the hoods pulled up over their heads, it was not obvious that they were not enchanters anyway. The only thing that gave them away was their height. Lex in particular was not tall enough for the coat and the end of it dragged in the snow in a most irritating way. He would just have to hope that if anyone did notice this they would assume that he was a lucky crone with a kind master who had graciously allowed her to wear one of the coats, although that in itself was unlikely.

But although the ice storms worked in their favour in emptying the harbour, they did not make it very easy to disembark the boat. Their rather brutal departure from the docks at Gandylow had broken off the gangplank, so the only way to disembark the ship was to have it hover just over the docks and then climb down the ladder that ran down the side.

Lex was agile and quick and had little trouble in making his way to the bottom of the frozen ladder. Schmidt, however, did not find it so painless. The ship was immensely tall and the ladder was at least five storeys high. Then there was the fact that the rungs were frozen solid, and cold metal, as Lex had found out when he tried to lick the ice from a frozen pole as a child, was painful to the touch and stuck to the skin if you weren't careful.

It took the lawyer an age to descend the ladder and his hands were trembling by the time he stepped onto the harbour, both with the cold and with the strain of having to navigate a frozen ladder down the side of a giant ship in the midst of an ice storm. He hadn't complained, hadn't voiced his fears at any time but, now that he was standing on the harbour, the sight of his trembling hands irritated Lex, reminding him of another old man and reawakening that terrible fear of being *old* and unable to control your body . . . or your tongue . . .

'You took your time!' Lex snapped. 'We're going to be late!'

Old age . . . Lex was never growing old. He had made that promise to himself a long time ago, after he had seen what the years could do to a person . . . what they could take away from you. No – one way or another, Lex fully intended to leave this life before any such thing could happen to him. Notoriety was something to be worked towards when you fully intended to end your days in the hangman's gallows.

'Late for what?' the old lawyer said, glaring at him.

'We need to be at Mahara's Tower before nightfall,' Lex replied.

'Why?' Schmidt said, narrowing his eyes suspiciously.

'Because that's when they're going to announce the Game,' Lex smirked.

He would have liked to be able to linger more over this delicious revelation, relishing Schmidt's horror, but time prevented it. Still, to his immense satisfaction, Schmidt looked like someone had just kicked him in the gut. '*Game?*' he croaked.

'We've been chosen, sir,' Lex said with his sweetest

smile. 'By Lady Luck herself. Come on, we need to get moving.' And he turned away and strode off.

Although Lex had never been to Khestrii before, he was familiar with the Black Tower of which Lady Luck had spoken, for it was a famous landmark on the Globe. It was said to have been created by Thaddeus, God of Illusion and the enchanters' patron deity, for his poor sister Mahara after she declined immortality for the sake of her human lover. The couple had been rejected by Gods and humans alike for their sacrilegious union and had lived together in isolation in the tower Thaddeus had built for them – some said out of compassion and some said out of spite – a prison or a haven? At any rate, upon the eventual death of the couple, Thaddeus had sealed the tower and no one had been inside since.

Even through the ice storm and the dimming light from the rapidly-setting sun, Lex could see it. Ice and frost had turned the tower's tip white; icy fingers reaching halfway down its length before relinquishing their hold back to the black marble. Lex hardly noticed the buildings and streets as he strode towards the tower. The sun had almost set and they could not be late. There might be a penalty or something if they were.

When he at last reached the towering turret, Schmidt wheezing along behind him, Lex was a little concerned that her Ladyship was not there to meet him. The Black Tower stood upon a huge, perfect circle of ice, with a black marble path leading straight to the door set at its base. Instinctively feeling that this was what he must do, Lex made his way across the black path, slipping and sliding where the marble had frozen over. Schmidt did not follow him, perhaps uncertain of his legs on such a treacherous surface, but stood watching at the edge of the ice circle. As Mahara's dead sun disappeared over the edge of the horizon, Lex lifted the golden knocker and slammed it hard into the black marble door. The echoes rang back to them across the surface of the ice before they were plucked from the ground by the Gods and taken to the top room of Mahara's Black Tower.

Lex stared round in wonder, still buzzing with the exciting alien sensation of having been transported in such a way. In contrast to the tower's exterior, the interior was made entirely of white marble. The Goddess of Luck looked most appropriate there in her white dress; her mass of blond hair piled up on top of her head, threaded with pearls.

The top of the tower was an unusual shape, being formed of three circles placed in a triangle so that the outer walls were curved and there was a triangular space in the centre, about ten feet across, beneath which there was no floor and you could see all the way down to the centre of the ice circle over two hundred feet below. The strangely curved walls around them reached above their heads to form a perfect point, confirming Lex's impression that they were at the very top of the tower. And suspended directly above them was a large crystal ball, rather like a smaller version of the ones Lex had seen in the gaming stadiums.

'Well done, Lex. I thought you weren't going to make it in time for a minute there.'

'By the skin of my teeth, as usual, my Lady,' Lex said, bowing graciously.

'*L-Lex?*' came a voice from behind them. 'Is that you?'

Lex froze at the sound of the familiar voice. He, Schmidt and the Goddess of Luck were standing in one of the three white circles. Others stood in the remaining two, although Lex had not yet had time to take them all in. But he knew that voice instantly, even though it had been more than a year since he'd heard it, for it was an exact copy of his own. Slowly, he turned round to face his twin brother.

'Hello, Lucius.'

Not a flicker of surprise or displeasure crossed Lex's face although, at that moment, he felt both in equal measure. Lucius Trent stared at him across the length of the circular chamber and said nothing. He looked pale and a little sickly. Lex had always been the healthier of the two. Lucius's brownish-blond hair was longer than Lex's, reaching down almost to his chin and curling slightly at the ends. Even though Lex had only been with his brother for all of thirty seconds, he could already feel his lip curling in that old expression of contempt. He stifled the impulse quickly. He was disciplined now – he did not let his emotions show on his face any more . . . It was just that Lucius was so *wet*. In every sense of the word.

So much so that Lex had often found it insulting that they shared the same genetic makeup.

It would have been nice to say that Lex and Lucius had got on once. That the things that happened later were what drove the two of them apart. It would have been nice to say it, but it would have been untrue. Lex and Lucius may have been identical twins, but they were at opposite ends of the personality scale. And that was why they did not get on – and nor had they ever.

'What are you *doing* here?' Lucius asked, looking miserable.

'Getting ready to play the Game,' Lex replied with an easy shrug. 'Or should I say, getting ready to *win* it? What are you doing here?'

'I was—'

'Shut up, Trents. I'm going to announce the Game, now.'

Lex looked at the speaker, who was standing beside Lucius, and his mouth fell open in shock, for it was Jezra – the God of Wit and Daring! Lex had, of course, seen him in paintings and statues, and he had glimpsed him from afar once in the Gods' box at one of the stadiums, but he'd never seen him up close in real life before. His straight blond hair was shoulder length and he had a rather hawkish nose and very intelligent blue eyes set beneath fair eyebrows. He was wearing his customary pale blue high-necked jacket and stood with a kind of gangly grace. Although he was not good looking – for his nose was too long and his eyes too sharp – he *was* clever. He was conniving and scheming and shrewd and devious. He was, in fact, everything that Lex had ever tried to be. And to see him standing beside his useless brother put a bad taste in Lex's mouth beyond all description.

At Jezra's words, everyone quickly dropped to one knee. Lex distinctly heard Schmidt's knee click painfully as he knelt down stiffly. The Gods, in the main, were happy to leave people to themselves much of the time. But when they did appear – at the Games, at ceremonies or on special days of celebration – they did expect to be treated as deities and were not above throwing the odd lightning bolt to emphasise the importance of respect if need be.

'As the current Gaming champion, it is my right to commence this Game and pick the first round.'

As Jezra spoke, his image appeared inside the huge crystal ball suspended above them and Lex knew that it was being broadcast to all the other crystal balls in the stadiums in all the major cities throughout the Globe, including the Wither City. The stadiums tended to be informed of an imminent Game announcement at very short notice – sometimes half an hour or less.

The last time there had been one, Lex had been on his way to work when excited people had started running to the stadiums, pushing and shoving in their eagerness to get there and not miss the start. Lex had longed to go with them and, indeed, had been sorely tempted for some moments to ditch work. But then he had realised that a lot of the younger clerks would be doing just that. If Lex dutifully turned up to the office on a day when many of the staff were skiving off, it could only make him look good. So he had dragged his feet to the dry old law firm, pasted the usual enthusiastic smile on his face and tried to look like he was enjoying sitting at the reception desk when everyone knew full well that there would be no clients that day. He had sat there and thought longingly of the hustle and bustle of the stadiums, the buttery smell of freshly roasted popcorn, the shouts of bookies and the replies of gamblers . . .

He had no worries about getting a front-row seat this time, he thought with a surge of triumph. There was to be no mere observing with the other spectators, this time he was to be an actual player himself! As Jezra went on, Lex had to resist the urge to stuff his fist into his mouth so that he wouldn't shriek with glee.

'I, Jezra, God of Wit and Daring, and the current Gaming champion, hereby commence this Game between we three deities: the Judge, God of Emptiness, shall be using as his player the prophet known as Alistari.'

Lex glanced at the opposite circle and saw the black-robed prophet standing beside the feared, nameless God known only as the Judge. A tall, imposing figure – he was dressed in grey, golden-edged robes and he wore a golden mask shaped with a human's features. Of all the Gods, the Judge was the only one who refused to show his true face in the Lands Above. No one knew whether he took the mask off in the Lands Beneath, but one thing they did know was that even the other Gods seemed to be a little afraid of him. It was said that his face must be so hideous, so grotesque, so monstrous, that he didn't want humans to see it. But in some ways that expressionless golden mask was even more terrifying. The gold lips did not move when the Judge spoke, and there was only the thinnest slit for the eyes to look out of. You couldn't see them. Not unless you really stared, in which case you might have caught a faint glimpse of . . . something . . . behind that mask . . . But no one wanted to look the Judge in the face too closely for fear of what they might see.

Stood beside the Judge in the circle was a black-robed, black-masked prophet, covered in black from his boots to the ends of his gloves and the hood drawn up over his face. The only parts of him that were visible were the blind whites of his eyes, staring out blankly from behind his mask, and the thin lines of his lips. Prophets always wore a lot of black, possibly because they didn't like people looking at them when, being blind, they couldn't look back.

All blind people became prophets eventually, for their lack of sight was compensated by the advanced sense of precognition that allowed them to see where they would be a few seconds from now, almost like a bat sending back echoes to itself. Prophets were also dumb – their tongues were cut out at birth to stop them from blabbing all the secrets they knew about the future. For it is a well-known fact that children are incapable of keeping secrets, and ones like that can do a lot of damage. The prophets were then shipped off to an isolated town in the desert inhabited only by other prophets for it was felt that they belonged with their own kind. Technically there was nothing to stop the prophets from leaving once they grew up, but very few ever did. They disliked the ordinary human population – perhaps it had something to do with the whole cutting-out-the-tongues business. At any rate, they mostly kept themselves to themselves.

At Jezra's mention of his name, the prophet bowed stiffly. Lex could practically hear the thunderous applause from the stadiums even though the nearest one was many miles away.

'I, Jezra, God of Wit and Daring, shall be using the farm boy, Lucius Trent,' Jezra went on.

Lex felt almost sick with envy. Of all the Gods, Jezra was the one that Lex had always admired the most – the one whose church he had been a member of before Lady Luck bribed him into hers. Jezra was the God of Wit and Adventure and Daring and Recklessness and yet he had chosen Lucius – *Lucius* – Lex's vapid, spineless, gutless, *wet*, perpetually placid brother as his playing piece! Why? Why, why, *why*?

At the mention of his name, Lucius glanced up from his kneeling position, saw his own frightened image staring back at him from the crystal ball and hurriedly ducked his head once again to stare in petrified fear at the floor. No thunderous applause for him, Lex thought with a gleam of satisfaction. Spectators could spot a loser a mile away.

'And Lady Luck, Goddess of Fortune shall be using the thief, Lex Trent.'

Lex leapt to his feet and bowed with a flourish. He had the look of a winner, he thought with satisfaction when he straightened up and saw his image inside the crystal ball. All right, he was small and a bit on the thin side, but he was determined – surely anyone could see that just by looking at his face! He was probably the favourite to win already! He dropped back down on to one knee as Jezra continued, 'The first round of the Game, then, shall be Sky Castles.' He glanced round at the players and added with rather a smirk, 'Players be aware that there are no rules and that we will do all we can to prevent you from reaching your goal. Your lives may depend on how capable your Gods and Goddesses are.'

Lex glanced doubtfully at his own dim-witted Goddess. Would flighty, unreliable Luck really be able to triumph over Jezra's sharp intellect or the Judge's cold determination? You'd have to be very lucky indeed to triumph against such opponents. But Lex had always been lucky, even before the Lady came along. And, more than that, he was a winner. He didn't play games to come second place. In fact, the words 'second place' didn't even register with Lex's inner vocabulary. Why play a game if you didn't fully intend to win it?

'The round commences at sunrise tomorrow,' Jezra said.

And with that the crystal ball in the centre went blank, and the announcement was concluded. The Judge disappeared from the tower without a word, taking his prophet with him. Lex and Lady Luck were left alone with Jezra and Lucius.

'Well, well, well,' Jezra said, eyeing Lex up and down. 'If it isn't the famous thief himself.'

'It is an honour and a privilege, my Lord,' Lex replied, bowing deeply.

'You seem to bear more than a passing resemblance to my own insipid player,' the God of Wit remarked with a slight sneer in Lucius's direction.

'Only on the outside, my Lord Jezra, I assure you,' Lex said quickly.

'You really should have seen it coming, Jezra,' the Goddess of Luck smirked. 'Now you've gone and crippled yourself from the start.'

'I am familiar with your work, Mr Trent,' Jezra said, ignoring her. 'I am, in fact, something of an admirer of yours and I'm aware that you were once a follower of mine. It will therefore give me no pleasure to destroy you in the course of the Game. But I do not intend to relinquish my place as Master Gamesman simply because I have been lumbered with this incompetent country hick.'

He slapped his hand across the back of Lucius's head carelessly as he spoke and Lex saw, to his immense satisfaction, the expression on his twin's face become even more resignedly miserable.

'Until tomorrow then, my Lady,' Jezra said, nodding at Lex's benefactress.

She returned the pleasantry and the two deities disappeared from the castle, depositing their players outside in the snow at ground level once again.

'All right, how did you do it?' Lex asked irritably. 'How the hell did you get Jezra to pick *you*?'

'This is your fault, Lex, you idiot! Your Goddess tricked him! Jezra thought I was you! That's why he picked me!'

'Seriously?' Lex asked, feeling pleasantly flattered. 'Oh. Well that's all right then. For a minute there I thought I might have horribly underestimated you all these years. But where are my manners? Monty, this is my dear brother, Lucius. He was born two minutes before me and therefore believes himself to be superior in every way. And Lucius, this is my employer, Montgomery Schmidt, one of the few people in the Wither City who I never actually cheated or stole anything from, but he only seems to hate me all the more for that.'

Lucius winced at Lex's words but he politely held out his hand anyway. 'I'm very pleased to meet you, Mr Schmidt,' he said.

Lex pulled a face inside his head. *Wet!* It really was the only word. Schmidt hesitated a moment before shaking hands with Lucius, perhaps instinctively wary of anyone who bore such a close blood tie to someone as reprehensible as Lex Trent.

'I'm so sorry for any displeasure or expense my brother might have caused you, sir—'

'Don't apologise for me!' Lex snapped.

By the minute he was remembering more and more things he disliked about his brother. He took a breath to reassert his control. How irritating these little lapses were. He smiled brightly.

'You're being extremely rude, Lucius. Have you not noticed how cold it is out here?'

'Of course I have. It's Mahara's sun.'

'And have you not also noticed how frail and elderly my employer here is? You are keeping him outside in the cold with your bland chit-chat.'

Lucius glanced miserably at Schmidt, wondering whether he should apologise or not.

Taking pity on him, Mr Schmidt said, 'You have my sympathy. At least *I* am not related to him.' And he turned and strode away in the direction of the ship.

'So you *are* a thief,' Lucius said. 'What they said about you in there was true.'

'Yes, all true,' Lex agreed cheerfully, before catching sight of the white binding bracelet on his brother's wrist. 'Where's your companion then?'

'He's at the inn. Jezra said he didn't need to come for this.'

'Anyone I know?'

'It's Zachary.'

'I told you to fire him!'

'You have no say over anything that happens on the farm any more!'

'Nor do I want any. I only said it for your own good, but you never did listen to me. Anyway, I don't have time to stand here jabbering with you.'

He made to walk away but Lucius grabbed his arm.

'Aren't you even going to *ask*?' he said, incredulity and disgust battling for first place on his face. 'Aren't you even going to *ask* about him?'

'Why should I? Nothing you're possibly going to say will please me,' Lex replied, shaking off Lucius's hand.

'Yes. Well that's it, isn't it? You only ever want to hear things that are going to please you. Life's not like that, Lex.'

'Mine is. Now that I don't have any attachments.'

'He died last summer. You left him to die on his own.'

'You were there.'

'I wasn't the grandson he wanted and you know it. He might have been ill but he could still tell us apart.'

'Oh, don't talk rubbish! He didn't know who *he* was, let alone who we were.'

'You're wrong. I had to have locks put on his bedroom windows because he kept climbing out of them in the middle of the night to go and look for you.'

'You're making it up!' Lex snarled.

'How could you leave like that, without even saying goodbye to us? We didn't know where you'd gone or what you were doing and then all these stories started coming in about you being a thief and a criminal—'

'I'm going to win this Game and I won't cut you any slack just because you're my brother, so I'd watch my back if I were you!'

And Lex turned and stalked away, glad to be leaving Lucius behind. What bad luck that he should be involved in the Game, too. It could have been such fun without him. But it would be fun anyway, Lex promised himself. He was not about to let Lucius ruin anything for him. And he was most certainly not going to be made to feel guilty.

CHAPTER NINE

THE SKY CASTLE

'Eat your breakfast!' Schmidt snapped irritably, thrusting a stale end of bread towards Lex.

'I'm not hungry,' Lex said, brushing the bread aside. 'Worry about your own breakfast.'

He had never been able to eat before stealing, either. It wasn't nerves so much as a heightened sense of antic-ipated exhilaration.

'I'm not concerned about your health, you stupid boy, I simply don't want to experience another hideously distasteful body swap.'

'Oh.' Lex was annoyed with himself for forgetting.

'Eat your bread,' the lawyer repeated, throwing over the pathetic crust.

Lex caught it and sat down on the white furs, feeling disgruntled. It was not even light outside yet. They had to be prepared for the dawn when the first round of this gloriously divine Game would begin.

'So how does this work, anyway?' Schmidt asked from

where he was sat across the bridge, picking at his own slice of bread.

'What?'

'This Goddess thing. The Goddess of Luck clearly favours you. That's how you're able to behave so disgracefully and get away with it.'

'Spare me,' Lex sneered.

'So how far does it go?' Schmidt continued. 'I would have thought that even the most gutless, useless person could win a Game if they were lucky enough.'

'Well, yes, but you must remember that her Ladyship's brain is so much smaller than the other deities we are playing against.'

Jezra and the Judge, probably two of the most dangerous opponents possible. *Dangerous* . . . Lex's pulse quickened with pleasure just at the thought of it.

'Luck will take us so far,' he went on, 'but a chopped-off head is still a chopped-off head however lucky you might be, and her Ladyship is not always the most reliable—'

He broke off as the ship suddenly began to rise, leaving the now unfrozen sea behind as it shot up into the sky.

'What are you doing?' Schmidt demanded.

'I'm not doing it!' Lex replied.

In a matter of moments they had burst through the clouds into the streaming sunlight above. Lex jumped to his feet and strode to the window. There was a huge castle looming before them, anchored to a cloud and made – entirely – out of sand.

'It's a sandcastle!' Lex exclaimed.

He turned from the window, ignoring whatever questions Schmidt was firing at him, and ran out onto the deck to get a better view. As soon as he opened the mirrored door, the heat hit him with all the force of a decidedly physical thing.

'Heetha's sun,' he croaked.

'I'm afraid so, dear,' Lady Luck said from where she was standing at the railings. 'It's the most devilish bad luck. The sun is bad enough on the ground but at this height it could be quite dangerous. You are going to have to be careful.'

'Well, all the players will be affected just the same by it,' Lex said, joining her at the rails.

He had never experienced this kind of heat before. It felt like he was inside an oven and it was quickly becoming unbearable.

'Yes, dear, but I'm afraid that horrible little lawyer is rather going to disadvantage you.'

'What do you mean?'

'Your brother has Zachary, who is merely middle aged and healthier than Lucius is himself. The Judge's player has Theba, who I understand is a gangster of some kind but you have an *old man*. Old men struggle more with the heat, you know. I do hope he is going to be able to keep up. I do not intend to lose this Game, Lex.'

It was the first time that Lex had ever heard anything of menace in her Ladyship's voice. 'He'll keep up,' he said. 'Don't worry about that. So what is this, anyway?'

Lex asked, motioning at the huge sky castle looming before them.

'Wait for the others,' the Goddess said. 'Jezra and the Judge are coming here. We're the first to arrive. There's your brother now.'

Lex looked to where the Goddess was pointing and didn't bother to stifle the sneer.

'What is he *doing*?'

'He's trying to land that thing on your ship, I think,' Lady Luck said happily. 'This should be most entertaining to watch, Lex.'

Lex grinned as his brother tried to manoeuvre the drayfus onto the deck of the enchanter's ship. Drayfii looked like shaggy hippos with wings. They were extremely placid and obedient creatures. That was what made them good for farm work. And this one had probably been born and bred on the Trent farm. It did not understand sky castles and enchanted ships and it was clearly scared out of its wits. Lucius was trying to get it to fly towards the great silver ship but the creature was obviously unsure which was worse – the ship or the giant castle – and was hovering uncertainly between them, rolling its eyes in fright.

'They might drop altogether in a minute,' her Ladyship said smugly.

Drayfii were not used to long flights, especially with so much weight on their backs and in the glare of such a ferocious sun. Lex turned slightly as the door behind them opened and Schmidt stepped out, gasping at the force of the heat. He managed a stiff bow when he saw the Goddess on the deck and then exclaimed in horror when he joined them at the railings and saw the struggling drayfus. Its long shaggy fur must have been making the beast overwhelmingly hot and it certainly seemed likely that it would drop out of the sky at any moment now.

'Can't you do something, my Lady?' Schmidt asked. 'They're going to plunge to their deaths in a minute.'

But just as the beast stopped beating its wings, the most extraordinarily strong gust of wind threw the drayfus and its passengers over the side of the enchanted ship. The animal collapsed in a steaming, wheezing heap and the two people were thrown from its back.

'Now wasn't that a fortunate thing?' the Lady murmured, disappointed. 'That was cheating, Jezra.'

Schmidt hurried over at once to where Lucius was lying curled on the metal deck. 'Are you all right?' he asked, grabbing him by the elbow and pulling him to his feet. There was a nasty burn across Lucius's cheek, down one of his forearms and across the palm of one hand where his skin had made contact with the scorching surface of the steel ship.

'I'm okay. It's just . . . these burns,' Lucius whimpered, searching round in vain for something cold to press against his blistering skin.

'Go find him some ice or something, Lex,' Schmidt ordered.

'Ice?' Lex repeated incredulously, gazing around at the

heat haze and the towering sandcastle. 'What do you think I am, a magician?'

'You've explored the ship. There must be something cold in there. At least get them both some water. The heat out here is—'

'I'm not going to risk missing the beginning of the round,' Lex said firmly.

'I don't think you've quite got the hang of this Gaming business, lawyer,' the Lady said, gazing at him coldly. 'These two are the *opposition*. Any misfortune of theirs is beneficial to us.'

Schmidt hesitated, acutely aware of the importance of not angering the Gods. 'Forgive me, my Lady, but I merely meant to say that—'

'Morning, friends. What glorious weather with which to begin our little frolic,' Jezra said breezily, striding across the deck. Lex had not even noticed him arrive. He was dressed in the usual high-necked blue jacket. Like the Lady, he did not ever seem to wear different clothes. In fact, the Gods always looked the same when they took human form. It was also clear that they did not feel the sun as the others did. Jezra was wearing a lot of clothing, but he was not sweating and his long blond hair was dry and hardly moved in the heat haze.

'Here – you look like you could use a drink,' he said, reaching out to Lucius with a hand that was suddenly holding a tall glass of lemonade. It looked good. Lex could see the ice piled up inside. There was even a paper umbrella.

'I'd offer you one, Lex, but you know how these Games are.'

Lex nodded, feeling embarrassed at the spectacle Lucius was making of himself as he pressed the cold glass to the burns on his face and arm, spilling some of the drink in the process. Of course, the lemon in it only agitated the burns even more.

'What about me, your Lordship?' Lucius's companion asked.

He was a large, brawny man, in his forties with hair that was starting to grey. Zachary did not look like an arrogant bastard. But Lex knew that he was one.

'You're of no importance to me,' the God replied.

'What's he here for, anyway?' Lex asked. He couldn't stop the sneer this time, for all his new-found discipline.

'In case this one dies,' Jezra replied, motioning to Lucius with his thumb. 'That's what the companions are for; didn't you know?'

Lex rolled his eyes and said, 'Of course I know!' He had, after all, had the whole thing explained to him by his Goddess. But he suspected Schmidt hadn't known for he noticed out of the corner of his eye that the lawyer was looking distinctly uncomfortable at the revelation. 'I meant what is he doing *here*? I don't want him on my ship.'

'*Your* ship?' Jezra repeated with a soft laugh. 'My, my, that's a little presumptuous, isn't it?'

'Don't be so rude, Lex!' Lucius said.

'Oh, go to hell!' Lex snapped. Then he cursed himself

for the lapse of control. There was just something about his brother that was forever rubbing him up the wrong way. And of course, the fact that they were twins was an insult that he was sure he would never quite overcome.

'The Judge will be here shortly,' Jezra said. 'And then the first round will commence and you're welcome to try and gut each other like fish, if you like. But until then I'm afraid we all have to be civilised for just a little longer. Just out of curiosity, Lex, how *did* you manage to get this ship?'

'Wouldn't you love to know, Jezra?' Lady Luck said before Lex could answer.

'I don't pretend not to be impressed, my Lady, but you must be aware that there will be trouble to pay later. Still it will make the Game more interesting, I suppose.'

Lex turned at the sound of a door closing and realised that his employer was no longer on the deck.

'Where's Schmidt?' he asked.

'I think the heat might be getting to him,' Jezra said, smirking at the Goddess. 'It looks like the scales may yet be balanced after all, your Ladyship. How careless of you not to explain to Trent how the Binding Bracelets worked.'

'It wasn't careless, Jezra. The companion backup is merely a technicality in Lex's case, so it hardly matters who he brought. Not only will he *live through* the Game but he'll come through it with barely a scratch on him. You know that he's a natural, or else you would not have let me trick you so easily into choosing his useless brother.'

Lex felt an immense swell of pride at that. The Gods

were *bickering* over him. After a moment, Jezra gave an almost imperceptible nod. 'Yes, well, we shall see.'

The swishing, leathery sound alerted them to the prophet's arrival. Lex looked up and saw a giant desert bat wheeling overhead. They were huge things, with a wingspan of over twenty feet, impervious to the heat, completely blind and yet able to smell water from several miles away. They were, in fact, the perfect creatures for such a climate. But they still could not compare to Lex's beautiful enchanted ship with its air-conditioned kitchens and bathrooms and wardrobes and he felt an immense sense of gleeful satisfaction at the fact that he was so far ahead of the others before they had even begun. He had been *born* for this kind of thing! The huge bat had ample room to land on the deck of the gleaming, metal ship, swooping down with an elegance that was in sharp contrast to the drayfus's botched landing. The prophet slid from the giant thing's back and stood there in silence, facing them. A thin, rather greasy man, about thirty years old, scrambled off after him and Lex assumed that this must be the prophet's companion – Theba, the gangster. He certainly seemed like a gangster. Lex didn't like the look of the shifty, resentful expression in the man's eyes one bit and made a note to keep an eye on him because he looked just the sort for foul play. And Lex should know, for it takes one to know one.

A bare second later, the Judge appeared beside the other two. He was dressed in the same grey robes and golden mask as before and, once again, he didn't utter a word to either of the other Gods or even his own player. It occurred to Lex that perhaps this was why the Judge had chosen a prophet – what with having their tongues cut out they were not exactly the talkative types either.

'Now that everyone's here,' Jezra said, stepping forward, 'we are ready to commence the first round. You shall all be provided with crystal balls for remote transmission during the course of the Game.'

He opened his fist to reveal the pocket-sized crystal ball, which he then held out to Lucius. Lady Luck held an identical one out to Lex and the Judge pressed one into the gloved hand of the prophet.

'Are we being broadcast to the stadiums now?' Lucius asked, peering nervously into his own dark ball.

'Of course not,' Jezra replied impatiently. 'We don't broadcast footage live. Haven't done for years. It's better for everyone all round if a bit of editing is done first.'

Lex managed not to snort. He knew it was vanity on the part of the Gods. They all wanted their players to look fearless. They did *not* want them breaking down in tears in the middle of a Game, so anything like that would . . . hit the cutting room floor, so to speak.

'Now, this,' Jezra gestured dramatically to the looming castle, 'is a sky castle, as you can see – a relic from the days of heroes. There is a broken mirror inside. I would like you to fix it. The first one to do so, wins.'

Lex said nothing, keenly suspicious of the seemingly simple task.

'Is that *all*?' Lucius asked in obvious relief.

'That is all,' Jezra confirmed, spreading his hands and smiling an honest man's smile that Lex did not trust one bit.

'Well, that doesn't sound too dangerous,' Lucius said, glancing at Zachary who merely nodded.

'From here on in, the help we can give our playing pieces is limited,' Jezra said. 'I trust we all understand that?'

The Lady and the Judge both nodded.

'After all, if we were to use the full extent of our powers,' Jezra went on deliberately, 'we would, of course, easily destroy each other's players but no one would actually *win*. And I believe that is why we are all here?'

Lucius was looking quite cheered at this but the distrust and suspicion that was rife in the air was quite obvious to Lex. The Gods were cheaters too, almost by definition.

'All right. Let it begin,' Jezra said.

He and the Judge disappeared and, at once, Lucius and Zachary were running towards their exhausted drayfus, and the prophet and Theba were running towards their bat and, after some persuasion on Zachary's part, the animals were rushing off towards the castle as if this was merely some kind of race.

'How simple minded,' Lex murmured.

'What do you mean?' the Lady demanded. 'Don't just stand there, Lex, get a move on; they're going to beat you!'

'Jezra is the God of Wit and Daring, my Lady,' Lex

said patiently. 'His round would never hinge on such a simple thing as fixing a mirror. There could be anything inside there. I certainly don't intend to rush in unprepared.'

'I suppose you have a point.'

'Don't worry, I fully intend to win this round,' Lex replied, his mind already going back to a story his grandfather had once told him about a huge castle that hung in the sky. Then he turned and sauntered back to the door, relishing the cold air that blew out from within when he opened it. He was a little worried about the heat. His own clothes were damp with sweat from the few minutes that they had been out on deck and he never had liked Heetha's sun, always doing his best to avoid it and it was even worse at this altitude. The sun could make you slow and sluggish. But the beauty of it was that Lucius was a total pansy when it came to heat and the prophet probably wouldn't fare too well with all the layers of black clothing he was wearing. He even had gloves for Gods' sake! The other players weren't prepared, they didn't have anything with them. Lex laughed softly. This was going to be all too easy.

'So what do we have to do?' Schmidt asked when Lex entered the bridge.

'Fix a mirror,' Lex replied briefly. 'Why don't you ask Lady Luck if you can stay here?'

'I'm not staying here!' Schmidt protested.

'Why not?' Lex asked, glancing at him in surprise. 'It's hot and dangerous out there, you know.'

'If you die then *I* will have to complete the Game by myself!'

'Oh that,' Lex said dismissively. 'Don't worry about that; I won't die. I'm going to win.'

'Convince yourself if you want to, but I'm not staying here. For all you know you might *need* a second person in there.'

Lex hesitated. It was a possibility. 'I suppose you're right. Well, you'd better hurry up and get ready if you want to come.'

'I *don't* want to come!' Schmidt snapped. 'But I don't have any choice, thanks to you! I should be at Lucas, Jones and Schmidt right now preparing for the Johnson case. If you've got some kind of death wish . . . if you want to die, then that's your business, but I'm absolutely astounded that anyone could be so outrageously selfish as to drag somebody else unwillingly into such—'

'Oh give it a rest,' Lex said mildly. 'I didn't know how the bracelets worked. I can assure you that I would much rather be playing this Game on my own. But I won't be slowed down by anyone. Meet me on the deck in fifteen minutes.'

The sky castle had a row of steel rings set into one side. From the deck, Lex could see the drayfus and the desert bat already tethered, at a safe distance from one another, to a couple of these rings. Although they were clearly meant for animals, Lex saw no reason why the ship could not be safely anchored there too and, as they approached, a rather delicious idea occurred to him. He closed his eyes and revelled in the sensation of the boat shifting in response to his thoughts. It made him feel *God-like*.

'You're going too close to the drayfus, Lex,' Schmidt said from where he was standing beside him. 'Pull back.'

Lex ignored him but opened his eyes to watch the entertainment. The drayfus had been resting on the platform, but it raised its large head now, watching the impending ship in alarm.

'Pull back!' Schmidt ordered.

'Shut up; you're ruining the moment.'

'You're going to hit it!'

'I'm only going to scare it. Just watch; it'll be fun, I promise.'

As the ship got closer, the drayfus at last staggered to its feet and tried to fly away. Unfortunately, it was tethered to a steel ring. But whilst the ring might have been made of steel, the castle was made of sand. Sandcastles, as every small child knows, are not built to have huge slavering beasts tethered to their walls. After some moments of agitated and terrified straining, the ring tore away from the side of the castle in a shower of sand and the drayfus flapped off, probably profoundly relieved to be free.

Lex laughed. 'I told you it would be fun.'

There were many doors into the castle. Most of them were huge, grand, ornate things. There was one door in particular, around the front, that was clearly the main door and Lex guessed that Lucius and the prophet would have entered via this one. Schmidt headed for it automatically but Lex ignored it and set off round the back in search of the obligatory, innocuous little back door. He smiled when he found it.

'Are you sure that's right?' Schmidt asked, coming up behind him.

'Oh, no, it's all wrong,' Lex replied. 'They won't be expecting us to use this door, so hopefully this route will have fewer traps.'

'Traps?' Schmidt asked sharply. 'I thought we just had to fix a mirror?'

'Yes, but there will be traps, trust me. Keep your eyes open.'

Lex grasped the metal handle and dragged open the door to reveal about twenty people all rushing madly towards them . . . Well, not quite. None of the people were moving. They were statues – frozen in a desperate rush towards the door, with expressions of abject terror on their carved faces. As if they were being chased . . .

'What a curious choice of décor,' Schmidt remarked.

'Hmm. Curious,' Lex responded at once, taking particular care to keep his voice level, for the lawyer clearly did not realise that these were no mere statues but something much, much more sinister . . . One might call that an irresponsible attitude on Lex's part. After all, if Schmidt wasn't warned about what was in the castle with them then he would not be adequately prepared to defend himself . . . But they'd be all right as long as they stayed in the cold rooms.

The long sandy corridor stretched away into the castle – the walls, ceiling and floor were made entirely of sand, with wooden brackets on the walls holding flickering torches to provide some light. And there were doors all the way along the corridor – blue or red, which meant that Lex's hunch had been right. He put down his bag and pulled out two fur coats.

'Here,' he said, holding one up for the lawyer.

Schmidt stared at him. 'What on *earth* did you bring *coats* for? The heat would kill us!'

'Just put it on,' Lex replied distractedly.

The top, bottom or centre? The broken mirror was bound to be in one of those places. As the top of the castle would be the hardest place to reach, Lex was guessing that it would be there. And to reach the top, they would have to pass through the blue doors, avoiding the red ones very carefully.

Lex pulled on his own coat, swung the bag back onto his shoulders and moved towards the shiny blue door, hardly hearing Schmidt's complaints in his greedy preoccupation with what treasures he might find in the course of the Game. He pulled open the blue door and Schmidt fell silent as he stared over the top of Lex's head at the huge icy room before them. Light poured in from the massive windows and cold air rushed towards them, shards of frost clinging to their clothes and hair. The entire room was made of ice, including the huge spiral staircase that curved upwards. Lex smiled smugly at the look of amazement on his employer's face. 'Put the coat on,' he repeated.

'How did you know?' Schmidt asked, struggling into the coat as Lex stepped carefully into the room, testing the floor as he went. 'How did you know the castle would be ice inside?'

'It's not entirely. The blue doors lead to ice and the red ones lead to sand and lava.'

'But how did you *know*? I don't remember sky castles appearing in any of the recent Games. You haven't done this before, have you?' Schmidt asked suspiciously.

Lex sighed. 'My grandfather told me, okay?'

Alistair Trent had been a great Chronicler in his day. Fifty years ago, Adventurers were still exploring the Lands Above, but now that enough information had been gathered to create a comprehensive map, people no longer went exploring like they used to, because they could learn about faraway places by reading the Chronicles in the library.

Of course it cost a lot of money to raise an exploratory expedition and so there had only ever been gentlemen Adventurers. The only way for less well-off men to go was by selling their services as a writer, Chronicling the adventure as it happened and then donating the book to the library once it was over. Alistair Trent had been on many different adventures as a young man with several different Adventurers, including the famous Carey East. Lex and Lucius had often delighted as children in the stories Alistair would tell them and, when Lex had first moved to the Wither City, he had spent many an evening in the library reading the Chronicles his grandfather had written, marvelling that the man who'd raised them had really done all those incredible things.

'Just be quiet and follow me,' Lex went on. 'There isn't time to explain everything to you as we go, so I'm afraid you'll just have to trust that I know what I'm doing. We need to get to the top,' he said, pointing to the staircase. 'Preferably without breaking our necks.'

It wouldn't be easy. The stairs and balustrade were made of ice. That would make the stairs almost impossible to balance on and the balustrade painful to grip without gloves. Lex reached into his pocket and drew out a pair of the thick gloves that he had found with the coats on the ship.

'There are gloves in the coat pocket,' he said to Schmidt, squinting up at the staircase and trying to work out how high it was. Three storeys perhaps? He walked over to the base and gazed up thoughtfully.

'So what's your plan?' Schmidt asked, coming up behind him.

'What?'

'How are you going to cheat to get up there?'

'Cheat?' Lex smiled. 'I'm afraid that when it comes to stairs, Mr Schmidt, there *is* no way to cheat. They just have to be climbed.'

'But they're made of ice, you stupid boy.'

'Yes.'

Lex considered the stairs for a moment longer, trying to think of something that would make the climb easier or, failing that, at least make it possible.

'Why don't we fly up?' he asked at last.

'Good idea, but for the one obvious flaw.'

'There's a desert bat tethered outside, didn't you see it?'

'You want to *steal* the prophet's *bat*?' Schmidt asked, aghast.

Lex wrinkled his nose in distaste. 'I do wish you'd stop using that word. We would only be *borrowing* it.'

'Isn't it enough that you've already lost your brother's drayfus?'

'No, it's never enough, Monty. You wait here, I'm going to fetch it.'

'It won't work, anyway. Desert bats have a very low tolerance to the cold. Besides which, they're incredibly vicious towards anyone who isn't their handler.'

Lex stopped halfway to the door and turned back around. Schmidt silently cursed himself. Why had he spoken like that? Now the insufferable little know-it-all's eyes were positively *ablaze* with curiosity.

'You're right. How do you *know* that?' Lex asked, walking back to the stairs. 'I didn't know that desert bats were required reading for lawyers.'

'I don't *know*, I just assume. It is a logical assumption,' Schmidt said defensively.

Lex said nothing. But Schmidt realised that he knew he'd just clumsily tried to hide something from him. And Lex knew that Schmidt knew that he knew. What a nightmare this whole situation was!

'Well, it looks like you're right,' Schmidt said briskly. 'The stairs will have to be tackled the old-fashioned way.'

★ ★ ★

'For Gods' sake, why can't you keep your damn balance for more than ten bloody seconds!' Lex snarled, almost tearing his hair out in exasperation.

They were just over halfway up the staircase, about twenty feet above the cold ice floor below. The going had been painfully slow for Lex. There is no fast way to ascend an ice staircase – no fraudster can alter this material fact, no matter how talented he might be. By clinging to the railings, they were managing to stay upright – most of the time – but slipping on the ice was unavoidable and the effort of climbing required the whole body to be constantly tensed. Lex was feeling tired himself but the fuss that the lawyer was making was absolutely disgraceful. He just *kept on* falling over! And what was worse, he was actually *letting go* of the balustrade when he did, so that a couple of times he had actually fallen down a few stairs before managing to stop himself.

'We seem to be taking one step forward for every two steps back!' Lex exclaimed. 'Why won't you just hold onto the rail when you slip? You'd stay upright then. I mean it doesn't take all that much intelligence to grasp that simple fact, does it?'

The lawyer was out of breath and Lex could tell from the way he was moving that he had hurt himself when he'd fallen. What an infuriating old idiot he was!

'You're slowing me down!' Lex hissed. 'Stop being so obstinate and hold on to the damned balustrade!'

Lex turned to continue the climb when Schmidt did something utterly unexpected. He pulled a pork pie out of his bag . . . and bit into it. The body switch was instantaneous. Lex sucked in his breath in startled pain. He was now standing further down the stairs in the lawyer's body. Every muscle seemed to be on *fire*.

'You greedy idiot,' he wheezed, stifling the familiar distaste at hearing himself talk with Schmidt's voice. 'We have to eat together, remember? Get back down here and finish the pie with me.'

'You think you can do so much better,' Schmidt said in an odd tone from above him. 'I'd like to see you prove it.'

Lex looked up, hardy believing his ears. 'You switched us on *purpose*?'

'Yes, I want to learn. Show me how it's done, Lex.'

'All right,' Lex retorted, never able to resist a challenge. 'All right, I'll show you how it's done, old man. Although really, for something so simple, I would have thought that a verbal explanation would have been more than sufficient.'

Lex stuffed the pork pie into his pocket and then gripped the banister in his gloved hand. Or tried to. He glanced down with a frown. The old man's hands were shaking. Lex silently willed them to stop. It didn't work. Scowling, Lex struggled his way up a few stairs before his feet inevitably slipped on the ice and, despite his best efforts, he was unable to retain a firm enough grip on the banister to prevent himself from falling over. He swore irritably and dragged himself back upright. After several more minutes, he was getting rather sick of continually bruising himself and called up to the lawyer who was now several stairs ahead of him, 'Okay, you've made your point.'

'My dear boy,' Schmidt called back, 'I haven't even begun to make it.'

And the lawyer quickened his pace, leaving Lex toiling further behind.

'Hey!' Lex shouted. 'Give me back my body, you bastard!'

When Schmidt continued to ignore him, Lex proceeded to shout insults in the most foul language he could think of before grudgingly deciding to conserve his energy for the rest of what was clearly going to be an exceedingly torturous climb. When he at last reached the top, Schmidt had clearly been waiting for him for some time – he was sitting at the top of the stairs with Lex's bag at his feet. Lex took a bite out of the half-eaten pie and then passed it to the lawyer. It was decidedly satisfying to see his employer wince on arrival in his own body once again.

'You made your point,' Lex growled, standing and picking up his bag. 'But I wouldn't do that again if I were you. Trust me, if it becomes a contest, I can make your life much more painful than you could ever make mine.'

'I believe you,' Schmidt replied solemnly.

'Glad to hear it,' Lex snapped.

He turned away to survey their new surroundings, calmly finishing off the pie as he did so.

'Well?' the lawyer asked coldly after a moment.

'It looks as if I may have made a rather horrible mistake,' Lex said.

They were standing on a large, circular upper floor.

That was all right; Lex had expected some kind of landing. But the problem . . . the real problem . . . was that there were no doors.

'It's a dead end,' Schmidt said flatly. 'We're going to have to get all the way back down those stairs again.'

'It was very kind of you,' Lex remarked, 'to allow me to finish the climb up here rather than tell me it was a dead end as soon as you found out.'

'What can I say? I have the soul of a teacher,' Schmidt sneered. 'I did not want to interrupt your lesson before it was finished, Mr Trent.'

'Well, I'm not going back down those stairs,' Lex declared.

'I beg your pardon?'

'Not after we've climbed so high. No way.'

'But this is a dead end!'

'Not for long,' Lex replied.

He put his bag on the floor and started rummaging through it. By the time he had pulled out a sledge-hammer, a huge ice pick and a rather bemused-looking penguin, Schmidt was beginning to realise that this was no ordinary backpack.

'What the hell is that thing?' he asked.

'Magic bag,' Lex said. 'I took it from the ship. It's bigger inside than out. Isn't it cool?' he said with a grin. 'Just think, if you hadn't thrown my old bag away I never would have found it.'

'Your penguin's leaving,' Schmidt said, for want of anything more sensible to say.

Lex glanced up with a frown as the creature shuffled off down the stairs, its feet slapping loudly on the ice.

'I didn't pack him. I guess there's a few things in here that the enchanter left behind.'

'Look, you're not seriously thinking about hacking your way through the wall with those things, are you?' Schmidt asked, gesturing to the ice pick and sledgehammer.

'Oh, don't be stupid,' Lex replied mildly. 'I was looking for this.' And he pulled from the bag a tall, pointed enchanter's hat. It was silver with the usual embroidered moons and stars.

'That's what your brilliant mind has come up with, is it? A hat? Thank the heavens, all our problems are solved!'

'Or soon will be at any rate,' Lex muttered.

He lifted the hat over his head but froze when Schmidt cried out in alarm, 'You're not thinking of *wearing* it, are you?'

Lex looked puzzled. 'Why not? Is silver not my colour?'

'The enchanter will be angry,' Schmidt warned.

'What the enchanter doesn't know,' Lex replied cheerfully, 'won't hurt him.'

And he lowered the hat onto his head, grinning at the way Schmidt flinched as if he was expecting flames to burst from its pointed tip.

'You worry too much, Monty.'

'Well, what good will it do you, anyway?'

'The enchanters keep some of their power in their hats,' Lex said, glancing at him. 'Don't they, sir?'

Schmidt raised an eyebrow. He was testing him! The little brat was testing him!

'Do they, Lex?'

'Yes,' Lex replied. 'They do. I thought you might have known.'

'It's not my business to understand the ways of the enchanters any more than it is yours! But these hats were not made for humans. We are not used to magic the way they are. It might be dangerous to—'

'Thank you, Mr Schmidt, consider your duty of care towards me discharged. I have been duly warned. Now, let's see about these walls.'

Lex looked at the curving ice wall that surrounded them on the circular landing. There was no way of knowing what lay beyond. They might be able to break through into another part of the upper castle or they might blast through to find nothing but more solid ice before them or a gaping drop to the floor below. It would be safer to go back down the ice staircase and start again somewhere else. Explosions are never a good idea when the super-structure of a building consists almost entirely of sand.

Lex did not know exactly how to use the hat, or even if he *could* use it, but it was certainly worth a try before resorting to the ice picks. He held out his hands, palms facing towards the walls, the way he had seen the enchanters do, and spoke the first magic word that came into his mind. '*Alakazam!*'

The wall imploded.

Which was ultimately a good thing, but the way the

floor trembled was a little worrying. Schmidt and Lex both slipped over on the ice, despite clinging to the banister. A large crack appeared down the middle of the floor and icy dust rose up from it and fell from the ceiling. For a moment, with the ice trembling beneath him, Lex was forced to seriously contemplate the possibility that the entire staircase would collapse. Fortunately, however, moments passed and the staircase remained more or less intact. What was more, it was clear that the explosion had gone right through the wall and out the other side to where they now had a clear view of a long sand bridge. Heat was pouring out from the gap in waves and Lex could see that the icy floor nearest the wall was already beginning to melt. Without speaking to one another, Lex and Schmidt very carefully and tentatively dragged themselves towards the door, wincing as the ice groaned when they passed over the crack down the middle.

When they at last reached the safety of the sandy floor on the other side, Schmidt rounded on Lex, almost foaming at the mouth. 'Alakazam? *Alakazam?* Did you have any idea at all what you were doing back there? Take that hat off before you kill somebody!'

'What's your problem? It worked, didn't it?'

But he raised his hands to the hat anyway, intending to remove it. 'Uh oh,' he said, tugging at the hat. 'I, uh . . . can't get it off.'

'Can't get it off?' Schmidt repeated, looking horrified. 'Can't get it *off*?'

'Can't get it off, yes, that's what I said!' Lex replied,

feeling irritated and just the tiniest bit alarmed. It must have been because he'd used the magic on it. After all, the hat had come off fine when he'd tried it on before.

'I warned you not to put it on. Here, let me try,' the lawyer said, gripping the hat and trying to pull it from Lex's head.

'Oh, never mind the hat for now,' Lex said after several rather undignified moments of pulling and tugging. 'We'll deal with it after this round.'

'I don't like it,' Schmidt said.

Neither did Lex but he wasn't about to admit his discomfort to the lawyer. The truth was that he had only ever expected to be wearing the hat for a few moments. He felt vulnerable with it stuck to his head like this . . . almost as if the enchanter might be able to *sense* the fact that he was wearing it. For all Lex knew, the enchanters might indeed possess such a sensitivity. And there was no getting away from the fact that he had *stolen* the enchanter's ship. He shivered involuntarily. He had always intended to steal something from an enchanter one day – some tiny little thing that probably wouldn't be missed for a very long time, if it was missed at all – but a huge, powerful ship stuffed full of valuables was something altogether different and, for an instant, Lex experienced the disquieting fear that he might be in over his head this time. He shook these fears off hastily. What was done was done and he must keep a clear head for the Game.

He turned his attention to their new surroundings. They had broken into one of the sandy rooms and at the moment the heat was making a pleasant change from the frozen iciness before but Lex knew that that would change pretty quickly. They both stripped off their fur coats and stuffed them into Lex's magic bag. It was a relief to feel sand underfoot again. Unlike the previous room, this one had no windows, but the same flickering torches in brackets were on the walls, just as they had seen in the corridor on the way into the castle. There was a sand bridge stretched across the length of another huge room, suspended some thirty feet in the air with nothing but more sand stretched out beneath them. Lex didn't particularly like the look of that bridge. There were no railings to hang on to and no obvious pillars supporting it. But they had to get across to the other side somehow and the sand staircase behind them only led back down, not up.

'Well, at least the sand should be easier to walk on,' Schmidt was saying. 'I don't know why we didn't just go through the sandy rooms to begin with; anything's got to be easier than trying to walk on ice.'

But ice is solid, Mr Schmidt, Lex thought. *Sand is not.* He didn't speak aloud. After all, that would not have been at all conducive to persuading the lawyer to cross the bridge. Besides which, he had already spotted another couple of stone people down there . . .

CHAPTER TEN

THE BROKEN MIRROR

Moving between the hot and cold rooms as they progressed through the castle was in itself uncomfortable, but infinitely preferable to being frozen or toasted alive. There had been a couple of heart-stopping moments in the hot rooms when the sandy floors had given way beneath them and they had been forced to sprint for the nearest exit. Lex had thoroughly enjoyed this, of course, finding the thrill of almost plunging to his death utterly exhilarating, but Schmidt had not seemed quite so entertained and had quickly grasped the importance of avoiding the sandy rooms where they could. Despite the thrill, Lex tried as hard as he possibly could to avoid the hot rooms for he did not want Schmidt to guess the truth behind those stone statues and start panicking and upsetting everything.

But then they found Theba and the secret was out.

They had just come out of an ice room and into another sandy corridor when they found him – frozen in stone like all the others. Lex tried to hurry Schmidt past him before he could notice but the sharp-eyed lawyer was not to be deceived.

'Gracious me, that's the prophet's companion!' he exclaimed in horror.

'Ah ha.' Lex made a weak attempt to laugh it off. 'There is a certain resemblance.'

'It's no resemblance, it's the spitting image!' Schmidt snapped.

'So it is,' Lex replied. 'Astonishing. Come on, we can't hang around here all day.'

He was most eager not to linger in the sandy rooms any longer than was necessary, but the damned lawyer was still ogling at the statue as if it were the most extraordinary thing he'd ever seen in his life. It was, indeed, identical to Theba in every way. The thin gangster with the greasy hair had a terrified expression on his face and, now that Schmidt looked at the other stone people in the corridor around them, he was obviously realising that they all wore the same expression. The penny finally dropped.

'Medusas!' he croaked.

Lex sighed. 'It seems that way. The prophet must have escaped the attack because he's blind.'

Schmidt was instantly panic stricken as Lex had known full well that he would be.

'We've got to get out of here at once!' the lawyer exclaimed, already looking round for possible exits.

'I'm not going anywhere,' Lex said coldly. He uncurled

his fist to reveal the mirror he had concealed there. 'And I have the only mirror. I've been using it to look around corners. Everyone knows a medusa can only turn you to stone if you look directly at her. So if you want to move safely through the castle then I suggest you stay with me.'

Lex turned on his heel and walked away, not giving Schmidt any time to wrestle with himself. There were medusas in the castle – the sensible thing was to push on quickly and not stand about in the open *discussing* the danger. Schmidt obviously came to the same conclusion, for he hurried after Lex almost at once.

Unfortunately, the supply of blue doors seemed to have entirely run out and so they had no choice but to continue moving through the sandy rooms and corridors, checking around each corner with the mirror for medusas first. Medusas liked heat and hated the cold, which was why Lex had known that, in the icy rooms, they would be safe from them.

Lex and Schmidt had taken their coats off but even then the heat was unbearable. Sweat trickled down their skin, dampening their clothes, and despite taking frequent gulps of the water Lex had packed, they felt permanently dehydrated. Soon the water was almost all gone and Lex – with a considerable lack of good grace – was forced to give the last bottle to Schmidt for the old lawyer was clearly feeling the heat even more than Lex.

They made to carry on down the next corridor when Lex's foot crunched on something lying on the floor. It was – quite unmistakably – a human bone. The floor ahead was littered with them.

'Medusas don't eat people, do they?' Schmidt croaked hoarsely.

Lex shook his head in silence and tiptoed forwards through the bones before Schmidt could suggest turning back. When he got to the end of the corridor, he could hear a munching, crunching sort of noise that made the skin at the back of his neck prickle. There was really no point in even using the mirror, for anything making that sound was not something that they were going to want to try and get past. They would have to find an alternative route. But Lex couldn't help himself – he had to *see* what it was before creeping away. So he raised the mirror in his hand and used it to look around the corner.

His heart sped up with excitement and dread for what he saw in the little glass was a minotaur – huge, horned, covered in tough, red skin, with great yellow fangs, sitting in what appeared to be a kind of den, gnawing happily on a human bone that had long ago been stripped of flesh.

Lex stared, fascinated, for a moment before lowering the mirror and turning back around to Schmidt. The lawyer stood only a few paces away but it was obvious from the expression on his face that he had seen what Lex had seen. He was shaking slightly as he turned around back the way they had come and Lex just hoped to the Gods that Schmidt would have the sense to avoid treading noisily on any bones, thereby giving them away.

Thankfully, although the lawyer moved quickly he also moved silently and Lex caught up with him and grabbed at the back of his shirt just as he was about to round a corner.

As it turned out, it was a lucky thing that Lex stopped him because when he raised the mirror he almost dropped it in his shock at seeing a medusa – fearsomely ugly with snakes for hair – inside the corridor they had just come from and walking towards them. There was nowhere to run. They were trapped – a minotaur on one side, a medusa on the other. Certain death, for sure . . .

Whilst Schmidt stood with his mouth hanging open in stupid horror, Lex stared around desperately for some means of escape. But the only things in the little corridor were bones and two frozen statues of large, muscled gladiators with helmets, armour and huge, bejewelled swords. They were about as strong and impressive-looking as any two people could be and yet they had both come to an unfortunate end. What chance did an unarmed elderly lawyer and a skinny teenager possibly have? There were no doors, no stairs, no windows, no weapons . . .

There was one chance and one chance only so Lex grabbed Schmidt's arm and dragged him towards the two gladiator statues. Schmidt thought at first that Lex's plan was to hide behind them, which seemed unlikely to work considering the noise they'd just made, clattering through the bones. But then – to the lawyer's horror – Lex grabbed a bone up off the floor and smashed it repeatedly against one of the statues, shattering the silence with the din and raising his voice to shout, 'We're in here!'

Then he dropped the bone and crouched down, dragging Schmidt with him. *Mad*, the old lawyer thought numbly, *he's gone completely mad*. He covered his eyes, cringing in fear at the noise of the thundering hooves of the minotaur running into the room followed almost at once by the hissing medusa. Then the hooves stopped abruptly, the monster was cut off mid-roar and Lex was leaping to his feet, out from behind the protection – such as it was – of the statues.

Schmidt could barely register what was happening. The boy was a goner for sure and Schmidt would soon be next. There was the terrible hiss of fifty or so snakes baring their fangs and then there was utter silence, broken a moment later by the sound of Lex . . . laughing . . .

Schmidt slowly lowered his hands, still crouched on the floor amidst the bones, wondering if he was going mad or was perhaps even dead already . . .

'You can come out now, sir,' Lex called nonchalantly. 'I've dealt with the minotaur and the medusa. It's quite safe.'

Half in a daze, Schmidt picked himself up off the floor and walked round from behind the statues to see Lex looking even smaller than he really was, with the medusa on one side and the minotaur on the other. Both the monsters had been turned to stone.

'How did you . . . ?' Schmidt trailed off dumbly.

'Oh, it was easy, really,' Lex replied, his voice rich with

glee, an insufferably self-satisfied expression on his face. 'By luring them both here at the same time I got the medusa to deal with the minotaur by turning it into stone. Then I simply jumped out at the medusa behind the mirror, causing her to look right at her own reflection and turn herself into stone as well. It's easy when you know how.'

Schmidt didn't know whether to be impressed or livid. After all, it had worked and they were both still alive but . . . 'A hundred things might have gone wrong!' he hissed.

'Might have gone wrong to other people, you mean,' Lex replied with a smirk. 'I'm lucky, Monty. My plans are always flawless. Come on, we can't dawdle about here. The race isn't over yet.'

Fortunately, once they walked through the now-empty minotaur's den, they came almost at once to a winding spiral staircase that led them straight up to the very top of the castle without further incident. They had made good time, without any seriously debilitating accidents to slow them down, and so it was an extremely bitter and entirely unexpected shock to Lex to discover that they were not the first to reach the broken mirror. Lucius and Zachary were already there.

This was one of the ice rooms – although only the floor was ice – the walls and ceiling were made entirely of glass, letting in pools of yellow light that splashed brightly off the ice and the broken mirror in the centre of the room. The other effect of the glass walls was, of course, to act as an uncomfortably effective reminder of how very high up they were. Lucius and Zachary were both sitting on the floor near the mirror and Lex could sense that they had been there for some time already.

'How did you get here before me?' he demanded from the doorway. The only apparent route was straight through the minotaur's den and Lex couldn't imagine Lucius strolling through that bone-filled place even if he had been lucky enough to be there at a time when the minotaur was not.

Zachary and Lucius both looked up, alerted to his presence for the first time at the sound of his voice. Lucius frowned at him. 'Why are you wearing that stupid hat?'

'It makes me look taller,' Lex said.

'It makes you look stupid,' Lucius replied.

'Well, I think your haircut makes you look like a girl but what can I do?' Lex snapped. 'How did you get here before us?'

'Don't tell him,' Zachary said as Lucius opened his mouth to respond.

Lex narrowed his eyes at the farmhand. How he hated the man.

'Shut your mouth before I shut it for you!' he snarled.

'What the hell is your problem?' Lucius said, scrambling to his feet. 'Can't you keep a civil tongue in your head? What do you think Gramps would have said if he'd heard you talking to Zachary like that?'

After the last, slightly scary, incident with the ice, Lex

had not intended to use the magic in the enchanter's hat again. But now he found he couldn't help himself. He directed his most frosty stare at Zachary and drew himself up as far as he could.

'If you don't tell me how you got here within the next five seconds,' Lex said calmly, 'I shall turn you into a ferret.'

He raised his hand to point at the farmhand, meaning only to reinforce the point but as a new and inexperienced user of magic with a complete lack of rudimentary control, the mere act of pointing had the immediate effect of turning Zachary Finnigan into a sleek, white, rather weaselly-looking ferret. There was a moment of utter silence before the ferret started to squeal.

'Oh my *Gods*,' Lucius whispered, staring at Lex. 'You're wearing an enchanter's hat, aren't you? Are you *insane*?'

Lex ignored the question. He was grinning in pure delight at the animal. What a profoundly satisfying moment it was!

'Doesn't it suit him?' he gloated. 'You know I always said that Zachary probably should have been born a weasel. In fact I even . . . thought tha—' Lex faltered, staggering back a few steps.

'Your nose is bleeding,' Lucius said, staring at him.

Lex raised a hand to his face and found that Lucius was right. Suddenly he wasn't feeling so good. The room seemed to have become very hot, despite the ice.

'I'd better take a look at this mirror,' he said, as an excuse to sit down.

'Are you all right?' Lucius asked anxiously.

'Yes,' Lex said irritably, pressing a tissue to his nose. 'Stop fussing.'

'I told you you shouldn't have used the hat,' Schmidt said. 'The enchanter can probably sense you when you're wearing it. He'll want it back.'

'Well, turn Zachary back and then take the hat off,' Lucius said.

'How did you get here before me?' Lex repeated.

Lucius sighed. 'We climbed the castle from the outside. The side where the shade is. We came in just below this room, okay?'

Lex frowned. That would certainly have been quicker, being much more direct than weaving through the hot and cold rooms, dodging minotaurs and medusas from the inside. And sandcastles were easy enough to climb since hand- and footholds tended to be present naturally and could be knocked in where they weren't.

'What about the heat?' Lex asked suspiciously. 'And how did you cope with your fear of heights?'

'With difficulty,' Lucius sighed. 'Now turn Zachary back.'

Lex gave a hard laugh. 'I don't think so!'

'But you said if I told you how we got here—' Lucius began to whine.

'I made no such agreement. You *assumed*. An assumption that turned out to be incorrect. But you're my brother, Lucius, so I'll tell you what I'll do . . . ' Lex put his bag on the floor and rummaged through it, drawing out a length of string. He then lunged for the ferret, tied one end of the string around its neck and passed the other end to his brother. 'Just to make sure you don't lose him,' he smiled.

'You can't leave him like that,' Lucius insisted. 'Turn him back!'

'And risk having some kind of brain haemorrhage? I don't think so.'

'Unsatisfactory as this whole situation is,' Schmidt broke in, addressing Lucius. 'Considering the danger inherent in using enchanted hats and the fact that this enchanter will be looking for us, it probably would be best if your friend remained . . . in his present state for now.'

'I'm glad we're all agreed,' Lex said, before turning his attention back to the mirror. It was one of Lex's highly advanced skills to be able to tune out anything that was being said that was likely to displease him, and he now totally blanked out the irritating sound of Lucius's whiny voice complaining on Zachary's behalf – as well as the racket the ferret was making – as he studied the mirror and applied his mind to the problem.

It was quite a small mirror, set in a silver frame and broken into five pieces. The breaks were all clean and the mirror remained resting in its frame. Lex had fully intended to use the hat to fix the mirror but he shrank from that now. The incident a few minutes ago had made him more uncomfortable than he would care to admit. He had *felt* the magician's anger. Well, perhaps anger was too mild a word to use – *towering rage* might have been more fitting. Yes, he did not want to die an old man but neither did he want to die quite yet. There was no doubt in his mind that he had seriously pissed the enchanter off and he could not risk that he might catch up with him. But how else to repair the mirror without using magic?

'What have you already tried?' he asked.

'What?' Lucius asked, cut off in mid flow.

'To fix the mirror. What have you already tried?'

'It's already fixed.'

'No it's not, the glass is all broken.'

'The pieces were all outside the frame and I put them back. I thought that was all I had to do.'

'Did Jezra come to tell you you'd won?'

'No, but I—'

'Then you haven't fixed it.'

Of course you had to look quite closely to see that the mirror was in fact broken, for the breaks had all been so clean that only very thin cracks appeared to mark where the pieces joined one another. And there was no obvious way to get rid of those, not without using magic. Lucius had merely *repaired* the mirror, he hadn't *fixed* it. A broken mirror was a broken mirror, however carefully glued together it might be. Any task set by Jezra would never be as simple as that.

'Did you see the prophet on your way up?' Lex asked.

'I think he's out of the round. He got stuck in some of the quicksand downstairs. I don't know what happened to Theba.'

Lex sensibly didn't enlighten him and knelt down by the mirror to tip out the broken pieces.

'What are you doing?' Lucius asked.

'Do you remember what Gramps told us about sand-castles?' Lex asked as he rummaged through his bag. 'He said that the corridors were sometimes guarded by mino-taurs. And – if you were really unfortunate – by medusas.'

Lex drew the mirror out of his pocket. 'I brought a mirror, just in case,' Lex said. 'In fact, I killed a medusa with it just a few minutes ago.' He noted Lucius's squeak of horrified awe before going on, 'And – as luck would have it – it seems to be exactly the same size as the one Jezra has left for us.'

Lex brushed away the broken pieces of the first mirror and carefully slotted his own one into Jezra's frame. It was indeed a perfect fit.

'So Lex Trent wins again,' a soft voice said.

Lex glanced up to see Jezra gazing down at him. 'I always win, my Lord.'

'Thirty-two minutes,' Jezra said, gazing coldly at Lucius. 'Thirty-two minutes you were here on your own before the others arrived and yet you were not able to solve this painfully easy puzzle.'

'I am sorry, Lord Jezra,' Lucius tremored. 'But I had no way of fixing the mirror because I didn't have a second one like Lex did and I—'

'Lex,' Jezra said. 'Assume for a moment that you had not had that second mirror in your bag. What would you have done next?'

'I would have thought of some other way, my Lord,' Lex said promptly.

'Please demonstrate.'

Lex had had many happy moments in his seventeen years, but this one had to be in the top ten. Top five, even. He had always been something of a show-off at school. Far from being embarrassed, he had actually *enjoyed* it when the teacher had picked on him to show the other students how something was done. Every teacher's pet knows that smug, contented glow. It was a thousand times better when a *God* was asking you to demonstrate your skills. Lex calmly glanced round the room, taking in anything that might be useful.

'Well, discounting the rest of what's in my bag,' he said, 'my first thought would have been to use the ice.'

'Use the ice, how?' Jezra asked steadily.

'Melt it,' Lex said: 'And pour the water into the frame so that the still water created a reflection. Just as effective although my way was quicker.'

Jezra smiled slightly, grasped a fistful of Lucius's hair and, ignoring the alarmed yelp, forced his head towards Lex so that Lucius was looking straight at his brother.

'Thirty seconds,' the God whispered in Lucius's ear. 'In less than thirty seconds your brother got what you couldn't get in more than thirty *minutes*. An appalling lack of resourcefulness on your part.'

'I will do better in the second round, my Lord,' Lucius trembled.

Before Jezra could respond, Lady Luck appeared in the

tower and instantly threw her arms around Lex in a suffocating hug. 'My dear boy, you were phenomenal! Better than I had even hoped! Why, it would hardly even matter if you hadn't been the one to fix the mirror after the way you defeated the medusa and the minotaur *simultaneously*!'

'It was nothing, my Lady,' Lex replied, airily, as she released him. 'I only wish there had been more of them. It would have made it more interesting.'

Schmidt rolled his eyes at the conceited bragging but Lady Luck just beamed even wider. In another moment, however, the smirk was wiped off Lex's face when Jezra spoke to Lucius.

'If you pay very close attention to your brother over the next few days as his guest then perhaps you will learn something.'

'Guest?' Lucius repeated.

'*Guest?*' Lex said, in much the same tone as if the God had said 'sex slave'.

'On board your great ship,' Jezra said, turning to Lex, a slightly malicious smile on his face. 'You frightened away the drayfus. Lucius and his . . . ' the God glanced at Zachary, 'and his ferret will therefore travel onboard your ship with you to the next round.'

'That hardly seems fair!' Lex protested. 'It was Lucius's fault for leaving the drayfus there! Why should I be punished for *his* mistake?'

'Now, now. Play nicely, children,' Lady Luck said lightly. 'I have agreed to this arrangement with Jezra, Lex. Lucius will travel with you to the next round.'

'But that just isn't fair!' Lex fumed. 'I'm the one who stole the ship, I should reap the benefits!'

'If it makes you feel any better, Lex, the enchanter is after you now that you've used his hat. If he catches up with you he will likely punish all persons on board the ship, so I'm afraid that, as well as reaping the benefits, Lucius may also pay the price for what you've done.'

Jezra picked up the end of string that was Zachary's makeshift lead and handed it to Lucius.

'Have fun,' the God said to the two distinctly unhappy brothers.

CHAPTER ELEVEN

MAGIC HATS AND NASAL LICE

Lucius was clearly afraid of the enchanter's ship. Of course, Lex had not helped matters when he had described, in great detail, some of the horrible things he had discovered on the lower decks.

'—and I distinctly heard the rustling of a giant spider coming from one of the rooms,' Lex went on maliciously. 'And there are trapped ghosts down below and lost, twisted children and—'

'Oh shut up, Lex! Just shut up! I don't care! I haven't slept or eaten properly in three days! I just want to have some food and then go to sleep for something more than four hours at a stretch! Do you think you could manage that, Lex? I know winning this stupid Game is the only thing you care about right now, but I'm not exactly a threat to you am I? Do you think you could just steer your way clear to sharing some of your food with me and then leave me alone for a few hours?'

'I seem to recall your saying that you would never ask

any favours of me ever again,' Lex said coldly. 'I thought that was our new agreement.'

Lucius sighed. 'I wasn't hungry then.'

Lex remained silent for a moment, making a show of hesitating, of thinking it over before standing up and instructing Lucius to follow him to the kitchen.

Lex had never had any interest whatsoever in the law. He had applied for the student scholarship programme back at the farm because of its notoriously heavy workload. They plied you with textbooks and assignments and, later on, they set you up with internships at law firms. Being bogged down in precedents and case law gave Lex a viable excuse for not helping his brother to care for his grandfather. That was the crux of it. It took a special kind of person to care for a sufferer of the soulless wake. It took a selfless, patient, gentle kind of person and Lex simply did not have it in him.

'I have to go and help Zachary with the new drayfus,' Lucius said, sticking his head into Lex's bedroom one day. 'Can you feed Gramps for me?'

Lex winced. *Can you feed him for me?* As if he was a child who couldn't do anything for himself. Considering the circumstances, the analogy was an apt one but still Lex felt angry when he heard people talk that way. Not angry at Lucius as such . . . just angry.

'Can't you see I'm studying?' he snapped, gesturing to the open textbook.

Lucius gave him a black look. 'He's waiting. I've got

him settled down in his chair. It's vegetable soup and bread today. Be generous with the butter when you do the bread and if there are any crusts then give them to him, they're his favourite. And make sure the soup isn't too hot because he might burn his mouth and—'

'I think I can manage it, thanks!' Lex snapped.

'All right,' Lucius said with a shrug.

Lex turned his attention back to his textbook once his brother had gone, intending just to finish the paragraph he had been on. Then he decided to finish the page. He might as well finish the chapter. There was nothing terribly depressing about automatic resulting trusts, and they delayed the inevitable moment when he would have to go out and deal with his grandfather. Lex subscribed to the ostrich philosophy – if you buried your head in the sand deeply enough and pretended that a horrible situation was not really happening, you could almost convince yourself that it really wasn't, and that took the edge off a little.

Unfortunately, Alistair Trent was hungry and had become bored with waiting. When he went into the kitchen to find Lucius, he somehow managed to knock the soup off the stove and burnt himself quite badly. Lex heard the noise from his room and rushed straight out to the kitchen, but it was already too late. He tried to calm his grandfather, implored him to hold his arms under the cold running water but it was no good and it was not until Lucius came and took over that the situation ceased to escalate. And then a little later there had been the most blazing row between Lex and his brother.

'I ask you to do one tiny thing for me!' Lucius raved. 'And look what happens!'

'You treat him like a child!' Lex accused. 'You can't deny it!'

'Of course I don't deny it! To all intents and purposes he *is* a child!'

'How *dare* you say that!'

'You know it's true,' Lucius said, trying to be conciliatory. 'Do you think *I'm* enjoying this?'

'Yes!' Lex snapped. 'I think you're enjoying it very much! You always were jealous of my relationship with him! You always wished that you could be as close to him as I was, only you never could because you just weren't interesting enough for him! And now whenever he wants something he goes straight to you like a child; how gratifying that must be for you!'

Lucius never had been very good at confrontation. He would always cave in rather than prolong the argument, which only irritated Lex all the more. Why couldn't he have some backbone for once?

'All right, Lex,' Lucius had said quietly. 'Fine. I won't ask any more favours of you, all right? Just go ahead and concentrate on your studies.'

'I'll hold you to that!' Lex replied, quite determined that no makeshift reverse psychology was ever going to work on him.

Then, one evening, something happened and Lex snapped. He just couldn't take it any more. So, after everyone had finally gone back to bed, he packed a bag and left, without saying goodbye and without looking back.

'What about Zachary?' Lucius asked, breaking in on Lex's thoughts. He stood clutching the ferret to his chest as he gazed fearfully round the huge kitchen.

'What about him?' Lex asked.

'He's hungry, too.'

Lex sighed and waved his arm to encompass the room. 'Help yourselves.'

There was a large metal table in the centre and a pantry that curved round two of the walls, stuffed from top to bottom with food, not all of which looked like it was supposed to be for humans.

'I'll leave you to it,' Lex said, turning towards the door. 'I need to figure out how to get this hat off.'

'You're not leaving us, are you?' Lucius asked in alarm.

'Why not?'

'I'll never find my way back without you!'

Lex sighed and sat down at the table.

'Thank you,' Lucius said.

Lex bit back the cruel retort. Why was he *thanking* him? Why did he always have to be so *polite*? It wasn't as if Lex was going out of his way to accommodate him. Lex hated genuine politeness. Calculated politeness could serve a purpose sometimes but real, *genuine* politeness . . . that was something for hypocrites. Lex sat back and watched as Lucius fetched some food from the pantry for himself and then found a saucer and poured milk into it for Zachary.

'No ferrets on the table,' Lex said lazily.

'You know he's not a ferret,' Lucius said with a touch of impatience.

'No ferrets on the table,' Lex repeated. 'It's my ship, I make the rules.'

'It's not your ship,' Lucius sighed, picking Zachary up and putting him on the floor. 'What happened to you, Lex? What happened to all your fine ideals about being a lawyer one day? You could have been wealthy and comfortable and respected. What could possibly have persuaded you to throw all that away?'

Lex shrugged. 'It wasn't exciting enough,' he said. 'You wouldn't understand. I never really wanted to be a lawyer.'

He had never truly had any fine ideals either. Very few people really did. There were almost always dark, gritty, secret motivators lurking behind the glossy golden surface. Lucius did not understand this.

'I think it's terrible,' he said stiffly, picking at a cold slice of ham.

'I know you do. That's why my life will be extraordinary and exciting and bigger than I am. Whilst your life will be tedious and meaningless and flat. I'm making the best of what I've got. You're just drifting meaninglessly through. It's such a waste.'

'Well, we can't all be adventurers,' Lucius said coldly. 'Someone has to do the drudge work. Anyway, it's kind of hard to have this discussion with you whilst you're sitting there with that ridiculous hat *stuck* to your head.

You look like an idiot. And you've put all of us at risk by wearing it.'

'What can I say? I do like my hats,' Lex drawled. 'But I had better do something about this one. Take your ferret, we're leaving. You can finish eating that on the bridge where Schmidt can babysit you.'

'I wish you'd stop referring to Zachary as a ferret,' Lucius sighed, carefully picking up the little weasel with both hands. 'You might hurt his feelings.'

'We wouldn't want that,' Lex murmured, eyeing the ferret with what some might have described as a murderous glint in his eye.

The sneeze was sudden and violent and seemed to catch even Lucius by surprise. Since his hands were both occupied holding the ferret, he was unable to cover his mouth. This was exceedingly unfortunate for Lex since it resulted in a spray of spit landing on his upper arm. This in itself would not have been overly problematic – nothing a bar of soap and a bit of scrubbing couldn't have solved. But the real killer of it was that, amidst the spit, was one small insect with rather a lot of legs and long feelers on its head. Lex yelled in pure horror when he saw the thing and started waving his arm about desperately in an attempt to shake it off. But the bug knew exactly what to do and within moments it had crawled up Lex's neck, across his face and, despite his efforts to knock it off, had disappeared straight up one of his nostrils.

'Nasal *lice*!' Lex spluttered in outrage. 'You *idiot*, why the hell didn't you *warn* me?'

'I'm sorry, I thought they'd all gone!' Lucius cried, wringing his hands hopelessly.

'Thanks a lot! Thanks a sodding lot, you moron!'

Nasal lice were one of the many reasons that Lex disliked farms. Excluding nostrils, the lice habitat of choice was a special kind of hay of the type used to feed the drayfii. That was why protective clothing was always supposed to be worn when handling the hay. The lice were not dangerous – just exceedingly unpleasant, especially if, like Lex, you had a fetish about being clean. They could lay up to twenty eggs a day but an infestation rarely lasted more than a week. The body had a very efficient, if *embarrassing* way of getting rid of them. Sudden, *violent* sneezes. Lex thought of Schmidt and was suddenly even angrier – *I daresay I would become accustomed to the lice given time*, the lawyer had drawled. So Lex had started life as a farm boy and Schmidt was an expensive lawyer in an expensive suit, but that didn't mean that Lex wasn't *clean*. But now, because of Lucius, he would have to go through several miserable days of feeling dirty again.

'Why weren't you wearing the protective suits?' Lex raged at his twin.

'I was, but there was a rip down by the leg and I didn't notice it till afterwards. Look, I'm sorry; I know how much you hate lice, but it will only be for a few days.'

'Don't say *anything* to Schmidt,' Lex ordered. 'Not a word!'

★   ★   ★

After escorting Lucius and Zachary back to the bridge, Lex trailed about the ship looking for the enchanter's wardrobe. He was sure the rooms moved about. It had been near the bridge before but this time he searched right across to the other side of the ship before he found it.

This room, like the bridge, seemed to be made of ivory. There was a large full-length mirror that took up almost a whole wall and Lex stood and examined his reflection for a while. The hat certainly added to his height. And although it clearly clashed horribly with the rest of his clothes, it did give him something of an impressive appearance. Despite the unease he felt over the enchanter, Lex couldn't find it in himself to regret putting on the hat. Lex liked power. He *craved* it in the aftermath of having felt so powerless for so long.

Lucius had tried to keep the special days special – birthdays and so on – but Lex had sneered at him for that. What was the point of dressing Alistair Trent in his best suit and putting out special food and pretending things were normal when it was nothing but a grotesque farce? Lex and Lucius had fallen out about it over the harvest weekend. Lucius had been in the kitchen pouring out three tankards of Grandy, for he couldn't let his grandfather drink anything with alcohol or caffeine in it now. Alistair had been sitting at the dining-room table waiting patiently for his food, unspeaking. Lex was also sitting at the table waiting but, whilst Lucius was still able to talk to their grandfather by speaking as if to a child, Lex couldn't do that. At last, unable to take the oppressive silence any longer, Lex had gone into the kitchen to find Lucius.

'Why are we *doing* this?' he'd asked.

'We always celebrate the harvest,' Lucius replied, looking up in surprise.

'But he doesn't even know what harvest *is* now, so what the hell is the point? I can't do this; I'm going out.'

'Lex!' Lucius said, and Lex stopped for he had never heard anything even approaching steel in his twin's voice before. 'Sit down,' Lucius said through gritted teeth. 'I know he doesn't understand any more. I look after him every day so, believe me, I know! But this isn't for him, it's for me. You pretend nothing's wrong every day so you don't have to help me. Fine. Okay. But *I* need this celebration, all right? I'll pretend everything's fine today and you can pretend all the other days of the year. Now go back to the table and *sit down*.'

And Lex had returned to the table, albeit with a certain lack of good grace. But that was in the past. Lex didn't take orders from his brother now. In fact, he didn't take orders from anyone. He tilted his head before the mirror, examining his reflection from different angles. The hat suited him. But it was a dangerous thing, he reminded himself. He had no choice but to try and remove it. It was the only responsible thing to do. Responsibility was so boring.

Lex turned in surprise as the door opened behind him. Of everyone onboard he had been the only one brave enough to explore beyond the bridge, so he was not expecting Schmidt to walk in on him.

'Why aren't you babysitting Lucius?' Lex asked.

'Did you know he was allergic to nuts?' Schmidt asked.

'Well, of course,' Lex said, turning back to the mirror. 'It's an allergy we share.'

'Then why did you let him eat that casserole? Didn't you know it had nuts in it?'

'I knew,' Lex said, smiling. 'Has his face swelled up yet?'

'Why do you hate your brother so much?'

'I don't hate him. I'm just not favourably inclined towards the constant sound of his voice. Lucius is a chatterbox. The swelling will shut him up,' Lex said, glancing at Schmidt's reflection in the mirror. 'Trust me, I was doing us both a favour. Why did you leave him, anyway?'

'I'm looking for the kitchen,' Schmidt said, sounding none-too-happy about it. 'He said if he didn't get a glass of water mixed with lemon then he could suffocate.'

'Oh. Well you don't seem to be in any great rush. I take it you don't overly care for my brother's company, either, if you're willing to risk liability for his death.'

Schmidt rolled his eyes. 'Despite what your brother told me, he did not seem to be in any immediate danger. And despite whatever contempt I might feel for you, I don't seriously believe you to be a cold-blooded killer.'

'Perhaps I didn't realise he'd eaten nuts,' Lex suggested.

'It seems to me that not much gets past you without your noticing it,' Schmidt grumbled.

'Thank you,' Lex said. 'Now tell me how to remove the hat.'

'What makes you think that *I* have any idea?' Schmidt said defensively.

'You knew about the prophet's bat and the dangers of using the hat. I don't know where you learnt about those things, but I do know it wasn't from any law book.'

'It was a law book,' Schmidt insisted. 'I learnt about the bat and the unsuitability of enchanted hats for humans from *reading*. I have had some strange cases to try over the years and my legal research has sometimes taken me into the realms of the strange and the bizarre.'

Lex gave a slight shrug and tried to pull the hat from his head again, for the look of the thing, before turning back to Schmidt. 'The enchanter is looking for us. I felt him when I used the hat and he felt me. He is, as we would expect, very angry indeed. You heard the Goddess of Luck earlier. When he catches up with us, which he will do very quickly if I don't get this hat off, he will not stop to apportion blame, he will simply punish everyone on board his ship and that includes you. He won't cut you any slack because you're elderly or because you're a lawyer or because you're a Withian citizen. Enchanters are above the law, Monty. We tricked his crone and we *stole* his ship. You played your part in that even if you played it unwillingly. I know that you know how to remove this hat. I can *sense* it just as you could sense that I'm a fraud. We're all at risk whilst I'm wearing it. Tell me how to take it off.'

Schmidt looked at him for a moment, an expression of pure hatred on his face until, making up his mind at last he said, 'Try holding your breath for twenty seconds.'

Half suspecting that he was being made a fool of, Lex did as Schmidt had suggested. After exactly twenty seconds, the hat fell off.

'You certainly didn't get *that* from any book, Monty,' Lex said quietly, letting out his breath in relief.

'Go to hell,' Schmidt hissed before stalking from the room and slamming the door behind him.

'Not today,' Lex murmured softly to himself as he replaced the silver hat back on the rack alongside the others.

The journey on board the enchanted ship continued on the basis of a kind of disgruntled, resentful truce between Lex, Schmidt, Lucius and the ferret. Lucius was exceedingly hurt over the whole nut-allergy affair and somehow managed to bring it up every time he saw Lex – which had not been often over the last few days for Lex spent little of his time on the bridge. He always took care to return at night, though. He knew well enough that the ship was not safe. He really had been joking when he told Lucius that he'd seen ghosts and lost, twisted children down below, but that joke backfired on him when he remembered it late at night and became extremely uncomfortable at the recollection of his own ghost stories.

He had gone out on deck one night with the intention of enjoying the air and the soothing sound of the ship cutting through the sea and the smell of the foam. But it had been unnaturally quiet for, of course, this was no ordinary ship – it flew, it did not sail and, as such, there was no sound of water, no white foam trailing in the ship's wake. Nothing but a slightly unnatural silence. It was a warm night so Lex sat down with his back against the wall, looking out towards the prow. He could enjoy smelling the ocean on the sea breeze, even if he could not hear all that much of it. Lex had always loved ships, especially at night. They were their own little worlds, separate from everyone else, hidden away in the middle of the ocean.

He dug in his pocket for the crystal ball and re-watched the first round. It had been broadcast to the stadiums about an hour after it had actually been completed and now the footage was stored on their individual crystal balls so that they could watch it whenever they liked. Lucius had not watched it even once but Lex had seen it over and over again. It annoyed him that the footage of Lucius climbing the wall of the castle had been edited to look more impressive, with lots of nail-biting shots of how extraordinarily high they were, and all the parts where Lucius had complained, whined or wept had been cut altogether.

The Gods called the little crystal balls *Divine Eyes* and Lex therefore assumed that they somehow recorded what the Gods saw. After all, there were no cameras in evidence, following them about during the course of the Game, but the Gods had some way of watching everything that went on even though they weren't physically there. It therefore seemed that, somehow, they also had a way of recording the images they saw so that they could be played back later.

The muted, tinny sound of glorious music came softly out of the little ball when it got to the part where Lex leapt out from behind the statues to freeze the medusa. He could imagine the music booming across the giant stadiums and the cries of awe from the spectators. The grand music, combined with lots of fearsome shots of both the medusa and the minotaur, as well as the fact that this part had been broadcast in slow motion, made the whole thing look even more dashing and courageous than it really had been.

'It wasn't as impressive as all that,' Schmidt had snorted when he'd seen it.

'That's easy for you to say,' Lex replied smoothly. 'Seeing as you were the one cowering behind the statues whilst *I* was the one who heroically saved both our lives!'

To his immense satisfaction, Schmidt did not have anything to say to that. But Lex had taken to smugly watching and re-watching the footage in his crystal ball when he was alone late at night up on deck. He wanted to appear careless and nonchalant about it and felt that image would be somewhat ruined if the others saw him vainly ogling himself in the ball over and over again.

Lady Luck had smugly told him that he was the favourite to win already, with both Lucius and the prophet trailing far behind him. The defeat of the medusa and minotaur had created quite a stir and, already, enterprising merchants had produced a limited edition action figure of Lex fighting the monsters. The Goddess had brought him one in delight when she visited the ship yesterday. Lex took the three figures out of his pocket and examined them in the moonlight. Action-figure Lex did not look all that much like him as he was practically the same size as the minotaur – tall and broad and with a brave, fearsome expression on his little plastic face. Lex didn't mind, however. You knew you'd made it when they turned you into an action figure.

He put them all back in his pocket and gazed out over the dark sea, feeling well pleased with himself. *Look at me now, Gramps,* he thought. *This would be an adventure worthy of your stories.* Lucius's news that Alistair Trent was dead hadn't particularly saddened Lex for he had known that it must have happened by now and he also knew that his grandfather would have wanted it. He was not a man made for half-lives. He had been a respected Chronicler and had only given it up when he had come home to raise Lex and Lucius after their parents died.

'Sorry we cut your adventures off short, Gramps,' Lex had said one day when he'd been about six. 'You'd have had loads more without us.'

'Well . . . some things are more important,' Alistair replied lightly, running a hand through his thick silver hair as he sat down on the bench. He'd been chopping wood for the last hour but Lex had just brought him a tankard of beer, so he was having a well-earned break.

'I want to be a Chronicler one day,' Lex said.

'Oh no,' Alistair replied with a smile, picking Lex up with his strong hands and putting him on his knee. 'You'll be an Adventurer yourself. Don't settle for writing the story, Lex. Accept nothing less than actually being the story and maybe one day *The Chronicles of Lex Trent* will be on the bookshelves next to Adventurers I wrote about myself.'

Lex had almost squirmed with pleasure at the suggestion. 'You said it takes a certain type of person to be an Adventurer,' he prompted, hoping for further praise.

'Yes. You need certain qualities.' Alistair glanced at his grandson. 'But you've got most of them in spades already, which is damned remarkable considering you're still only a little sprat. I'm completely confident that you'll do the Trent name proud one day, my boy . . . '

After a while, Lex fell asleep. He started awake some time later feeling cold and stiff and, for a moment, unsure of where he was. Then he remembered and was suddenly filled with the desire to get down below with Schmidt and Lucius where there were warm furs and the comforting sounds of other people breathing. He was about to stand up when he noticed the creature moving about on the deck. It was a moon-goblin – a strange, thin, melancholy creature made from moonlight. Lex froze, hoping the thing hadn't seen him. Although mostly harmless, moon-goblins could be dangerously unpredictable when they were upset. This one was crying, wandering morosely about the deck, gazing out at the black sea, staring up at the stars and then wandering about again. Lex could hear its muffled sobs as it shuffled around. No one knew why the moon-goblins were such a sad species or what it was they cried about. This one had probably had its curiosity roused at the sight of the enchanted ship flying over the ocean. After a few minutes, it climbed over the outer railings, let go, and was blown away by the wind. Lex lost no time in scrambling to his feet and getting off the deck and back to the bridge as fast as he could, doing his best not to think about lost, twisted children.

It was with relief that he slipped into the bridge, firmly closing the door behind him. The light from the stars and moon shone in through the panoramic windows and illuminated Schmidt, Lucius and the ferret curled up in the warm blankets that had been piled around on the floor. As soon as Lex stepped into the room, Lucius sat bolt upright. 'Is that you, Lex?' he whispered fearfully.

Lex cursed inwardly. He knew he'd been quiet. Still, at least Lucius had had the sense to whisper – the last thing he wanted was for Schmidt to wake up and start telling everyone off.

'Of course it's me,' Lex said quietly, tiptoeing over to his own designated sleeping space beside Lucius.

'Where were you?' Lucius asked. 'I was worried about you when you didn't come back. I thought something might have happened. I thought you might have had an accident or fallen overboard or—'

'Gods, will you listen to yourself? You're like an old woman! Shut up and go back to sleep.'

'I suggested to Mr Schmidt that we make up a search party just in case something had happened to you,' Lucius went on, unperturbed. 'But he said that he would never be that lucky.'

Lex chuckled softly.

'It's not funny,' Lucius said huffily.

'Schmidt knows that I'm controlling the ship with the ivory Swann in the basin over there,' Lex said nodding towards it. 'So if the ship is still moving then that means that I am still alive and still on board, all right?'

'Oh. All right, but I wish someone had told me before. Where is the ship going, anyway?'

Lex groaned softly. 'Don't you ever stop talking? You know where the ship is going; the Goddess of Luck said that her round would take place in the Golden Valley.'

'Well, I don't see what we can possibly do there,' Lucius grumbled. 'There's nothing there but—'

'*Wealth*,' Lex said gleefully.

When the Lands Above had at last washed its hands of royalty and the assassinations and bloody feuds that went with it, the last kings had gone to the Golden Valley, taking much of their acquired wealth with them. The western kings took horse-drawn carriages that stretched on for miles, journeying with them across the continent to the promised land where there would be no subjects baying for their blood and no relatives plotting to kill them. The eastern kings did much the same but for the fact that their carriages were pulled by elephants rather than horses. The kings had been allowed to take people with them but strangely they had all chosen to take servants rather than family. Kings had grown to be instinctively distrustful of relatives, especially since many of them had got their own titles by sneaking a drop of poison into Uncle's brandy one night. So they took gold and servants instead of loved ones. It was said that the Golden Valley did now truly glitter, due to the amassed wealth of the land's exiled kings.

'I want to see that gold,' Lex whispered. 'It must be the most amazing sight.'

'But it isn't *worth* anything,' Lucius grumbled. He pulled out a note of m-gold and held it up to the moonlight. 'We use paper money, now.'

Lex snatched the note from him and examined it as best he could in the dark. Paper money! He sneered at the sight of it. What intrinsic worth did it have? What intrinsic beauty did it possess? There was nothing rare or unique about paper notes. Lex tossed it back to his brother dismissively.

'And I thought people weren't allowed to go there now, anyway,' Lucius said.

'The Gods want us to go,' Lex said. 'Isn't that enough?'

'Well, yes, I suppose. I'm glad to see you've maintained some respect for the Gods.'

Lex suppressed a smile. If Lucius could only hear how he spoke to Lady Luck when it suited him. Although, to be fair, he probably would not have tried it with any of the other Gods.

'Go to sleep,' Lex said. 'We'll get there tomorrow or the day after and I want to be ready.'

CHAPTER TWELVE

THE GOLDEN VALLEY

'Rise and shine!' Lady Luck exclaimed in a horribly cheerful voice for such an early hour.

Schmidt and Lucius were already awake from the sounds of things, but Lex was not a morning person and under normal circumstances would have buried his head under the pillow with a groan. But because he was currently in the middle of a Game he sat bolt upright and said, 'It hasn't started already, has it?'

'No dear,' Lady Luck replied. 'There's still another hour to go.'

'Well then, what the heck are you waking me up for?' Lex snapped. 'I only need half an hour to get ready! I could have had a whole extra half hour of—'

'You've made the headlines again, dear,' the Goddess interrupted him. 'I thought you might like to have a little gloat over breakfast.'

Lex saw that she was holding a newspaper out towards him and, because there was nothing he liked better than having a little gloat over breakfast, he snatched it from her eagerly, expecting to see something about the current Game. He was therefore surprised to see the headline: *Shadowman Strikes Again!*

At first he thought it must be something to do with the museum break-in back at the Wither City. But then he noticed the date printed at the top of the page and saw that this was not an old newspaper at all. In fact it had only been printed that very morning and was about a different theft altogether. It appeared that the famous Blue Diamond had gone missing from the jewel vault in one of the Bandy Towns, and Shadowman calling cards had been left at the scene of the crime. Lex stared at the page, dumbstruck and horrified.

Being the nosy snoops that they were, Schmidt and Lucius came over at once to peer over Lex's shoulder at the front page. They both gave predictable, and rather irritating, gasps and then Schmidt said, in an outraged voice, 'So *that's* where you were when you went missing yesterday! Hand over that diamond, Lex, right this instant!'

'I'd sooner give myself a lethal dose of poison than hand a precious diamond over to you!' Lex snarled. 'But, as it happens, I don't have it. Which you would know if you had an ounce of common sense in your thick head!'

The Bandy Towns were on the edge of the Wild West and they boasted the most impressive collection of jewels anywhere on the planet (with the exception of the Golden Valley). They also happened to be about four thousand miles away.

'How do you think I got there, eh? You must think I'm a truly awesome magician with spectacular, *superhuman* powers to be able to achieve such a magnificent feat! I suppose I should be flattered.'

'All right, Lex,' Lucius said, in what he obviously thought was a soothing manner. 'There's no need to be offended. You can't blame Mr Schmidt for jumping to the wrong conclusion. After all, you *have* stolen things before, and even if you've turned over a new leaf now, you—'

'I have *not* turned over a new leaf, you twit!' Lex said, swatting Lucius's hand away from where he'd been trying to pat him on the shoulder. 'I *am* the Shadowman! I'm not upset because Schmidt thought this was my doing,' – he waved the newspaper around – 'I'm upset because it wasn't!'

'You mean you didn't steal the Blue Diamond?' Lady Luck said, finally catching up with things.

'No! Someone is impersonating me!'

'Oh. Well, I suppose it's natural to get copycats – after all, you are becoming quite notorious.'

'But it's *my* notoriety! How dare someone steal it like that?'

The irony of that sentence was not lost on Lex. But Schmidt looked very much like he was about to start pointing it out for the benefit of everyone present, so Lex screwed up the newspaper, threw it away from him and, before Schmidt could say anything, went to the window and said loudly, 'Where the heck are we anyway?'

But as soon as he saw the sight below he needed no answer. Lady Luck gave him one anyway: 'We're in the Golden Valley.'

And Lex decided that resolving this Shadowman business would have to be postponed. In fact, he was already seeing how this could be of benefit to him. Presumably the authorities back at the Wither City would know that he was playing in a Game by now. And so he had an alibi for this most recent theft. He could once again deny being the Shadowman. The so-called 'witness' Schmidt had found would be discredited. Lex would say he fled the Wither City because he was scared of the upcoming trial, not because he was guilty as sin. Yes . . . there might just be a way out of this yet.

As soon as the Game was finished he would get stuck right back in with his thefts and his scams, but he would drop the Shadowman and come up with something else. A new name, a new identity and a better calling card next time – one that could not possibly be replicated by some contemptible copycat who wasn't original enough to come up with his own alterego.

But for now all that could wait. He was in the Golden Valley. Finally he was going to see it with his own eyes. He left the others dawdling about in the observation room and legged it up to the deck.

Humans liked being kings for it made them feel closer to Gods. There had been a time, before the physical split of the Lands Above from the Lands Beneath, when humans all over the Globe had started proclaiming themselves as royalty, commanding over anyone who would listen and making their own crowns out of twigs and coloured glass and beads and anything else they could find. In the end, the Gods had been moved to put a stop to it. There could only be so many kings, they said. To limit the number, the Gods presented humanity with twenty crowns. Only the wearers of these twenty could be considered true kings – the missing link between divinity and humanity. And so the bloody battles commenced until the day when the kings were kicked out once and for all.

Lex had heard stories of these twenty crowns. His grandfather had even seen one once, from a distance. They were not made from gold, it was said, but from something even more beautiful. Just the joy of being able to *brush* one with his fingertips would have been immeasurable to Lex.

As an appreciator of beauty, it had always been Saydi's sun that Lex had loved the most, for, as Goddess of Beauty, she was a deity after Lex's own heart and she could do the most breathtaking wonders with her sun. Sometimes she cooled its rays enough for a soft, powdery snow to fall whilst the sky remained blue and bright, and at others she painted the sky with rainbows and golden-hued warmth or scented the air with honey and pollen and summer. Saydi seemed to understand that, in order for beauty to be appreciated in full, it must not impact on comfort and so her sun always heralded the most amenable weather on the Lands Above. There would never be any sunstroke or frostbite whilst Saydi's sun was in the sky and Lex would have loved her for that alone. He recognised her sun as soon as he stepped out onto the deck of the enchanted ship on the morning they arrived at the Golden Valley. The air was clear and cool and beautifully fresh. It seemed incredibly sweet and oxygen rich – as to normal air what distilled spring water is to sewage. The gentle, golden light from the sun had liquefied in its purity and was splashing down upon the deck in soft smatterings of what the people knew as sun drizzle – a kind of golden rain that gently warmed the skin rather than wetting it.

The day was beautiful, as one would expect from Saydi. But what Lex had not been prepared for was the utterly astonishing sight of the Golden Valley. He had always had a greedy streak, even as a child, but he had never realised until now just how savage greed could be. His fingers *itched* at the sight of what lay below.

'Like it?' Lex's Goddess asked, appearing at his side.

Lex nodded speechlessly.

'Saydi's sun adds magnificence to an already spectacular sight,' Lady Luck said.

The valley was full of white palaces. Lex loved palaces and fully intended to own at least ten before he died. They were made out of white gold and were of all different shapes – the western kings preferring spires and turrets and sparkling turquoise moats, and the eastern kings favouring jewelled domes and carved images of spirit-hosts and huge glittering stone elephants. There were fountains and emerald walkways and a vast enchanted forest for the kings to hunt in.

'Can I have it?' Lex asked – because if you don't ask you won't get. 'Please?'

Her Ladyship laughed. 'The Golden Valley belongs to kings, Lex; you know that. You can't have what's down there unless you happen to be royal.'

She turned away from the railings with a strange little smirk, telling Lex that he'd better go and get ready before he ran out of time. So Lex went back down to the observation room and ate a hurried breakfast with Schmidt before checking and rechecking his bag and then going back up to the deck with the others.

The prophet arrived a few minutes later, landing his desert bat on the deck of the ship, looking a little bedraggled after what must have been a long and harrowing journey. The Judge appeared on the deck beside him instantly.

This was Lady Luck's round and although Lex had pestered her for some kind of hint as to what to expect, she had staunchly refused to tell him anything until everyone had reconvened at the Golden Valley. Lex was currently in the lead, of course, having won the first round as well as losing Lucius his companion. To Lex's delight, Lucius had actually made a little *halter* for Zachary, complete with nametag and shiny, sparkly studs. Although not usually *completely* stupid, Lucius did seem to have something of a blind spot when it came to small, soft animals, no matter how sharp their teeth might turn out to be. The ferret looked ridiculous in the halter and, what was more, it was quite clear that Zachary knew it. He had tried to bite Lucius when the halter was first put on before finally being persuaded to wear the thing and thereby bid farewell to whatever last scrap of dignity he might have been vainly hoping to retain. The ferret was now slumped moodily at Lucius's feet in such a stance of hopelessness and embarrassment that Lex almost . . . *almost* felt sorry for it.

The Goddess of Luck cleared her throat and glanced round at everyone, looking well pleased with herself. 'As we all know,' she began, 'royalty is blind. It is not based on intelligence or valour or merit. It is based on blood. It is based on *luck*, in other words.'

'Royalty is *valueless*, in other words,' Jezra said contemptuously.

The God was in a foul temper that morning and it was not difficult to understand why. Jezra was a master gamesman but in this case it seemed all too clear that not only was he going to *lose* but he was going to lose *spectacularly*. If he had nurtured some faint hope that Lucius might turn out to be more like Lex than people thought, he had been sadly disappointed.

'There are twenty royal crowns left on the Globe as I'm sure we're all aware,' the Lady went on, completely ignoring Jezra's petulant comment. 'At the end of this round Lex will be one of the Globe's Kings.'

She paused, hoping for a dramatic outburst of protest

from the others, but a slight raising of the eyebrows was the only response she got from Jezra; the Judge's face was hidden behind his expressionless mask; Lucius looked like he couldn't have cared less about anything that was being said; the prophet was incapable of speaking and no one was too sure about exactly how much Zachary could understand in his current . . . state.

The Goddess of Luck sighed, apparently deciding that everyone's lack of enthusiasm had rather taken the fun out of the thing. 'All right, there's a crown hidden in the depths of the Royal Forest.' She pointed down at the valley below. 'First one to put it on is King.'

Once again, apart from Lex's broad grin, the others seemed distinctly unimpressed.

'Was there a royal death last night of which I am as yet unaware?' Jezra asked, in an exaggerated tone of politeness. 'Because if not then where has this crown come from?'

'I was granted special permission to create one for the purposes of the Game,' Lady Luck said sweetly.

'By who?' Jezra demanded. 'The only God who could give you that permission would be—'

'Goban,' Lady Luck said with a smug smile. 'God of Royalty. Yes, he gave me his permission. Do feel free to ask him if you don't believe me, but I think we'd all like to get on with the Game now.'

'Well, what use is it anyway?' Jezra asked, throwing up his hands. 'When the winner will only be subject to an instant and permanent exile?'

The smile faded from Lex's face, for Jezra was right. All kings were exiled to the Golden Valley and were never allowed to leave. It was hoped that one day they would eventually die out although the royal bloodlines seemed to have been doing well so far.

'Goban has agreed that, in this case, the royalty will only be temporary. The winner will be allowed to leave the Golden Valley after they have removed the crown.'

'I must say there seems to be a lot of rule bending going on!' Jezra said sharply. 'Aren't you even going to say anything?' he said, rounding angrily on the Judge. 'Are you just going to let her do this?'

The Judge spoke out from behind his mask then for the first time since the Game had begun. It was a deep, velvety voice that sent shivers down Lex's spine. 'If Goban has given his permission, I do not see that there is anything we can do.'

After a moment when it looked like it might go either way, Jezra bit his tongue and was silent though the expression on his face made Lex distinctly uneasy. This was the God of *Wit* and *Daring*. Ultimately, the Goddess of Luck was no match for him in the Games, for luck could only last so long. Jezra was becoming angry and it was Lex Trent upon whom he was likely to turn his anger.

'What do you think I should pack?' Lucius fussed once they were back inside the ship.

'Pack whatever you like,' Lex said dismissively. 'What do I care?'

'But Lex!' Lucius whined. 'You've got more of an idea about what to expect than I have. I might run into trouble down there.'

'I very much hope you do,' Lex said, stuffing food into his bag. 'We're not on the same side.'

Lucius sighed. 'All right. Well, I'll just take some food and water then but if I—'

'No, you don't,' Lex said sharply as Lucius reached out for the sugary energy cake on the middle shelf. 'That's my food.'

Lucius stared at him. 'But you've got more than enough here for everyone!'

'That's hardly the point,' Lex said. 'We're *competing* against each other, Lucius, you twit! I'm not going to do anything that might help you.'

'Well, it's not like I'm going to win, is it?' Lucius replied huffily.

'Lucius,' Lex said, turning towards his brother, 'loath as I am to offer you any kind of advice at this stage, you'd better at least *try* to win or else Jezra is going to be very angry with you indeed.'

'Can I at least take some water?'

'No!' Lex snapped, his voice turning hard. 'If you were anyone else I would have sabotaged you by now. I've suppressed the urge to do that out of respect for the fact that we're related, but I won't go so far as actually *helping* you. I'm far too good at Games for that sort of weakness. I'm ready now, so I'm going to go ahead and start. Stay on the boat for as long as you like, but don't take anything that doesn't belong to you. Come on, Monty,' Lex said to Schmidt who was lounging by the kitchen door.

With a shrug, Schmidt turned and followed Lex out along one of the mirrored corridors. 'You really are a mean little sod, aren't you?' he remarked as they came out onto the deck. 'You lost him his transport and his companion and yet still you would begrudge him having just a few bottles of water.'

'I've done him a favour,' Lex grunted. 'Because he had no drayfus, he got to come with me, which means he's well rested for this round rather than exhausted as he would have been if he'd travelled here on the drayfus, and to be perfectly frank, he's better off without any companion at all than he was with Zachary.'

'What do you have against the man, anyway?' Schmidt asked curiously.

'He thought he could tell me what to do,' Lex said simply.

Eventually Lucius had asked Zachary to move into the farm house to help out on the occasions when Alistair became agitated. And Zachary had duly decided that this gave him the right to interfere in private family matters whenever he felt like it.

'I know you're busy,' he said one day, after rudely barging into Lex's bedroom where he was trying to study. 'But if you could just help Lucius sometimes with your grandfather it would help him enormously—'

'Sod off,' Lex said, without looking up from his text-book. 'I'm trying to learn how to be a lawyer here.'

'Alistair won't be with us much longer,' Zachary said quietly. 'So if you don't make time for him now, you won't get another chance to say goodbye.'

'Let's not talk as if he's already dead, shall we?' Lex asked in a loud voice. 'I realise you're earning yourself some serious brownie points with my brother right now but that doesn't give you the right to forget your place. You're a *servant*! And you'd do well to remember it if you don't want to lose your job!'

Lex was pleased to note that Zachary reddened slightly at that. 'You can't fire me,' he said stiffly. 'I'm employed by your grandfather, not by you.'

'Yes, but he'll kick the bucket soon, won't he?' Lex asked, standing up suddenly. 'Then guess who'll inherit the farm? When he's gone, I shall make it my personal responsibility to see that you go, too!'

Zachary narrowed his eyes angrily. 'I know you were very close to Alistair,' he said at last. 'But he would be ashamed of you and the way you're behaving if he could see you now.'

After an uncomfortable spasm of shocked, angry guilt, Lex lunged forward, knocking things over in his haste to hit Zachary in the mouth. Lex didn't tend to get involved in physical fights because he knew he wouldn't win them. He wasn't stupid – Zachary was a large, broad-shouldered forty-year-old farmhand and Lex was a skinny fifteen year old who'd never done a day's hard labour in his life. Fortunately Zachary did not hit him back, although he very much looked like he wanted to. He just stalked away, one hand held to his bleeding lip, and never said another word about it. But the already strained relationship was certainly not improved by that incident.

'Now shut up so I can land the ship,' Lex snapped at Schmidt. 'I fully intend to find that crown before the prophet does.'

He stomped off to the prow, took a couple of deep breaths to collect himself and then closed his eyes and threw out his arms in a dramatic pose because he knew it irritated the lawyer. He concentrated all his thoughts on visualising what he needed to do and then slowly and expertly brought the great ship down to the valley floor. He was very adept at controlling the ship already and it landed gently with barely a tremble of impact.

'Is there nothing I can't do?' Lex asked, turning back to Schmidt with a broad smile, all irritation now properly suppressed.

Lex made Schmidt go down the ladder first this time so that he could go after him, treading on his fingers where necessary to speed him up a little. It went without saying that Lucius wasn't a threat, he was still messing about inside the ship, but the prophet was already in the Royal Forest and Lex knew it would be dangerous to underestimate him just because he'd lost Theba and then made a silly mistake with the quicksand in the last round. After all, he was the Judge's player, so he couldn't be totally incompetent. When he jumped down onto the ground, Lex ignored the glare the lawyer was giving him as he pointedly rubbed his bruised fingers, and set off down one of the emerald pathways towards the forest.

Winning the first two rounds of the Game was not as important as winning the third one. The last round was the most dangerous and the real decider of who won the Game for the points accumulated during the first two rounds were wiped clean before the third round even began. The only thing those points were actually good for (aside from earning the player a good reputation and some adoring fans) was that they gave the winning player a headstart for the all-important third round. Therefore, Lex could have conceivably lost both the first two rounds and still won the Game overall if he was able to triumph in the third round despite the disadvantage of a late start. But it was not just about winning the Game in the *end*; it was about winning the Game all the way *through*, and Lex would have felt that way even if a royal crown hadn't been involved. But now that he knew about it, he was, if possible, even more determined to win than he'd been before.

All the paths in the Golden Valley were made of pebbled emeralds that had been embedded into the ground and sparkled underfoot. Lex wondered how easy it would be to prise some of them up and decided to give it a go on the way back if there was time. The emeralds would fetch a handsome price back in the Wither City or anywhere else in the Lands Above.

Some of the kings came to the windows of their palaces as Lex and Schmidt passed to stare out at them curiously before disappearing hurriedly back inside again. They did not get many visitors in the Golden Valley since it was a forbidden place to all but royalty and their servants under usual circumstances, and inbred fears of assassins resurfaced as soon as the kings caught sight of strangers. They probably wouldn't even stop him if he started chipping gold off the walls outside as long as he didn't actually try to get in. It would be so painfully easy, it would be almost sacrilegious not to line his pockets before he left. Lex promised himself that he'd see what could be done about that after he'd found the crown.

He paused at the entrance to the Royal Forest. It was kept well stocked with deer for the kings to hunt. But it was also enchanted. There were talking trees and it was also said that many fairy godmothers retired to the forest because the only people who lived in the valley were kings and they were a contented lot, having already fulfilled their life's dreams. This was probably the only forest on the Globe where the fairy godmothers were not likely to be bothered by any poor woodcutters or lost children whining about wishes.

'There probably isn't anything all that dangerous here,' Lex said. 'But magical things are unpredictable, so keep an eye out anyway, all right?' He adjusted the straps of his bag and crept into the dark creepiness of the forest, revelling in the uneasy familiarity of it whilst the distinctly unhappy lawyer followed on behind him.

★ ★ ★

Lucius fastened Zachary's halter and made his way up to the top of the ship using the coloured length of string Lex had set up for him. To say that Lucius was feeling miserable would have been to put it very mildly indeed. He had found the Game much easier when Zachary had been there to reassure him. Since his grandfather's death, Lucius had come to rely very much on Zachary's help with the day-to-day running of the farm. He would have been lost without him and had found his presence immensely comforting in the first round of the Game. But Lex had taken even that small comfort away in a childish moment of petty spite and Lucius couldn't help but resent him just a little for that. Lex always had been one to hold a grudge and he would never forgive Zachary for all the bitterness of the past.

Zachary hadn't been himself since becoming a ferret, even trying to bite Lucius on more than one occasion when he'd gone to stoke him. Lucius didn't even want to be part of this Game – he had always been rubbish at these competitive things and he was very aware of Jezra's anger and it worried him. He'd had no choice but to take part or Jezra would have turned him into a wooden chessman – a lowly pawn, knowing Lucius's luck. The only good thing about the Game was that it had given him the opportunity to see his brother again. He hadn't realised how much he'd missed Lex until he'd seen him again in Mahara's Black Tower in Khestrii. He was half hoping that he might be able to persuade him to come home after the Game but even Lucius realised that this was probably a futile hope. Lex was far too set on his own path to be talked off it by anyone.

He opened the door and stepped out onto the deck, revelling for a moment in the beauty of Saydi's sun and the gentle warmth of the sun drizzle that flecked his skin within moments. But then he froze as he heard Jezra's voice from the level above. Lucius had no wish for his already disgruntled God to see how late he was, having left at least twenty minutes behind the others, so he started to creep towards the ladder, hoping to slip down over the edge without Jezra noticing, but then he heard his brother's name being spoken and froze.

'It can only benefit both of us to get rid of Lex Trent, my Lord,' Jezra said softly. 'I beg you to reconsider.'

There was silence for a moment before Lucius heard the Judge. 'How can you know that Lucius won't get to the crown first and bewitch himself instead of Lex?'

Jezra gave a contemptuous snort, which seemed to be all he considered necessary for an answer. 'I accept that I am going to lose this time, my Lord,' he said. 'The Goddess of Luck tricked me into choosing Lucius Trent and as such I realise I'm going to be utterly handicapped for the rest of the Game. All I care about now is seeing her Ladyship lose and I will thwart her any way that I can. So we have a common goal in this. All I ask is that you keep the prophet back in this round and let Lex find the crown first. I managed to bewitch it without Lady Luck's knowledge. As soon as he puts the crown on, a poison will pass into his system and that will be the end of Lex Trent as far as the Game is concerned.'

Lucius couldn't help the harsh intake of breath and clapped his hand over his mouth hurriedly. He waited for the Judge to admonish Jezra for such a vile act of cheating, but after a few moments the Judge said, 'Very well. I will keep my player out of this round. I very much hope your plan works, Lord Jezra.'

Lucius suppressed the squeak of horror that rose in his throat. He draped Zachary around his shoulders and scuttled down the side of the ship as fast as he could, taking great care all the while to ensure the scheming Gods above didn't see him. Once he was on the ground, he tucked the ferret under his arm and ran down the emerald path towards the Royal Forest as fast as his legs would carry him.

CHAPTER THIRTEEN

THE DRAGLINGS AND THE WICKED WITCH

'You must have some idea where the crown is,' Lex said to the tree impatiently. 'Don't you take any interest at all in what goes on in the forest?'

The grand old tree regarded Lex disdainfully. 'Little human,' it said majestically, 'human crowns are of no importance to us whatsoever. It's not here; I suggest you look elsewhere.'

'But you must have seen where the Goddess put it or at least be able to direct me to the general area,' Lex insisted.

'Why should I?' the tree asked lazily. 'What's in it for me?'

'Well, not getting chopped down by me for a start,' Lex snapped.

'Lex,' Schmidt warned.

At Lex's last words, the trees surrounding them in the

dappled green grove seemed to rustle their leaves in a distinctly threatening way and the light from Saydi's sun became a little darker. No sane person wants to be surrounded by a group of large, strong, rather put-out enchanted trees when they're lost in the middle of an enchanted forest. It's not a happy situation.

'You do not even begin to possess the strength that would be necessary to damage us, little boy,' the tree said, evidently less than impressed with Lex's scrawny frame.

Lex frowned, irritated. Okay, so he wasn't exactly the bulging-with-muscles type and no teenage girl was ever likely to exclaim in delight after ripping his shirt off. But he was clever. He did have that. And you did need to be clever to lie convincingly.

'I have a magic axe,' Lex announced, pleased to note the alarmed rustling from the trees.

'No you don't,' the tree scoffed. 'Only magical people have things like that.'

'You know that enchanted ship that flew overhead an hour or so ago?' Lex asked. 'I stole it. I'm the one who flew it here. I made a list, you see, of things I'd never done before. Escaping from prison was one of them. So was stealing an enchanted ship. I've never cut down a magic tree either.' Lex eyed the tree before him with renewed interest. 'Do you think if I cut the bark up into little bits I could sell it back in the Wither City?' Lex asked, turning to Schmidt. 'Actually, come to think of it, I might be better off cutting down all these trees and taking them back to the ship and just forgetting about the crown altogether. I bet they'd fetch an absolute *fortune*. I'll get started,' Lex said, shrugging the bag off his shoulders and rummaging through it in search of the non-existent magical axe. 'You go back to the ship and get the other axe and then come back and—'

'No, no,' the tree said hastily. 'Look, we don't know exactly where the crown is. All we know is that the Goddess left it due north from here.'

'How far?' Lex asked.

'Towards the middle of the forest.'

'Thank you. To show my gratitude for your help I shall spare you,' Lex said graciously.

'You are most noble, young Adventurer,' the tree said gratefully. 'May your Chronicles fill many shelves.'

Schimdt gawked at Lex as he turned and strode due north out of the glade. How did he *do* that? Schmidt couldn't help feeling a little envious. It would be nice to be able to wrap anyone around your finger in that way.

'I know what you're thinking,' Lex said when Schmidt caught up with him. 'If only I would use my power for good instead of for evil, right?'

'Something along those lines, I suppose,' Schmidt said. 'You could have been a very fine lawyer, Lex.'

'Because I'm inwardly contemptible, you mean?'

'No! Because you're quick thinking. As it is, you're the kind of person who gives the legal profession a bad name. The law used to be something noble once. It was what separated us from the animals and the magical peoples. We had *rules* – certain lines we were not allowed to cross.

Lawyers were like policemen. We were like guardians. And then people like you came along and started twisting everything so that justice wasn't what was being aimed for at all any more. It's a disgrace! It's an absolute *disgrace*, Lex!'

Lex gazed at the old lawyer in surprise. He could tell that Schmidt was already regretting what he'd said. 'Well, I never got the chance to twist anything,' Lex said mildly, 'seeing as I never qualified. There's only so much damage you can do to the noble legal profession when all you ever do is file papers and make the coffee. So I can only assume you weren't talking about me. So what is it, Schmidt? Do you have some dirty, dark little secret lurking in your past? How very mysterious. I shall make it my duty to find out what it is.'

'You're letting your imagination run away with you,' Schmidt said dismissively.

Lex opened his mouth to rub more salt into the raw wound when his nose began to fizz and he rummaged desperately for a handkerchief, only just managing to find it and press it over his face before the ferocious sneeze came. Luckily, Schmidt was already stalking huffily ahead, so he didn't see the nine or ten nasal lice thrashing around in Lex's tissue. Lex shook them out onto the ground in disgust and then hurried to catch up with the long-legged lawyer.

Apart from the obvious enchanted trees, the only other things they had seen so far were the deer that lived in the forest and the odd fleeting glimpse of woodland spirits flitting between the trees. Both were gentle and neither were likely to pose any threat to them, but still Lex was watchful. It would be very easy to get lost in a place like this and there were stories about the things that lived in enchanted forests. If Lex lost this round he could still win the Game if he did well in the third round. But this was extra special to him now because of the crown. Not only would he get to see and touch a genuine royal crown, but his temporary royalty would mean that his name would be added to the Royal Monument in the centre of the Wither City. That would be immensely satisfying. It would piss Schmidt off for one thing. And it would earn him a kind of immortality. Children had to memorise the names of kings at school and he loved the thought of being partially responsible for the hair-tearing frustration of that exercise.

The Royal Monument was something of an anachronism in a way but it was tradition and people clung to tradition like leeches because it made them feel safer in changing times. Any man who had been a king, even if only for a few minutes, would have his name inscribed on the Monument and passed down through the years. Hundreds and hundreds of years from now, people would look at the Monument, reading through the names and Lex Trent would be there – set in stone at last. Lex was absolutely determined to have the crown for himself and he was more than happy to cheat to get it. He *deserved* it because he was the only one who would fully *appreciate* it. It was not just about winning the round now, it was about tasting royalty just for a moment and the immortality that went with it.

They headed on deeper into the forest, towards the centre. Lex was feeling a little uneasy about the prophet. Everyone knew that prophets were dangerous because they could see the future and so were sometimes able to manipulate it. They couldn't speak so they couldn't utter spells or enchantments but it was difficult to outwit a prophet when they could see what you were going to do. And then of course there was Jezra who was even more pissed off than the prophet.

The forest itself was not overly dangerous. But it was maze-like and they kept finding themselves getting turned around. It was as if the forest did not want them to travel too deeply inside. And then there was the whistling. A strange, ominous high-pitched whistling that seemed to be coming from something on the forest floor around them. The sound was making the lawyer look distinctly uneasy so Lex didn't trouble himself to tell Schmidt that the whistling was in fact caused by harmless duckigs – strange little creatures that looked somewhere between a duck and a pig. Lex knew there wouldn't be anything overly dangerous in the Royal Forest for although the kings rather enjoyed hunting down gentle, harmless deer, they were not favourably inclined towards being butchered themselves . . .

. . . Now, usually, Lex would have been quite right about that but, to make the round more interesting, Lady Luck had deliberately chosen a day when she knew that the kings were to hold a royal hunt. Although usually they only hunted deer, today they had the extra special treat of hunting a wicked witch. Lady Luck knew this because that morning she had made a gift of the witch to the kings, knowing full well that they would instantly set her loose in the forest to hunt, for – with the possible exception of taking royal mistresses – there is nothing in the whole world that any king loves more than a good hunt and a grisly kill.

Lex and Schmidt had been in the forest for only half an hour when they saw the kings go thundering past on horses, elephants or rhinoceroses depending on the ethnicity of the particular king. Fortunately, they did not notice Lex or Schmidt – who crouched down to watch from behind some bushes where they could get a good view without being disturbed themselves. But Lex's heart couldn't help but sink a little. The kings were all waving huge swords and screaming war cries, but they weren't even the worst part of it – it was what they were hunting with that concerned him. For the kings were preceded by a pack of rabid draglings. The baby dragons were about the size of large dogs and came in a variety of colours from blue to green to yellow to orange. They were all slavering at the mouth – or at the snout – driven half insane by the maddening scent of the evil witch . . .

When the last king – a fat one trailing behind on a huge elephant – had loped noisily past them, Lex turned his head to meet Schmidt's gaze. He felt just as horrified as Schmidt looked, but couldn't help breaking into a broad smile at the expression on the old lawyer's face.

'Why are you grinning?' Schmidt snapped.

'Because you're not! Don't worry, sir. I won't let them get you.' He reached out to pat the lawyer's hand comfortingly.

Schmidt snatched his hand away and said irritably, 'Let's just get on with it.'

So they got on with it – albeit with a lot more caution, for the forest had just become a much more dangerous place and they realised that without even knowing about the witch.

When the kings split up shortly afterwards, it became practically impossible to move about the forest, for as soon as they took a step in any direction they would see a king thundering through the trees up ahead.

'I think we'd better find somewhere to hide until they've passed,' Lex said reluctantly. He didn't want to have a repeat performance of what had happened in the sky castle by getting trapped between kings, for he didn't know that he'd be able to pull another miraculous escape out of his hat this time.

'Very sensible,' Schmidt said approvingly. 'I agree entirely.'

That almost made Lex change his mind and, indeed, he was right on the verge of saying that perhaps they would continue just a little bit further before finding somewhere to hide when a pack of four draglings burst out of the nearby trees, closely followed by a ferocious-looking

king on an even more ferocious-looking rhinoceros. The king saw Lex and Schmidt at once, gave a great bellow of anger and raised his sword over his head, screaming about assassins as the whole lot came charging towards them. Lex and Schmidt turned as one and raced into the forest as fast as they could.

They didn't have much of a head start and Lex knew that the draglings would be upon them at any moment. Attempting to outrun them was quite, quite hopeless. But, as luck would have it, as they stumbled and slid their way down a leaf-covered slope, Lex tripped on a raised tree root, crashed into Schmidt and sent the pair of them rolling down the hill where they landed right beside the narrow mouth of a cave.

'In here quick!' Lex exclaimed, heaving the lawyer back to his feet and dragging him into the cave from where they had a perfect view of the king thundering past a bare minute later.

Fortunately, draglings are unable to detect the human scent and so could not tell that Lex and Schmidt had left the path. They were, in fact, a totally ineffectual animal with which to hunt, which was why the kings very rarely caught anything. They liked the draglings because they were colourful and impressive and the sort of creature a king was expected to hunt with. And it was worth it even if it meant they didn't catch their prey, for although the kings really loved to finish the hunt with a bit of blood and gore, the main attraction for them was that they got to ride along screaming and waving their swords.

Lex and Schmidt watched as first the scaly, lizardy draglings raced past, slavering madly, followed a moment or two later by the wheezing rhino, eyes rolling in anger at the way the insane king in his billowing royal blue robes was sticking his spurred heels mercilessly into its sides. In another moment they had stumped out of sight and Lex said to Schmidt with a smile, 'If he carries on like that he's likely to get impaled on the horn of his own rhinoceros.'

Before Schmidt could reply, a voice from the cave behind them made them both jump. It was a sly old voice, practically dripping with greed.

'Why, it appearth that dinner hath walked right into my cave all by it-thelf.'

Lex and Schmidt turned around and out of the gloom stepped the wicked witch the kings were hunting. She had green skin, long, greasy black hair, a hooked nose with a large spot on the end of it that looked as if it was about to burst at any moment and her almost-blind eyes had a milky white sheen. She slowly smiled, displaying the revolting remnants of her decaying, yellowed teeth, although most of them were missing – which quite possibly explained the lisp. Lex could smell her bad breath from where he stood.

'*Urghh!*' he exclaimed in obvious and horrified disgust. As someone who was an absolute stickler for cleanliness, the contents of that rotting mouth were enough to make Lex feel sick. He turned on his heel with the intention of walking straight out of the cave and back into the forest. Better to risk insane kings and rabid draglings than this . . . But there were bars blocking his way. And when he turned back he realised that they were all around him, trapping them both. The witch had conjured up a cage – one of her gnarled, bent old hands with disgustingly overgrown fingernails was still stretched out towards them. She gave a dry cackle that made the hairs on the back of Lex's neck stand up.

'Dinner ith therved,' she giggled to herself before turning away and promptly starting to build a cooking fire from the sticks and twigs that littered the floor.

'I thought you said there was nothing *dangerous* in the forest?' Schmidt hissed.

'There isn't, usually,' Lex replied defensively. 'She must be what the kings are hunting.'

'And you call yourself a lucky person?' Schmidt snarled. 'Things just seem to go from bad to worse whenever you're around!'

'Oh, settle down,' Lex said calmly. 'I have every confidence that I shall be able to talk my way out of this. If you're extra-specially polite to me, then I just might save your skin as well. Again.'

He turned away from Schmidt and studied the cave. It was always sensible to study your surroundings first – see what might help you and what might hinder you . . . The cave was a deep one – stretching far back into the rock. There were obviously large trees above it, for Lex could see the thick roots entwined throughout the walls. Sunlight shone in from a hole in the ceiling and it was beneath this that the witch was assembling wood for a fire, attempting to whistle while she worked but – due to her lack of teeth – mostly just spitting on the sticks. There was a large black cauldron behind her, set on top of a metal tripod, presumably to hold it above the flames and, on the floor, were an assortment of rather dirty vegetables, which mostly seemed to be turnips and carrots.

'How long have you been living here?' Lex said, for if she had only been set loose in the forest that morning, then it seemed rather odd that she had stopped to collect vegetables and a cauldron from somewhere before finding a place to hide from the kings.

'A few dayth,' the witch replied cheerfully, 'before the Goddeth took me to the kingth.' She shrugged. 'All they did wath thet me looth, tho I came thtraight back here and – lo and behold – my dinner came in right behind me. Wathn't that a fortunate cointhidenth?'

'Most fortunate,' Lex replied. 'But I see you already have quite an assortment of vegetables there to eat. Wouldn't you rather just make do with them and allow me to reward you handsomely for letting us go free?'

Lex could see at once that this line of reasoning was going to be quite, quite useless. The witch was already shaking her head vehemently. 'There'th nothing like a good thlab of meat!' she said gleefully as she pointed a gnarled finger at the pile of wood. A green spark leapt from her filthy fingertip and in a matter of moments caught onto the sticks so that they crackled away cheerfully.

'Ethpecially little-boy meat – that'th alwayth the juithi-etht and I haven't had any in thuch a long time!'

Lex scowled. 'Not that I suppose it matters much at this stage but – just for the record – I am *not* a little boy!'

'You mean you're a big boy?' the witch replied, practically salivating at the mouth in anticipation as she dragged the cauldron towards the fire – water slopping over the edges as she did so. 'Exthellent. Now I than't have to wait and fatten you up a bit before eating you. Oh, what a featht I thall have!'

'Skinny as a rake,' Lex said hurriedly. 'Not a scrap of meat on me. A walking skeleton would give you a better meal.'

But the witch was cackling to herself and not listening to him.

'I have a vast array of treasures in my magic bag here,' Lex announced. 'You can have your pick of anything in it if you will let us go free.'

'I thall have everything in your bag little boy, oneth I have feathted on your flesh!'

Lex swallowed. She had a point there. How could he possibly hope to bargain with anything that was inside the bag when it was as good as hers, anyway? He eyed her critically as she sat herself down beside the vegetables and started peeling the carrots with a dirty old knife. Despite being armed, she didn't look very strong – he might be able to push her over when she opened the cage and then make a break for it. But witches were not like crones – they had dangerous magic of their own and she

226

was bound to have some sort of fail-safe in place to ensure that Lex did not escape. For all he knew she would cast a spell so that he willingly climbed right into the pot himself . . . Lex shuddered at the thought. He feared he could hear the water bubbling already . . .

He pulled himself together and desperately tried to think. If anyone was going to eat him, it was *not* going to be someone with teeth like that. An idea occurred to him and he said, hopefully, 'You'll never be able to eat me, you know. Not with those teeth. You can't possibly chew meat with hardly a single tooth in your head. You'll find me tough as old boots.'

The witch carefully laid a peeled carrot on the ground. 'I chop my food into very tiny pietheth. Like thith.' And she lowered the knife and chopped through the carrot so quickly that in no time at all there was only a handful of bite-sized chunks on the floor. She scooped these up and dropped them into the cauldron with a splash. 'I can eat you,' she said with an obscene grin. 'Jutht ath long ath I cut you up thmall enough firtht.'

Lex swallowed hard. He didn't like to admit it, but he was beginning to feel a little frantic. Turning his attention away from the witch, he looked at the cage instead, hoping to find some weakness, but the bars appeared to be made of bone and were quite solid. There didn't seem to be any chance of breaking them or squeezing out between them. It was all beginning to look a bit desperate.

'Whereabouts do you come from?' he said. Lex had learnt long ago that, when in doubt, the thing to do was to keep people talking about themselves. Sooner or later they were bound to give you something that you could use against them.

'What are you doing?' Schmidt whispered, digging Lex sharply in the ribs. 'How is making chitchat with her going to help?'

'I don't see you coming up with any ideas!' Lex said irritably, shoving the lawyer away. 'A fat lot of use you are, just standing there criticising me! Keep your bony fingers to yourself!' But then his head snapped back to Schmidt and he stared at him for a moment as if he'd never seen him before. Then a grin slowly spread across his face. Schmidt did not like the look of that grin. He didn't like the look of it one bit.

Lex turned his attention back to the witch, looking at her intently. Just how blind was she? She must have some sight for she was cutting up carrots without any problems and yet her eyes were that milky-white colour so she obviously couldn't see at all well . . .

'I can see there's no talking you out of it,' Lex said loudly. 'You're going to eat me and that's that.'

'That'th that,' the witch agreed, nodding her head over her carrots. There was a neat little row of them lined up in front of her already.

'Yes. But what are you going to do about the stick? Cut it up and use it for your spells, I suppose.'

'Thtick?' the witch said, looking up suspiciously, her hands stopping their peeling. 'What thtick?'

'Why, this one, of course,' Lex replied, jabbing his

thumb at Schmidt. 'I found him on the forest floor. The kings knocked him off his tree during their hunt and I was going to return him. I mean, it never hurts to make a friend of a magic tree, does it? I knew he had to be from a magic tree because—' He broke off abruptly because the expression on Schmidt's face was putting Lex in imminent danger of laughing and it was very important that he didn't. He pulled himself together, cleared his throat and went on, 'It's not every day you come across a walking, talking stick.'

He clapped his hand over his mouth to muffle the snigger as the witch scrambled hastily to her feet and scuttled closer to the cage. She wasn't quite close enough for Lex to touch her or try and make a grab at her, but she was near enough that he could see the sheen of grease on her green skin and the ever-so-faint glimmer of fear in her milky eyes as she squinted intensely at Schmidt's tall, skinny frame.

'That'th not a magic thtick!' she said at last. 'Magic thtickth talk.'

Lex looked back at Schmidt. The only words he'd spoken since they were trapped had been whispered ones that the witch clearly had not heard. Lex opened his mouth to order Schmidt to say something but then hesitated. He was himself a natural actor and could embrace any role that was presented to him instantly – as such he knew he could have done a beautiful impression of a magic stick. But Schmidt was a dry old lawyer and was already looking rather panicky at the prospect of trying to pass himself off as anything other than what he was. Perhaps it *was* better that he shouldn't talk, for he might somehow end up giving the game away and ruining everything.

'Can ordinary sticks wave?' Lex asked, with a pointed look at Schmidt who awkwardly raised his arm and waved it around a bit.

But the witch, although she squinted at them intensely, was apparently unable to see this, for she said, 'I don't thee anything. That'th no magic thtick. You're jutht trying to trick me with an ordinary one!'

She was about to return to her carrots at any moment, Lex could tell. There was nothing for it. Desperate times and all that.

'Well, come on, magic stick,' Lex said with an air of impatience. 'Speak up! Tell her what you are.'

Schmidt scowled at him for a moment before clearing his throat and – looking exceedingly uncomfortable – said stiffly, 'I am a magic stick.'

The witch gave a great squeal of alarm and Lex – because he couldn't resist it – said, 'What *makes* you a magical stick?'

'I can walk and talk,' Schmidt replied through gritted teeth.

Lex allowed himself to burst into laughter. It hardly mattered now, for the witch had clearly been taken in by it and, Lex had to admit, Schmidt's dry, old voice did sound a bit like the sort a stick might have.

'The joke's on you, witch!' Lex exclaimed gleefully.

'Even as we speak the magic trees are tightening their roots around your cave. They want their stick back and they're very angry with you for imprisoning him like this. Soon the roof will cave in altogether!'

With the usual lucky timing that Lex seemed to be blessed with, there was a thundering from above – probably caused by an elephant-riding king going across the roof – and several clumps of mud were shaken loose to land on the witch's shoulders. She screamed shrilly and suddenly the cage was gone and she was practically pushing them towards the exit.

'Out, out!' she gasped. 'Get out at oneth. Tell the magic treeth to thtop – I'm letting you go! Leave my cave alone!'

A moment later they found themselves back out in the dappled sunlight of the forest floor and the witch was barricaded securely in her cave. They set off in a random direction, eager to be as far away from her as possible. They were a reasonable distance away before Lex allowed himself to burst into laughter – partly because he was genuinely amused and partly because he wanted to add as much as he possibly could to Schmidt's humiliation. The lawyer was not used to being put in undignified situations and – unlike Lex – he had not already been called all the names under the sun. Referring to him as a walking, talking stick was funny because, as far as Lex was concerned, there was a very large element of truth to it.

He was a little disappointed that Schmidt didn't rise to the bait, but instead merely stood there in dignified silence, watching him patiently. Lex had a good chortle anyway, determined not to let the lawyer ruin his fun, then he straightened up and said with his most smug expression, 'You're welcome!'

'On the contrary,' Schmidt replied calmly. '*You* are welcome.'

Lex shrugged. 'A team effort, I should say. I was the brains of the operation and you were . . . well, we all know what you were!'

Still grinning, Lex looked around for the first time, taking in his surroundings and trying to get his bearings. The forest was silent. There was no sound of hooves or hunting horns or screamed war cries. All was quiet once again and it occurred to Lex that perhaps the kings had given up by now and gone home. After all, they enjoyed hunting but not enough to persuade them to miss their lunch, and the midday sun was now high in the sky. Time was flying by and they would have to get a move on if they wanted to get to the crown before the prophet. But . . . but . . .

. . . There had been draglings before. And Lex knew that where there were draglings there would be a dragon lurking about somewhere, and where there was a dragon there was a dragon's lair, and where there was a dragon's lair there would be *gold*. Could there possibly be time to—

'Control your greed!' Schmidt snapped.

Lex looked at him in surprise. Had he actually been thinking out *loud*?

'I can tell what you're thinking!' Schmidt sneered at

the expression on his face. 'You're not very complex, Lex, I'm afraid.'

'You're quite right, Schmidt. The crown should be our first priority. But after that – if there's time, of course – I think I may go dragon hunting.'

CHAPTER FOURTEEN

MATILDA

Lex and Schmidt came across no more kings as they made their way through the forest, confirming Lex's belief that the hunt was probably over by now. But they did meet a couple of fairy godmothers who were out picking berries now that the forest was safe again. Their faces fell when they saw Lex, thinking that he was going to start pestering them for wishes (as any normal person would have done) so when he asked them where the crown was hidden, they were only too happy to point him in the right direction to get rid of him. Lex had no interest in wishes. What was the fun in simply being *given* something? The satisfaction came to a large extent from earning the thing . . . or, as in Lex's case, from pinching it. He smiled, hoping that Lucius and the prophet might stumble across a fairy godmother themselves and be slowed down, greedily thinking of things to wish for.

When they came across a third fairy godmother, Lex made a show of whining about wishes first in order to convince the godmother to take him straight to the clearing where she knew the crown to be. He smiled as she led them on, keeping his eyes fixed on her neat grey bun. Apart from the slight detour with the witch, he had made good time. The others were certain to have ensnared themselves in traps or run into trouble with the kings and draglings and Lex was sure that they would not have been able to extricate themselves anywhere near as smoothly or quickly as he had done. He was bound to get there first. So with these happy thoughts going through his head, Lex was clearly somewhat less than impressed to walk out into the clearing to find that the crown . . . had already . . . gone. The colourful banners were there, hanging from the surrounding trees, the velvet cushion where the crown had sat was there but there was nothing else.

'Where's the crown?' Lex said stupidly.

'Someone got here first,' Schmidt said with a smirk. 'Serves you right for being so cocky.'

'It's not cockiness,' Lex snapped. 'We've made very good time. No one could have beaten us!'

'The prophet left before we did,' Schmidt said with a shrug. 'You underestimated him.'

Lex shook his head impatiently. He knew he had taken the prophet's head start into account. The prophet was blind and dumb and as such he would not be able to get help from the forest's inhabitants. His precognitive ability would have helped him to some extent but he would still have had to circle the crown for some time before managing to zero in on it. This round should have been the easiest one for Lex since stumbling across the crown in the vast forest would be largely dependent on luck. And Lex was lucky even without the Lady.

'It wasn't the prophet,' he said.

'Lucius then,' Schmidt suggested.

Lex didn't even deign to respond to that, the notion was so ridiculous . . . although . . . it was true that his brother had managed to get to the broken mirror in the sky castle first and it wasn't like there was a riddle to solve this time. All he needed to do was put the crown on his head and surely even Lucius could manage that? Just as Lex's horror began to mount at the thought that his brother might actually have somehow *beaten* him, the fairy godmother bent over something on the ground beside the bare cushion and muttered an irritated exclamation.

'What is it?' Lex asked sharply.

'I'm afraid I know where your missing crown has gone,' she said glumly, turning around with a necklace in her hand.

Lex peered at the thing, at first thinking it was made of large misshapen white beads but on a closer look realising that it was, in fact, made out of small skulls.

Lucius very quickly became lost inside the forest. Because he was wandering through the outskirts he was never even aware of the hunt that was taking place in the thick of the wood and he was not overly afraid for his own safety because of the duckigs. Lucius was familiar with the creatures, having raised them on the farm and so he knew that they would not stay very long anywhere where there might be predators. Anyone who had ever had anything to do with duckigs knew that wherever the strange animals lived was likely to be one of the safest places on the Globe. They knew when danger was coming and they would always be gone before it got there. So he wasn't scared for himself. But he was terrified for Lex. With the prophet being held back, Lex was bound to reach the crown first and Lucius knew that he wouldn't think before putting it on. For all his supposed shrewdness, he would walk right into the trap, driven by that unquenchable greed. Unless Lucius could get there in time to stop him, Lex was going to be in very serious trouble indeed.

Lucius had no idea whatsoever about how to go about finding the crown. He needed help. He didn't trust the enchanted trees or many other magical creatures for that matter. But there was one magical people he knew he could trust implicitly and that was the fairy godmothers. He knew they were said to take up their retirement in the forest. He therefore had no choice but to find one and implore her to help him. They were kindly old ladies and he was sure they would not let him down. But he had not seen any yet. Lex would probably stumble across them without even trying but Lucius wasn't lucky like that. He needed to find their village. And the only way he could think to do that was to follow the duckigs. The duckigs liked people, and the fairy godmothers were bound to feed them sometimes. The creatures were therefore likely to stay as close to the fairy godmother village as they could and the more duckigs he came across, the nearer he must be. He had to reach that crown first, he had to! Otherwise, Lex's lust for power and riches might be the death of him sooner than he'd thought.

Lex stood and regarded the fairy godmother village. It was quaint in a boring kind of way. The godmothers liked their neat, pretty little thatched cottages and every house in the glade seemed to be exactly the same . . . except for one, huddled miserably on the outskirts. It seemed to be mostly made out of mud and sticks with a feeble patch of what looked like weeds growing outside in sharp contrast to the neat rows of flowerbeds the godmothers favoured.

'She doesn't realise she's a crone,' sighed the fairy godmother.

'I beg your pardon?' Schmidt said, staring at the pathetic hut.

'She calls herself Matilda. She thinks she's a retired fairy godmother like us. From what we've gathered, we think her enchanter dispossessed her for some reason and she's been alone ever since.'

'I thought crones couldn't survive without an enchanter?' Lex asked.

The fairy godmother shrugged. 'Matilda barely survives. She'd have died within a week in most forests but this one is kept safe for the kings to hunt in. She's quite unbalanced of course. We don't want her anywhere near us but we haven't been able to get her to leave. It's the most dreadful shame because that horrible little house of hers really spoils the neighbourhood and she goes through our rubbish at night, pinching things—'

'I don't suppose it occurs to any of you just to *give* her the things you throw away?' Schmidt snapped irritably.

The fairy godmother gave him a startled look and went on hurriedly, 'Crones are attracted to shiny things – I expect that's why she took the crown. She probably just stumbled across it when she was out looking for berries.'

'Well, we won't need to bother her for long,' Lex said breezily, reaching his hand out towards the fairy godmother for the skull necklace.

'For all you know she's already put it on and made herself Queen,' Schmidt said. 'In which case, you've already lost.'

'Crones can't be royal,' Lex said dismissively. If Schmidt had known anything about royalty he would have known that only humans could be kings and queens.

'Well, at any rate I doubt she's going to hand something like that over to you just because you ask her to.'

'Whoever said anything about *asking*?' Lex said with a nasty smile. 'Trust me, she'll hand it over.'

'I should warn you,' the fairy godmother began hesitantly. 'Matilida is . . . not like other crones—'

'Madam, she could be Queen Japunzel herself for all I care,' Lex said firmly. He was going to get that crown if he had to wrestle the old crow for it himself. 'Are you coming?' he asked, looking at Schmidt.

The lawyer hesitated and then shook his head. 'No,' he said stiffly. 'I'll wait here. But be civil to her, Lex.'

'I'm always civil,' Lex replied. He wrapped the grotesque skull necklace around his wrist, walked up to the house, found the front door and went straight in without bothering to knock. After taking no more than a couple of steps inside he'd already managed to tread on about three disgruntled cats who shot out of the hut, hissing. The remaining cats regarded him moodily from their various perches.

Lex stopped in astonishment once he was inside. He had never seen a house quite like it. Crones liked small spaces, they liked strings of skulls and creepy, grinning masks and more cats than windows. And this one was no different but she had clearly tried to make the hut seem like a fairy cottage and the clash of the two decors was more than a little disturbing.

What light there was came from the large hole in the pointed roof and one small window set high up in the wall. There were the usual skull-strings but these had been painted with sap from the cherry-drop tree to make them pink and sparkly. A thick, matted spider web served as a substitute for a lace doily in the middle of the table upon which stood a vase with a couple of dead roses in it. There was a bed the crone had managed to get from somewhere, presumably a fairy godmother chuck-out for it was clearly old and worn and very, very lacy. The crone's basket was perched on top of the bed, though, for crones did not like sleeping on mattresses – they would have to lie down straight then and their bent backs seemed to be more comfortable if they curled up in a basket. There were net curtains over the window but, like the bed, they were now so filthy as to be almost black. There was a mushroom ring in the middle of the room and in the centre of this sat Matilda herself. The fairy godmother had been right. Matilda was clearly not like other crones.

Physically she was much the same as all the others – an old lady with matted grey hair, a bent back and more than a few warts. But, at an angle on her grey head, was an old bonnet that she had clearly taken from one of the godmothers' trashcans and a grotty old apron was tied around her waist. There seemed to be a cat sleeping in the front pocket. The rest of her clothes looked as if she had simply smeared cherry-drop sap all over them in an effort to make her outfit more colourful. The result was a sickly sweet smell that mixed with the other odours of cat, old mud and decaying flowers in the tiny hut.

'Matilda doesn't do princesses and coaches any more, dearie,' Matilda rasped when she saw Lex silhouetted in the doorway. 'Matilda is retired. You must take your pumpkin elsewhere.'

'I don't have a pumpkin, you blind old woman!' Lex said irritably, unimpressed with being mistaken for a princess by anyone. 'I just want that crown you pinched from the forest. Where is it?'

'Matilda doesn't steal,' the old crow sniffed huffily.

Lex walked over to the bed and tipped the grubby blankets in the crone's basket out onto the floor, ignoring her squeal of protest. He looked through them with his boot and then kicked them away into a corner once he was satisfied the crown wasn't there. Then he turned the bed over and did the same with that as more cats shot out of the hut in alarm. He tried not to touch anything more than he had to, for it was clear that no cleaning ever went on here. The crown wasn't in the bed but where else could it be hidden? There wasn't anywhere to hide such a thing in a tiny, empty hut like this. Lex tried to control his frustration. He tried to prevent a snarl from curling his lips. But he could feel his anger mounting. He had had just about enough of old women for one day. And if this one hadn't interfered, he would have won the round long ago.

'I know. It's in the walls, isn't it?' Lex said with sudden maliciousness.

He stood back a little and kicked as hard as he could at the mud wall. It crumbled around the edges of where Lex's foot had struck it, dust rising up in a cloud and bits of twig and stone falling to the floor in a heap. It was clear that a few good kicks from Lex would be enough to bring the entire wall down. The crone was on him at once, tugging at his shirt and screeching in his ear. 'Do not wreck Matilda's home!' she wailed. 'It took Matilda so long to build! No one else would help her!'

'Then tell me where the crown is, you stupid old crone, and I'll stop destroying your house!'

'Horrible boy has no right,' she sobbed. 'No right! The crown belongs to Matilda!'

Lex aimed two more really hard kicks at the wall and this time he broke right through so that the wall partially crumbled in on itself and light shone into the hut. The crone screamed at him but still she wouldn't tell him where the crown was. The prophet wouldn't need anyone to tell him where it was for he'd be able to sense the magic in it. He'd be circling in on it even now whilst Lex wasted time messing about with this infuriating old woman. Jezra's opinion of Lex as a player would be diminished. He'd wonder why he ever went to such trouble to try and procure him. Gods would no longer argue over him and his name would never be etched in stone. And he would have won ages ago if it hadn't been for this vile, pathetic, thieving old crone.

'What the hell are you doing?'

Lex turned to see Schmidt's lanky frame in the doorway. The noise from the destruction of the wall had drawn the lawyer down to the hut. He had to bend almost double just to get inside. Lex ignored him. Time was precious and they had wasted more than enough as it was. So Schmidt didn't like his methods. Fine. That was why Schmidt would never be a winner like Lex was.

'Tell me where it is or I'll pull your whole house down!' Lex shouted, turning back to the crone.

'I've had enough of this!' Schmidt snapped, striding into the room and pulling Lex roughly away from the weeping old woman.

'Oh, get off me! Do you remember what happened last time you tried to protect a crone? She attacked you with a pair of walking sticks! She's a *thief*! She stole my crown! I thought you frowned on stealing, Schmidt?'

'Whatever else she is, she's an old lady and you will respect her for it!'

'Respect her for it? *Respect* her for it? Why should I respect her just for being *old*?'

'Because she knows things about life that you couldn't possibly understand, you arrogant brat!'

'Oh, spare me!' Lex said angrily, throwing the lawyer off.

'You'll be an old man one day, Lex. It'll come quicker than you think and you might regret all this then.'

'I don't intend to ever be old!' Lex snapped. 'I want to die young! I have it all planned out – I'm going to die suddenly, extraordinarily, doing some daring, villainous thing! I'm not content to just drift towards a slow, undignified death like you are!'

'You know, if it wasn't for your brother I would have thought that whoever brought you up did a very poor job of it indeed and clearly had no manners whatsoever themselves,' Schmidt said spitefully.

'My grandfather had impeccable manners!' Lex shouted and then cursed himself for rising to such obvious bait.

'Yes, well, I'm forced to believe you since Lucius must have got his manners from somewhere, although I suppose he might have just read about them in books.'

'Lucius!' Lex sneered. 'If my grandfather was alive today, Lucius would be just as much of a disappointment to him now as he was when we were growing up, because my grandfather was an Adventurer and a storyteller and he liked *excitement* like I do! And I am quite sure that he would have detested you, Mr Schmidt, because you are quite the most boring, uninteresting man I have ever met in my life.'

'Yes, perhaps you're right,' Schmidt said calmly. 'But if you really were the favourite, as you claim, I find it odd that Lucius was the one who cared for your grandfather when he became ill.'

That was the nub of it, really. One might think that his parents dying at such a young age, and then his grandfather succumbing to a horrible illness just a few years later might have changed Lex. But the truth was that he had always been this way. He had always had a terrible thirst for adventure as well as a generous dose of selfishness that must, by very definition, accompany all the truly great Adventurers. You can't be *'truly great'* if you let family ties and responsibilities hold you back. Lex knew it, and his grandfather had known it. Alistair Trent might have come back to raise his grandsons but that was only because there was no one else. He had not been around whilst Lex's father was growing up. Adventurers *had* to be selfish if they were to be any good, but no one ever seemed to be able to understand that. And Schmidt had no right to criticise Lex for leaving when his grandfather became ill. No right at all! What did Schmidt know about it? What did he know about what life had been like back then – how intolerable it had all been?

Lex glared ferociously at the old lawyer. 'So Lucius blurted out our life story, did he? He always did have a loose tongue. Yes, I left home when my grandfather became ill and I'd do it again. Do you know why? Have you *seen* the way old people are treated? They're treated like imbeciles half the time. If people aren't outright rude then they're condescending and patronising and that's worse! I left because I couldn't stand the sight of it a moment longer. He wouldn't have wanted us to see him that way. It was . . . it was undignified!'

'But, Lex,' Schmidt said softly, 'surely you're not saying that old people deserve a modicum of *respect* are you?'

Lex opened his mouth to give some clever retort but then froze and glanced at the crone with a scowl, realising that he'd contradicted himself. 'No, I'm not,' he sniffed. 'My grandfather was better than everyone else but this crone deserves nothing from me. And I'm warning you now that if you say one more word about him I'll put that enchanter's hat back on and turn *you* into a ferret, too!'

'I wouldn't advise it,' the lawyer said mildly. 'The hat will probably kill you next time you use it.'

'You're bluffing!' Lex scoffed.

'Perhaps. But you can't be sure, can you?'

'I'll risk it! It would be worth it!'

Schmidt shrugged. 'Go outside and I'll get the crown for you.'

'Oh, will you?' Lex sneered. 'Smuggle her out the back door and into the forest, more like. I'm not letting that old woman out of my sight for a second!'

'Then you'll never get the crown,' Schmidt said simply.

Lex laughed. 'How little you know me. Crones love their cats, don't they? There were some here a minute ago. I'm going to go out and start skinning them and when she's fed up with listening to the screams of her dying pets then perhaps she'll tell me where the crown is.'

Predictably, Matilda started the most ear-splitting wails at Lex's words – he'd never heard anything like it.

'Gods, is it really worth all this upset?' he asked, throwing up his hands. 'If you just tell me where the crown is, all this would be over!'

He shook her just a little to reinforce his point, ignoring the protesting clicks of bones that came from the old woman's body. But within moments, Schmidt had grabbed him by the arm, spun him round and smacked him hard across the face. Lex staggered back a few steps out of pure shock. Then the lawyer and the thief stared at each other for a moment in surprise, ignoring the screeching of the crone.

'Well,' Lex said at last, reaching up to wipe blood off his lip, 'which of us is being civilised now?'

'I'm sorry,' Schmidt said, and to be fair he looked it. 'I didn't mean to hit you that hard.'

'No, but I bet it felt good, didn't it?' Lex asked, smiling to show the blood on his teeth.

The lawyer winced. 'I'm sorry,' he said again. 'But you just don't know when to hold your tongue. You can't treat people like that.'

Lex shrugged. 'Go ahead and smack me around. It's

happened before and I'm sure it'll happen again. I've never pretended to be one of those strong, muscled types, so I can't stop you from hitting me if you want to, but if you think it's going to shut me up in any way or stop me from doing whatever I need to do to win, you're wrong.'

Schmidt sighed and turned back to the crone. Lex saw him whisper something in her ear. At once she stopped crying, looked up at Schmidt as if seeing him properly for the first time and, to Lex's astonishment, *hugged* him!

'Oh, Marvin,' she sobbed.

'Marvin?' Lex repeated. 'You two don't know each other do you?'

Schmidt said nothing but Lex could tell from his face that he was feeling very uncomfortable indeed.

'Oh, my Gods,' Lex gasped, as a horrific thought struck him. 'That's not your *mother* is it?'

'Of course she's not my mother,' Schmidt snapped. 'Now shut up so I can find out about this crown.'

'Don't let him kill my cats, Marvin! Don't let him do it!'

'No one's going to touch your cats, Matilda,' Schmidt said. 'Just tell us where the crown is and we'll be on our way.'

'I don't see what all the fuss is about, anyway,' Lex said irritably. 'What's the crown to her but a shiny thing? She probably doesn't even realise what it is. She can't make herself a queen with it, so what use is it to her?'

The crone wiped her eyes on the back of her sleeve, glared at Lex and then leant up to whisper something to

Schmidt. The lawyer frowned and then nodded. He straightened up and looked at Lex. 'She needs to keep the crown.'

'Why?' Lex demanded.

'You don't need to know why,' Schmidt replied impatiently.

'Well, it's irrelevant anyway because she's not keeping it. There's a prophet out there,' Lex said, looking at the crone. 'And he can sense magic. So wherever the crown is hidden, he'll find it eventually without any help from you.'

The crone gave a startled yelp at that and turned imploringly to Schmidt. 'Matilda,' he said, 'perhaps you could just let Lex put it on for a few seconds and as soon as he's done he'll take it off and give it straight back to you. How about that?'

'That's no good at all!' Lex said before Matilda could reply. 'I want to *keep* it! Do you know how *beautiful* those things are meant to be?'

'How does Matilda know you won't just take the magic crown from her if she shows it to you?' the crone demanded.

'Because I promise you that won't happen,' Schmidt said.

'But this isn't fair!' Lex wailed. 'It doesn't *belong* to her!'

'Well, she did find it and by your definition I would have thought that would constitute full legal ownership, Lex,' Schmidt replied sharply.

'Oh, all right,' Lex said, unwilling to waste any more

precious time. 'All right, she can keep it. Just get her to take me to it quickly before the prophet finds it.'

'It's still in the house,' Schmidt said.

'Where?' Lex stared round suspiciously. There just wasn't anywhere the crown could possibly have been hidden in the tiny space, unless it was on the crone herself. Lex grimaced with distaste at the idea of having to strip search the old woman.

'She buried it. It's in the floor.'

With a decided lack of good grace, the crone squatted down in the centre of the mushroom ring and started scrabbling around in the soft mud. Lex looked on, horrified as she slowly uncovered the crown.

'She buried it in *mud*?' he groaned.

'Why? What does it matter?' Schmidt asked. 'You can still put it on for a second even if it's not clean, can't you?'

'But I want to see how beautiful it is. I'm not putting it on my head like that,' Lex said, staring at the misshapen lump of mud the crone was offering him. 'It'll have to be washed.'

'Oh, don't be so childish, Lex. What does it matter as long as you win the round?'

'If I'm not allowed to keep it, I at least want to *see* it,' Lex snapped, snatching the dirty crown from the crone. 'Now where can I clean it up?'

'There's a water pump outside,' the crone said. 'Matilda is not supposed to use it but she can show you where it is.'

Lex gave a curt nod. This whole business was really starting to wear on his nerves. It was an undignified way to be crowned. It would have been much nicer if he'd found the crown in the quiet, sun-speckled glade as Lady Luck had intended instead of having to dig it out of a crone's muck before washing it at some miserable little pump. But the development with Schmidt had been interesting. Very interesting indeed. Although it had naturally hurt to be hit in the face, Lex was glad he had succeeded in making Schmidt lose his temper, making him lose control. It might be useful for the future. People were easier to manipulate when their control wavered like that. And guilt was always a useful thing to have tucked away somewhere. Lex's curiosity was even more aroused by the revelation that Schmidt knew this crone. Lawyers were not generally on speaking terms with magical peoples. It was frowned on by the Law Society, so this was another thing that Lex carefully filed away under *Potential Leverage*.

CHAPTER FIFTEEN

MUGGETS AND WHISKERFISH

The water pump was in the centre of the fairy godmothers' village. Their own guide had disappeared when they walked out of the crone's hut, probably frightened off by all the shouting. They were being watched with curiosity from various windows, but no one came out to take a closer look or to protest at the free use that was being made of their pump. Lex shooed away some loitering duckigs and then knelt down on his knees beside the pump. He deliberately made a show of washing his mouth out, spitting bloody water onto the grass and noting with satisfaction the rather mortified expression on his employer's face. Then he set to work cleaning the crown.

When he had finished, the three of them stared at it, enthralled, for several moments and the fairy godmothers in their cottages went to fetch their glasses so they might see it better from their windows. Lex had already known that the royal crowns were made from something even more beautiful and valuable than gold, but he hadn't known what exactly. Now he clearly saw that the crown was made out of star-silver. The Gods made these crowns out of the stars themselves, imbuing them with an ineffable majesty and beauty that gold would never have been able to achieve. Lex couldn't take his eyes off it. He wanted to be able to look at it always. There was no way he was ever giving this back to the crone; no way. They would have to prise it from his cold dead fingers first. It was simply shaped with no jewels or gilt adornment of any kind – it simply didn't need any. Now that it had been washed, the silver shone softly in Lex's hands, dappling his face with starlight. Lex could see his wavering reflection in the crown's surface as if he was looking into a clear, still unicorn lake. This was what he lived for – this, right here. The moments when he came face to face with beauty like this.

After they'd been gazing at it for a few moments, the crone began to fidget restlessly and started whining about getting 'her' crown back, so Lex stood up with a sigh, shushed her and then prepared to lower the crown onto its rightful place on his head. He froze in surprise when a madman burst from the trees, waving his arms and chasing a herd of startled-looking duckigs before him.

'Don't put it on!' the figure shrieked. 'Lex, don't put it on, it's *bewitched*!'

'What's wrong with Lucius?' Schmidt asked in surprise.

'Ha! He's too late, as usual,' Lex said with a grin as his brother sprinted towards him.

'You're too late, Lucius. I already found the— oompf!'

He broke off as Lucius crashed into him and the two of them went rolling over on the grass, the crown flying out of Lex's hand.

'You idiot!' Lex snapped, snatching it up again. 'You're too late; I've already won. I found it first.'

'Lex, please listen to me,' Lucius begged, still very much out of breath. 'The Gods are *cheating*!'

'Well of course they are; they want to win.'

'The crown is bewitched. It's a trap!'

'Eh?'

'It's a *trap*! I overheard Jezra talking with the Judge. He's bewitched the crown with some kind of poison to take you out of the running. He made the Judge keep the prophet back so that you'd find the crown first. Oh Gods, Lex, you have to believe me; I'm not making this up!'

'All right, calm down, I believe you,' Lex said calmly.

'You do?' Lucius beamed up from where he was still sprawled on the ground. He had been sure that Lex would think this was some kind of ploy – that his greed would overturn his common sense and he'd crown himself anyway. 'Thank the Gods.'

'Hmm,' Lex examined the crown in his hands thoughtfully. 'But is it really bewitched?'

'Lex, I swear I overheard Jezra saying that—'

'Yes, yes, I already said I believe you,' Lex said, waving his hand dismissively.

'Then you understand it's a trap?'

Lex glanced at his brother disdainfully. He noticed he

254

still had Zachary tucked under his arm. The ferret was hanging there resignedly. 'Of *course* it's a trap, Lucius; that's not the issue. The issue is working out exactly what the trap is.'

'But . . . I just told you . . . ' Lucius stammered.

Lex sighed. 'Jezra would have realised that you overheard him.'

'No, no,' Lucius protested at once. 'I was careful not to be seen. He told the Judge he realised he wasn't going to win. He said all he wanted now was to hamper you.'

'How can you be fooled so easily?' Lex sneered. 'This is the God of *Wit* and *Daring*. He's not going to accept defeat that easily. Trust me, he's still playing to win and if you overheard him it's because Jezra wanted to be overheard. It was a part of his plan.'

'Well, what difference does that make, anyway?' Lucius said.

'Jezra tricked the Judge,' Lex said patiently. 'He got the prophet out of the running before the round had even begun by making up this story about the crown being bewitched. He ensured that you overheard what he'd said so that you would run and tell me not to put on the crown. That much is clear. There'd be a stalemate and you and I would get an equal number of points for this round. A bold lie to frighten me out of winning the crown. If he knew you had overheard and were going to warn me, then he'd have no need to actually bewitch the crown, see?'

'You've lost me,' Lucius said.

Lex ignored him. Of course Jezra knew that Lucius knew. He had anticipated Lucius's loyalty; he knew the message would be passed on to Lex. And he knew that Lex knew his brother was a terrible liar and so had to be telling the truth. So Lex should be able to put the crown on safely . . . but there was that slight danger that Jezra himself might have been even cleverer than that and also anticipated Lex working out his scam, in which case the crown might be dangerous after all. Lex looked at the beautiful thing in his hand. He just *had* to put it on. The chances were that this was nothing more than a lie that Jezra had cleverly arranged for Lucius to deliver, for he must have let Lucius overhear deliberately. The whole thing had to be a bluff. Lex glanced at Schmidt. 'Well, you only live once, don't you, sir?' And before anyone could stop him, he lowered the crown onto his head, ignoring the others' yells of warning.

Nothing happened.

Everyone was staring at Lex in silent apprehension. A grin slowly spread across his face. 'You see?' he said. 'What did I tell—'

And then, without any warning at all, Lex turned into a fish. A whiskerfish, to be precise – with a small, blue, spotted body and long, ridiculous whiskers that fanned out from his face. For a moment everyone stared at the thing, thrashing around in the grass on top of a pile of Lex's clothes, the crown having rolled off a little distance. Schmidt was the first to recover. He picked Lex up and ran to the nearest fairy godmother cottage with him –

dropping him several times because he was thrashing so hard and almost treading on him once. He barged straight into the cottage, past the indignant fairy godmother and dumped Lex into the sink, which he quickly filled with water.

'Just what do you think you're doing, young man?' the fairy godmother said irritably from behind him.

Schmidt turned around in surprise. It had been a long time since anyone had addressed him as 'young man'.

'Isn't it self-evident, madam?' he snapped. 'My friend poisoned himself with whiskerfish poison and was suffocating out there.'

'Yes, but you might have knocked before barging in,' the godmother said huffily. 'It doesn't do to forget our manners over these things.'

'Oh, shut up,' Schmidt said wearily.

Lucius appeared in the doorway then and pushed past the irate godmother to rush over to the sink. 'Oh, is he okay?' he asked, wringing his hands. 'Is Lex all right, Mr Schmidt?'

'He'll live,' Schmidt said dryly. 'But for the next couple of weeks his life is going to be rather difficult, I'm afraid.'

The Goddess of Luck was not at all happy with Jezra over the whiskerfish incident. She was furious at the attack on her player and furious that Jezra had managed to bewitch the crown behind her back. Jezra was pleased to have caused her Ladyship inconvenience, but of course the plan had not worked as well as he'd hoped, for the whiskerfish poison he'd used was not lethal and Lex had still won the round. So really there wasn't anyone who was all that happy about what had happened. Except, perhaps, for Zachary. When Schmidt had asked the fairy godmother if she had anything with which they could transport Lex back to the ship, she had grudgingly given them a small plastic bag and Schmidt had scooped Lex up in this and given the bag to Lucius to carry. Unfortunately, they had only gone a few steps from the cottage before Zachary leapt up and punctured the bag with his sharp carnivorous teeth so that water started pouring out and Lex had to be rushed back to the fairy godmother's sink again, much to her tight-lipped irritation.

Then Schmidt and Lucius had an argument over whether Zachary had been truly trying to eat Lex or not.

'He only has a ferret brain,' Lucius whined. 'He can't understand. He probably thought Lex was lunch, or something.'

'Well, just keep an eye on him, would you?' Schmidt snapped. 'He's been a ferret for so long he probably can't remember being human. If he got hold of Lex he could kill him instantly.'

When they got back to the ship, Schmidt found a large transparent plastic container in the larder that had been used to store spider snacks. He tipped these out, filled the makeshift tank with water and poured the water from the plastic bag into it so that Lex fell into the tank where he could swim about agitatedly.

'What's going to happen to him?' Lucius asked anxiously,

pressing his nose against the side of the tank to stare in at his brother.

'For the next week or so he'll alternate daily between his usual charming self and this . . . little fish.'

'But what are we going to *do*?' Lucius cried, wringing his hands again.

'Oh, stop flapping, Lucius! There isn't anything we can do,' Schmidt said impatiently. 'We'll just have to wait for it to wear off. In the meantime, do you know anything about caring for whiskerfish?'

It was an aggravating thing to have to spend one day as a fish and one as a human, but the real problem of it was that whiskerfish needed to eat at least once every couple of hours and – as they had no teeth whatsoever – they needed soft, mushy food. But although Schmidt turned the larder inside out looking for seaweed, flotsam or sea cucumbers, he was unable to find anything of the sort. It was all starting to look rather serious because whiskerfish absolutely *had* to eat once every two hours or they'd starve to death. Lucius volunteered to mash up some bananas he'd found and put them in the tank, but whiskerfish-Lex wouldn't touch them and it looked, for a worrying few moments, as if he was not going to survive . . .

But then Schmidt found a box of muggets. Now muggets, as any fisherman knows, are made from a mixture of leech brains, jellyfish legs, maggot eggs and octopus tentacles, and are the best fishing bait ever created. They were seafood – of a type – and they were soft. It was also their only chance. So Schmidt dropped one into the tank, praying to the Gods that Lex would eat it. As it turned out, muggets were apparently divinely delicious to whiskerfish and Lex gobbled the thing up in no time. Based on Schmidt's calculations, they had enough to last two weeks as long as they were careful. The problem, though, was that whilst this mixture was perfectly delicious and sustaining to the whiskerfish, to humans it was a mildly poisonous combination that the human body was incapable of digesting – not that any sensible person would ever try, for the muggets tasted as disgusting as they looked and smelt.

Because Lex needed to be fed every two hours as a fish, Schmidt and Lucius took alternate night shifts. Then, on the days when Lex was human again, they caught up on some sleep whilst Lex spent most of the day throwing up over the side of the ship. He was always worse in the mornings, when the remnants of muggets he'd eaten the day before were still undigested in his body. Within twenty-four torturous hours he would just be starting to feel like he was merely ill as opposed to dying when he would turn back into a fish that gobbled muggets all day.

There had initially been some worry over the Binding Bracelets. When Lex had turned into a fish, his bracelet had obviously fallen off and been taken back to the ship along with Lex's other clothes. During his days as a whiskerfish he was unable to wear the bracelet and he and Schmidt were able to eat their meals separately without swapping bodies. But as soon as Lex turned back into a human the bracelet always shot straight back onto his wrist and it was these days that had really worried Schmidt for continuous puking had not put Lex in an eating mood and if Schmidt tried to eat anything without Lex, he would simply have found himself in Lex's body, meaning he'd have been the one to turn into a whiskerfish when the time came. It even occurred to the lawyer that Lex might refuse food on purpose, just for that reason.

It was therefore with a distinct sense of unease that Schmidt suggested to Lex on his first human day that he put a crumb of bread or something in his mouth at meal-times so that Schmidt could eat his own food without body-swapping. To his surprise, Lex had agreed with a disinterested shrug and said, 'If I'm going to be throwing up all day anyway I might as well throw up bread as well as muggets.'

It therefore appeared that, if swapping bodies on purpose had occurred to Lex, he wasn't going to act on it and, to Schmidt's relief, this remained the case even as the days went by and Lex became more ill.

'How are you feeling?' Lucius asked one afternoon as Lex staggered onto the bridge and dropped down onto his blankets.

Lex ignored the question. He felt like he would never be able to eat anything ever again. Being constantly sick drained away all his energy so that he couldn't believe he would ever want to do anything active ever again either. And the really disheartening thing of it was that he knew he would not even *begin* to start getting better until he stopped turning into a fish all the time. The idea of this going on for weeks was unbearable.

'Lex? I said, how are you feeling? Did you hear me, Lex?' Lucius persisted.

Lex would have shot him if he'd only had a gun in his hand.

'It's quite clear that he feels like drowning himself in his own tank,' Schmidt said from across the other side of the bridge. 'Why don't you just leave it at that?'

Lex felt a burst of gratitude towards his employer in that moment and made a silent vow to be nicer to him once he was recovered. At last he drifted off to sleep, but it seemed like mere moments later that Lucius was shaking him awake. 'Come on, Lex, it's time to get back down to your tank and have some more of those nice juicy muggets,' he said, trying to lend a supportive hand. Lex shook him off irritably, suppressing the urge to heave just at the very mention of the word *mugget*.

'Don't fuss me!' he snapped. 'Don't touch me! I can manage!'

'All right,' Lucius said, holding up his hands and backing away. 'Fine. Do it yourself. Here's your blanket.'

Lex snatched the blanket from his brother's hand and wrapped it around his shivering shoulders, glaring at Lucius from red-rimmed eyes as he did so. Then he turned and stalked from the bridge towards the kitchen where his tank was, with Lucius trailing along behind him. Lex actually preferred it when Schmidt was the one babysitting him. Schmidt didn't ask stupid questions or try to help him get dressed when he became human again – he just let him do it on his own.

Lex tried to stop himself from gnashing his teeth in annoyance when he walked into the kitchen and saw his tank sitting on the kitchen table with a slimy-looking mugget all ready for him. There was also a miniature castle in the tank, which Lucius had found on the ship somewhere and had insisted on putting there to make it seem more 'homely'. Lex picked the thing out with distaste and threw it down on the table. 'How many times do I have to tell you not to put that in my tank?' he snapped. 'It's demeaning. I'm not really a fish – you do realise that, don't you?'

'You like it when you're a fish,' Lucius sighed, picking up the tiny castle and replacing it in the tank. 'I think it makes you feel safe. You like hiding underneath that little drawbridge thing.'

Lex scowled and said nothing. The truth was that he found it hard to remember much of what he did as a whiskerfish. The only thing that mattered to his tiny fish brain was muggets. When he was human he would always promise himself that he was never going to eat another one of those awful things even if that meant he starved to death as a whiskerfish and Lucius had to flush his little fish corpse down the toilet the next morning. But when he was a fish again, it was like he was *addicted* to the bloody things and all he could think about was how much longer until he'd be given his next mugget. It was exhausting and Lex was thoroughly fed up with it. He was also less than comfortable about his tank being in the kitchen in case someone, in some fit of madness, decided to cook him for a midnight snack or something. But they couldn't move his tank to the bridge because it was too heavy with all the water inside. And they absolutely had to keep him away from Zachary, for the ferret seemed quite determined to eat him if he could.

'How many more days?' Lex asked, shivering as he pulled off his shirt. When you're ill and longing for warm sheets and blankets, having to get into a cold tank of water with no clothes on and eat slimy poisonous brains and tentacles really is the very last thing you want to do.

'Mr Schmidt said probably just a few more days,' Lucius said.

Lex would be interested to find out just how Schmidt knew so much about whiskerfish poison later. But for now, all he could do was concentrate on how ill he felt and how bitter he was that that beautiful, flawless, enthralling crown had been left behind in the dirty fingers of a mad old crone.

CHAPTER SIXTEEN

JEZRA'S PROPOSAL

At long last, eight days later, Lex was standing shivering in the kitchen, stripped down to his underwear, waiting to get into his tank, glaring ferociously at the slimy mugget already there when . . . absolutely nothing happened.

'You should have turned into a fish by now,' Schmidt said eventually.

Lex sat down on the chair, pulled his blanket tighter around his shoulders and said nothing. He didn't care any more. Fish, human, what did it matter? Another side effect of whiskerfish poisoning was that, for some reason, it made your hair grow. Lex's hair was now as long as Lucius's, and lank and greasy because he hadn't washed it since becoming ill. His skin had turned this greyish colour and he felt thin and everything *ached* . . .

Schmidt insisted they wait an hour to be sure Lex definitely wasn't going to turn into a fish again before letting him crawl into the small room near the bridge that he had taken over. Lex had moved in there a few days after the poisoning because there comes a point in any illness when you feel so awful that you just can't stand to be around anyone. Besides which, the panoramic windows on the bridge let in far too much light. Lex wanted a small, dark, silent room where he could curl up and just concentrate on not moving. *This will pass*, he kept telling himself. Jezra had weakened him but he was still in the running and – damn it – he was still going to *win*. Schmidt had been in charge of the ivory swan that drove the ship whilst Lex had been ill so that it continued to head towards their destination – the Ladder Forest where they would play the third and final round. They were now only a week away and Lex would be recovered enough to play by then.

'Try and eat some human food as soon as you can,' Schmidt said when they reached his room. 'With me, of course . . . ' He hesitated a moment before going on. 'Lex . . . why didn't you swap us on purpose?'

'What do you mean?' Lex asked, rubbing at his red eyes.

'Why didn't you swap bodies with me and make me share some of the illness instead of doing it all yourself?'

'I was feeling so ill it didn't occur to me,' Lex said. 'It's a good thing you didn't ask me that question a few days earlier, Monty.'

'Huh,' Schmidt grunted. But he didn't believe him.

'Look, do me a favour,' Lex said. 'Keep Lucius away from me for the next few days.'

The lawyer nodded. 'I hope you feel better.'

And he left Lex to crawl gratefully under his blankets at last.

Lex walked onto the bridge three days later, aware that he still looked pale and sickly but feeling much better now that all traces of muggets had left his system. At long last he could look at human food without feeling sick and he'd brought a couple of fruit sticks up to the bridge with him. He was ready to rejoin the others and find out what he'd missed. He was most displeased, however, on stepping onto the bridge, to have Schmidt look round at him from the window and say, 'Haven't you found Zachary yet, Lucius?'

Lex's mouth dropped open in pure horror at being mistaken for his pale, weedy brother. 'I'm not Lucius!' he spluttered indignantly.

'Oh, is that you, Lex?'

'Yes!'

'Feeling better?'

'Well, I was,' Lex grumbled, 'until you just insulted me like that.'

'Have you looked at yourself in the mirror recently?' Schmidt asked. 'At the moment I'm afraid Lucius is the healthier-looking one of the two of you.'

Lex scowled. 'I'm going to have a wash and cut my hair after this and then I'm sure I'll look much better. So where's Lucius?'

'Looking for Zachary. He keeps wandering off.'

'Good, I hope he falls overboard,' Lex said, throwing

one of the refreshing fruit sticks to Schmidt before taking a bite out of his own.

'I would have thought your recent illness would have made you a little more sympathetic to Zachary's plight,' Schmidt said, after biting into his fruit stick.

'Well, then you were entirely wrong,' Lex said with a shrug. 'Don't feel bad about it.'

The door opened then and Lucius walked in with a struggling ferret tucked under his arm. 'Lex!' Lucius exclaimed, dropping Zachary in delight when he saw his brother on the deck. To Lex's irritation he came over and tried to hug him. 'I'm so glad you're feeling better. You'll never have to eat another mugget again!'

'I hope not,' Lex said, trying to twist out of his twin's grip.

'Well, it was your own fault, anyway,' Schmidt pointed out helpfully. 'Lucius did try to warn you.'

'It was worth it,' Lex declared. 'I was a king for five seconds. My name will be on the Royal Monument in the Wither City now, Mr Schmidt. You'll have to check it out when you get back.'

'I'm sure you plan on seeing it for yourself, as well,' the lawyer said, watching him closely.

'Of course. But I'm not going back to the Wither City with you. You'd turn me straight over to the police and I'd get stuck in jail.'

'Well, you did break the law,' Schmidt said with a shrug.

'How long will Lex have to serve, Mr Schmidt?' Lucius asked, looking distinctly unhappy.

'Well that depends on the judge to some extent,' Schmidt said. 'But you've got theft, fraud, criminal damage, evasion of justice—'

'It would be about five years,' Lex interrupted.

'If you were lucky,' Schmidt said.

'I'm always lucky.'

'Five *years*?' Lucius said, looking horrified. 'Oh, Lex—'

'Shut up, Lucius. I'm not going to prison. They'll never catch me.'

'But do you really want to be running your whole life?' Lucius asked.

'Ha! Only if somebody's chasing me,' Lex grinned. 'It wouldn't be fun otherwise. Who's done what with my crystal ball, anyway? I want to watch the footage from the second round.'

Lucius dug it out of the pile of blankets and handed it over to Lex.

'Thank you,' he replied. 'Now I'm going to clean up and cut my hair. We're looking a little too similar for my liking. I'll be back later.'

He left the bridge and went down the corridor to the bathroom. It was a large ivory room with a huge circular bath in the centre. When he'd first found it, Lex had been put off from using the bathroom by the thick black toenail clippings that blocked the plughole. When he'd turned the taps on, he'd washed them all away but the image had stuck in his mind. The enchanter had clearly had something of an obsession about his feet, for Lex found a myriad of foot creams and lotions and – *urgh* – a whole bag of pumice stones neatly laid out in one of the mirrored cabinets. But now the thought of clean hot water outweighed Lex's distaste and he filled the tub to the brim, sloshing water everywhere when he stepped in. He couldn't help a groan of pleasure when he sat down and a whirlpool motion started up, pummelling his back and easing away all the aches and pains. The hot water was wonderfully soothing and slightly honey-scented and – whilst Lex would have preferred a more manly scent – being clean again felt indescribably good. He ducked his head under the water to wash his hair, getting rid of the horrible build up of grease at last. He'd always hated long hair, anyway, for it got in the way and gave him a wimpy look, but having lank, greasy strands stuck to his head was unbearable. Whatever else he might be, Lex was a stickler for cleanliness.

After he'd sat there for a while, he reached over for the crystal ball he had left at the side of the tub and leant back to enjoy the footage from the second round. Like the first one, it had been edited to make him look suitably impressive and he could just imagine it beaming out over the stadiums accompanied by *oohs* and *aahs* as Lex raced through the magic forest – an entire herd of draglings and a mad king in pursuit. The wicked witch footage in particular had been very heavily edited – Lex was sure her remaining teeth hadn't been as sharp as that in real life and she hadn't been so big either and she certainly hadn't chased after them when they escaped from her cave, as the recycled dragling-chase footage seemed to imply. The fairy godmothers' village and Matilda had been cut altogether and so had the whisker-fish transformation as none of that really seemed very dignified at all. The last image of Lex showed him standing with the gleaming crown on his head and a self-satisfied smirk on his face. He was still the bookies' favourite to win by a long shot, for he had already won both the first two rounds by a mile. But the slate would be wiped clean for the third round, so that it was anybody's Game.

When, at last, Lex managed to drag himself out of the bath, he wrapped a white towel around his waist and took a comb out of the mirrored cabinet. He carefully ran this through his chin-length hair to detangle it. When he was done he put the comb down on the edge of the sink and opened the cabinet door again to get the scissors. But when he shut the mirrored door, he jumped and almost dropped the scissors as Jezra's reflection swung into view. The God of Wit and Daring was standing just behind Lex by the now-empty bath, wearing his usual high-necked pale blue jacket, a lazy smile on his face.

'Hello, Lex. Feeling better?'

'I'm afraid so, my Lord,' Lex said, bowing stiffly.

He did not overly resent Jezra for what he'd done. Lex understood the need to win. But it was hard not to feel just a little bit bitter when looking directly at the person responsible for making the last two weeks of his life an utter misery. Especially when Jezra had always been something of a hero to Lex.

'It was nothing personal, you know,' Jezra went on, running a hand through his long hair.

Nothing personal? Of course it had been personal! But Lex just nodded. There was no sense in arguing with Gods. He turned back to the mirror and raised the scissors to his hair but froze at the sound of Jezra's sharp command, 'I wouldn't do that if I were you!'

'Why not?' Lex asked, looking at the God in the mirror, scissors still poised at the side of his head.

Jezra smiled. 'Because if you cut your hair then all those awful muggets you ate will have been for nothing.'

'I don't follow,' Lex said, putting the scissors down carefully on the side of the sink and then turning to look at Jezra. Something in the God's voice alerted Lex to the fact that Jezra was excited about something.

'You didn't really think my plan was to kill you, did you?' Jezra asked, and then, when Lex didn't answer, he continued, 'Lex, you're far too valuable for that. I'm not the kind of God who would destroy something he wanted just because someone else had it at the time. I would wait patiently, fully expecting to procure the object of my desire in good time.'

Lex stared at the God, a suspicion suddenly coming into his mind. 'You want to switch us?' he said incredulously as realisation dawned.

Jezra laughed. 'Yes, I'd like to pass you off as Lucius. What do you think?'

Lex turned and gazed at himself in the mirror. He did look virtually identical to his brother now that his hair had grown and his skin had taken on a sickly pallor. But Lucius was merely pale, he did not have the dark shadows under his eyes that Lex had or the greyish tinge to his skin and he wasn't as thin as Lex had become after a week spent eating nothing but muggets. Lex was about to voice these objections to the God but then he realised that they could all be overcome. There was a week to go before the last round and by then Lex would just look pale rather than sickly. And any weight he hadn't put back on could be disguised with the right clothing. A slow grin spread across his face.

'Will you play for me, Lex?' Jezra asked softly. 'Will you trick Lady Luck as she tricked me and win for me instead of for her in a beautiful, spectacular double cross?'

'My Lord, it would be an honour to win for you,' Lex said, still grinning at his reflection and silently thanking his whiskerfish poisoning for giving him such a perfect, flawless disguise.

It was not a very difficult thing for Lex to convince Lucius to go along with the scam, for Lucius was afraid of the Ladder Forest even before he knew what the round entailed. There was, to be fair, something a little bit ominous about all those old ladders of various shapes and sizes just stuck into the ground, like trees without leaves or branches. The Ladder Forest was an accumulation of spares to replace worn-out Space Ladders. This was very important for, without the ladders, the two halves of the planet would drift apart and the Lands Above would lose their Gods. Some even said that the ladders were *growing* – getting taller and older and darker by the year. And that little ones had started sprouting up, too. People stayed away from them in the main, and the tourists gave them a wide berth when they came to gawk at the Space Ladders.

'I got you into this,' Lex said charitably to his brother. 'And now I'm going to get you out.'

'What about the Gods, though?' Lucius whined. 'They'll be angry—'

'They *expect* cheating,' Lex said dismissively.

'I know but—'

'Look,' Lex interrupted, 'it's simple. All you have to do is hide in the enchanter's closet until the Game is over. You can manage that, can't you? Otherwise you'll have no choice but to go out into the ladders yourself.'

So Lucius had agreed to hide in the cupboard – taking Zachary with him since the ferret would have given the game away, for he wouldn't let Lex pick him up and would always bite him at the first available opportunity.

The timing was perfect, for by the time they arrived at the Ladder Forest, Lex and Lucius had identical complexions thanks to the whiskerfish poisoning. They didn't do the switch until the night before, so as not to give Lady Luck any more warning than necessary. Lex installed Lucius in the closet with Zachary that evening after dinner, then crept back to the bridge where Schmidt was about to lie down to sleep.

'Where's Lucius?' the lawyer asked when Lex walked in.

'I am Lucius, Mr Schmidt,' Lex said, slipping easily back into the respectful tone he had once used every day with his employer.

'Oh. Well, where's Lex then?'

'I don't know,' Lex replied, biting his lip and feigning worry as he glanced around the bridge. 'He said something about going to look for scissors.'

Lex had explained his hair by saying that he'd been unable to find any scissors. He had enjoyed complaining bitterly about his resemblance to Lucius over the past few days, allowing the lawyer to believe he was in a foul temper and proclaiming that he would find something with which to cut his hair if he had to turn the ship upside down to do so.

'Perhaps I should go and look for him?' Lex said, fiddling with his hands in an exact mimic of Lucius when he was worried.

'Lex will turn up,' Schmidt said. 'Don't worry about him. Just go to sleep. And by the grace of the Gods, this will all be over this time tomorrow and we can go back to our lives.'

'I hope so, sir,' Lex snivelled. 'I just want to go home to my farm.'

Lex hid a smile as he lay down to sleep. This was all going so perfectly. He was going to trick Lady Luck, he was going to win the Game, he was going to better *everyone*. Schmidt would be easy enough to fool, the doddering old twit. And afterwards Lex would be even more notorious and have the great Lord Jezra himself as his patron.

Lex had agreed to Jezra's proposal on the condition that he won the Game as Lex Trent and not as Lucius. He wanted to make his own name notorious, not his wimpy brother's. Jezra had been more than happy to agree to this, for it would enhance his own reputation once it was known that he had bested Lady Luck by stealing her player right out from under her nose.

The players were due to meet at the edge of the Ladder Forest at sunrise the next morning. When Lex supposedly didn't turn up, the round would simply commence without him and there wouldn't be a damned thing Lady Luck could do about it. Ha! How perfectly delicious it all was.

CHAPTER SEVENTEEN

ZOEY

Lex (as Lucius), Schmidt, the prophet and the Gods had been at the Ladder Forest for fifteen minutes when the Judge at last said, 'Lex Trent is not here. The round will commence without him.'

The Goddess of Luck fluttered her hands agitatedly. 'I just don't understand it,' she said. 'He should have arrived just in time, he always does.'

'You'll have to go on to the companion,' the Judge said with a dismissive wave of his gloved hand. 'The object of this final round is to locate the griffin that lives in the Space Ladders. The first of you to return its black feather to me, wins.'

The shock on Lex's face was genuine, for humans weren't allowed on the Space Ladders. It was expressly forbidden. Excitement bubbled up inside him and he wanted to laugh with delight at the mere thought of stepping out onto those ladders. But he had a part to play before the sharp-eyed Gods, so he gasped just as Lucius would have done and turned to Jezra with a wail. 'My Lord Jezra, I beg you! A griffin! It'll kill me; I know it will!'

'Hold your tongue!' Jezra snapped, smacking him round the back of the head. 'You disgrace me with your cowardice!'

Lex bowed his head in silence.

'Well, at least my player had the guts to turn up,' Jezra said to her Ladyship. 'I guess Lex Trent isn't as brave as you thought he was.'

'Lex is the bravest player I've ever had!' the Goddess stormed – Lex could hear the angry pride in her voice and couldn't help feeling just a little ashamed at the way he was repaying her. 'You've sabotaged him again somehow!' the Goddess went on.

'I'm afraid I can't take the credit for Lex's untimely disappearance,' Jezra said with a shrug. 'Perhaps that enchanter caught up with him at last.'

The Goddess blanched at the suggestion and opened her mouth to say more but the Judge interrupted her: 'Continue to dispute this between yourselves, if you wish, but as of now the round has commenced.'

With Lex supposedly gone, the players were all now to start at the same time, for a stand-in companion was forbidden to take advantage of the headstart that had been won by the player. The Judge disappeared and the prophet turned and set off in the direction of the Space Ladders.

'What are you waiting for?' Jezra snapped at Lex, aiming

a kick at him to get him going. Lex hurried off, leaving the Gods to argue.

'Well, there's one way to settle this,' the Goddess of Fortune snapped. 'You there!'

Schmidt looked up and caught the apple the Goddess threw him.

'I want to talk to Lex!'

'My Lady, if Lex really has been compromised by an enchanter then I'll become trapped in his place,' Schmidt protested. 'Punished for something I didn't do—'

'That's the price of being a companion!' the Goddess snapped. 'If Lex isn't here then you have to take his place. I only need a few minutes. Now do as you're told and swap places with him!'

Unwilling to bring a deity's wrath down upon himself, Schmidt reluctantly raised his hand and bit into the apple. Of course, Jezra and Lex had not been foolish enough to forget the Binding Bracelets when they were making their plans. They had simply factored them in. As soon as Lex got past all the warning signs that were stuck in the mud around the perimeter of the Space Ladders, he had taken some handkerchiefs out of his bag and gagged and blind-folded himself with them. Then he'd bound himself hand and foot with the rope – which had been no easy feat, considering the fact that he couldn't see. The ropes didn't need to hold for long – only a few moments, for Lex had broken off a piece of biscuit and put it on his tongue and he knew that the lawyer would automatically swallow this almost as soon as they changed places.

He didn't have to wait very long before he was suddenly standing before the two Gods in Schmidt's body, the taste of apple still in his mouth. 'My Lady,' he gasped. 'Help me, I don't know where I am! I woke up in this strange—'

And that was all he had time to say before Schmidt swallowed the biscuit and they changed back.

'You imbecile!' the Goddess raged at him. 'That wasn't enough time! What did you do, stuff the first piece of food you saw straight into your mouth?'

'I couldn't see anything,' Schmidt protested. 'He's tied up and blindfolded. I don't know where. I doubt Lex knows.'

'I told you the enchanter would get him,' Jezra said with a smirk. 'It'll take you a while to find him, you know. The Game will be long over by then.'

Then Jezra disappeared, apparently quite oblivious to the fact that the Goddess of Luck was staring daggers at him. After ordering Schmidt on to the Space Ladders, the Lady went to go and look for Lex herself and Schmidt was left standing alone at the edge of the Ladder Forest. The Space Ladders were usually a favourite tourist spot, and parents brought their children to see them stretching away into the dark, inky blackness, but today the area had been kept clear for the Game.

Schmidt laughed softly under his breath and then turned and strode towards the Space Ladders. It was normally forbidden to get too close – people were only allowed onto the carefully positioned viewing platforms. There were warning signs written on wooden boards and stuck into the mud all around, which tended to go along the lines of 'DANGER', 'TURN BACK', 'MORTAL PERIL' and so on. They got the job done anyway. Schmidt weaved between them and carefully rested his hands on the fence that guarded the perimeter. When he looked down over the edge, there they were – thousands and thousands of ladders stretching down towards the bottom half of the planet. It was a maze – there were just so many of them, so many different routes to take. The griffin could have made its home anywhere.

Schmidt couldn't see the prophet – his black robes camouflaged him perfectly in the dark skies of space. But he could still see Lex, standing below on one of the central platforms, obviously trying to decide which way to go from there. There were rope ladders, wooden ladders and a whole steel staircase all leading off from the one platform, going down in different directions.

'Hey!' Schmidt shouted over the edge.

He saw Lex look up. 'Mr Schmidt?'

'Wait there for me!' the old lawyer called.

Then he swung his leg over the fence and stepped onto the uppermost staircase. Lex stared up in horror as he realised that the old fool was actually intending to *join* him! That was no good – as Lucius, he would be expected to actually be *polite*! And *slow* and *useless* and to *lose*! He stood there, fuming, trying to remain calm as Schmidt slowly scaled the ladders to catch up with him.

'Mr Schmidt, this really isn't necessary,' Lex said once

the lawyer had joined him on the platform. 'I can't let you put yourself in danger on my account. Please, go back to the ship.'

'Nonsense, my boy,' Schmidt said, in the kindliest tone Lex had ever heard him use. 'I couldn't abandon you down here alone. Especially since Lex spitefully lost you your companion. Besides, I have to take Lex's place now that he's gone. We might as well go on together. Accompanying you is the very least I can do.'

Lex stared at the lawyer. He had not been expecting this. He'd expected Schmidt to be glad of the opportunity to escape the most dangerous round. Surely he couldn't be *that* fond of Lucius?

'I'm grateful for the thought, sir,' Lex said desperately, 'but I just couldn't . . . these ladders will be so difficult for you to climb and . . . The Gods won't like it if we go on together.'

'I hardly think that matters now, Lucius,' Schmidt said. 'We both know the prophet is going to win, so we might as well travel together.'

Lex just about managed to resist the urge to wring his hands in frustration. He simply couldn't think of any way around this without admitting to Schmidt who he really was. If they continued together, Schmidt would be sure to guess once he saw that Lex was not permanently cringing in terrified preoccupation with the Space Ladders. Then Schmidt spoke again with a smirk and Lex couldn't help but gasp when he said, 'It's okay, Lex, I know it's you. You can stop trying to think up a convincing lie.'

Lex's mouth dropped open in stunned disbelief. 'How did you *know*?' he demanded.

'I've known since last night,' Schmidt said smugly.

'*What?*'

'I've always been able to see through you,' Schmidt said, clearly well pleased with himself. 'I can tell the difference between you and Lucius. I admit the hair threw me at first, but I'm accustomed to it now.'

'Why didn't you *say* anything?'

'I wanted to see what would happen. So where is Lucius, anyway?'

'On the boat,' Lex said moodily. 'Hiding in the enchanter's cupboard.'

Schmidt laughed. 'Yes, that sounds about right.'

'Well, thank you for not telling her Ladyship.'

'I thought you might be forced to play a penalty round for cheating and that I'd have to accompany you,' Schmidt said dismissively. 'That's the only reason I didn't say anything.'

'Huh. Well, what do you think? Rope ladders or metal ones?' Lex pointed at the ladders leading away from their platform.

'The metal ones look more stable,' Schimdt said. 'Do you know where the griffin is?'

'No. She used to live on a big chunk of comet that got tangled up in the Space Ladders but she's probably moved on since then. I think the metal ladders look better, too.'

He walked over to the nearest one and started to make his way down it with Schmidt following behind.

'How do you know where the griffin used to live?' Schmidt asked.

'My grandfather told me.'

'Just what exactly did your grandfather do?'

'He was a Chronicler,' Lex replied.

Well, that explained a lot, Schmidt thought, remembering how Lex had seemed to know so much about magical sky castles and enchanted forests and the Golden Valley. Although Chronicling was now a dying profession, Schmidt knew that in the olden days well-read, well-educated men had often travelled with exploring Adventurers to Chronicle their adventures and expand their native libraries with knowledge about faraway lands. A lot could be learnt from reading the old Chronicles and the Chroniclers were well respected as explorers and glorified storytellers.

'From what Lucius told me about him, he sounded like a good man,' Schmidt said as they continued their rather treacherous climb.

'Yes,' Lex replied. 'He was.'

'I'm sorry about what happened to him.'

He sounded like he meant it, but Lex couldn't bring himself to reply. The subject was much too painful for him. Besides which, the climb was becoming more frightening now that they were getting further and further away from the Lands Above. The ladders felt less stable and it was colder. The space frost did not stick to their hands like normal ice, but it did cover them like chalk dust, making them sneeze as they went. The one and only blessing about Lex's whiskerfish problem was that it had completely eradicated his nasal lice without Schmidt ever managing to find out about them.

'I realise this is a stupid question, but do you have a plan?' Schmidt asked after about ten minutes. They were clinging to rope ladders by this time. 'Or are we just going to keep climbing down these ladders in the hopes that we'll eventually stumble upon the griffin?'

'I think she's over there,' Lex took one hand away from the ladder to point but hastily put it back when the ladder began to turn beneath his weight.

There was an area to the right of them that seemed to jut out beyond the main mass of ladders so that it had been far more ravaged by the elements and was coated in the chalky, glittering space frost.

'What makes you think that?' Schmidt asked.

Lex pointed down. 'The suns,' he said.

Griffins were attracted to brightness, although they were more comfortable in colder temperatures. Holli's sun had been rising when they went down into the Space Ladders. But Mahara's, Heetha's and Saydi's suns were all still down below the Lands Beneath, waiting for their turn to come up.

'That outcrop of ladders should give quite a good view of the other suns,' Lex said. 'Plus, it will let the griffin watch them rising and setting.'

'You don't seem very worried about the prophet getting there first,' Schmidt said. 'He did get a head start after all.'

'Yeah, but he won't be able to get the feather from the griffin very fast,' Lex said, grinning. 'There's only one way a griffin will willingly let you take one of its feathers and that's if you ask it very politely by name. I very much doubt that the prophet knows this griffin's name but, luckily for us, I do.'

'How do you know?' the lawyer asked suspiciously.

'Because my grandfather was the one who named her. She's called Zoey.'

'That's a ridiculous name for a griffin,' Schmidt said bluntly.

'I know,' Lex shrugged. 'It was my grandmother's name. He named her after her.'

'Oh,' Schmidt immediately looked uncomfortable. 'I'm sorry, I didn't mean—'

'No need to be sorry, sir,' Lex said, smiling at the lawyer's embarrassment. 'Zoey is – as you say – a ridiculous name for a griffin. I suppose my grandfather thought it was romantic to name a huge, hulking wild beast after the woman he loved.'

The climb down the ladders was . . . not a pleasant one. In fact it was a harrowing, terrifying, terrible journey, and Lex couldn't help but have the teensiest, grudging glimmer of respect for the old lawyer that he managed it at all. They both kept their eyes fixed very firmly on the ladder in front of them, taking it one rung at a time in an effort to fool their brains into believing that they weren't really dangling from a ladder between two halves of the same planet with cold black space pressing in against them. If this technique had been working in any small way, it ceased to do so rather spectacularly when Lex and Schmidt reached the bunch of ladders that jutted out in a cluster on their own. For then there were quite clearly three huge, brilliant suns glaring up at them from below.

They were standing on a wooden platform now, their feet leaving footprints in the deep, chalky frost. The Lands Beneath was a vague blur below them, although most of it was blocked from view by the mass of ladders. But they could now quite clearly see the three suns belonging to the two Goddesses and the one God. The sheer enormity of their size made them look closer than they really were. Lex had never seen more than one deity's sun in the sky at any one time and so had never noticed that they all looked slightly different. The first huge, fiery ball of heat was clearly Heetha, the God of War's sun. The second sun was so pure that it was almost white, sparkling like a perfect, heat-emitting diamond. There was no mistaking that this was Saydi's beautiful sun. Mahara's abandoned sun was not as bright as the others. Indeed its outer rim seemed to have cooled enough for space frost to settle on the surface, although there was enough heat left in the core for it to give out a feeble glow.

The sight of those gigantic, majestic suns burning away below them made both Lex and Schmidt feel tiny and unbalanced. The lawyer decided it would be prudent to sit down before he tipped over the edge and Lex followed his lead, sinking slowly to his knees, enthralled laughter bubbling up incredulously in his chest.

'Why would anyone *choose* to miss this?' he asked, gazing down at the spectacular sight below. 'How could Lucius actually *prefer* hiding in a cupboard to this? You must be glad you came now, Schmidt? What life would be complete without that sight in it? Come on, you must agree that this has made the whole thing worthwhile? I would have eaten muggets for a *year* to get to see this.'

'It is . . . humbling,' Schmidt agreed, gazing down at the suns.

Although Lex himself did not feel particularly humbled by the suns, he did feel an immense swell of pride that he had managed to get there. He was probably one of the only humans ever to have set foot on the Space Ladders. Even his grandfather had never been on the ladders themselves – he'd simply assisted Carey East in sending Zoey down to guard them after the previous griffin died of old age.

'Well, I think she's over there,' Lex said at last, pointing over to their left, where there were two wooden platforms, one on top of the other, connected by ladders on either side so that it looked like a square, wooden cave.

'You'd better stay back for this bit,' Lex said. 'I'll have to say her name quickly or she'll attack me. She'll think I'm a threat when she first sees me and it would only be worse if there were two of us.'

So the lawyer remained where he was whilst Lex scrambled up and over ladders to get as near to the makeshift ladder-cave as he could. When he was on a smaller plat-form only about twenty feet away, the griffin heard him and came to the entrance. She was a huge creature and looked just like the murals Alistair Trent had once taken Lex and Lucius to see in the underground church-cave where people from around the Globe still went to pay tribute to the magnificent beast.

The griffins came in several different colours and this one was white, with just a single black feather on her left shoulder. Her head and the front of her body were those of an eagle, with sharp golden eyes, curved clawed feet and white feathers covering her chest and wings. In contrast, her hindquarters were clearly those of a lion, with snow-white fur covering her from midway down her back to the end of her long tail.

The griffin had been worshipped on the Globe for a long time because of its role in the aftermath of the Great Divide. They kept the Space Ladders sacred by chasing away any people who might stray onto them. Climbing the ladders was dangerous enough but to have a griffin coming after you at the same time meant certain death since it would be only too easy to lose your grip and fall off altogether. Of course, in recent years, the presence of the griffin had become little more than symbolic, for everyone knew the Gods had forbidden humans to ever go onto the Space Ladders – they did not want people down in the Lands Beneath.

The griffin was clearly surprised to see Lex on the ladders but after a brief hesitation she stepped out into the open and stretched her wings threateningly. It was an impressive sight. The three suns below painted golden light across her pale wings as her beak snapped sharply at him in an aggressive warning. Before she could start chasing him away, Lex raised his voice and said clearly and calmly, 'Hello, Zoey.'

The griffin slowly folded her wings back at the mention of her name and didn't move as Lex slowly climbed the last two ladders to reach her. Carefully, he stepped onto her platform, very aware that she could knock him off it just by rearing up onto her legs. But his grandfather had said that the use of their real name and a proper show of deference would make the griffins docile and Lex trusted his advice. As a Chronicler, it had been very important for Alistair to be accurate in every detail because future generations were likely to rely on what he'd written.

Once he was on a level with her, he truly realised how big she was. Even Lex, who had never felt humbled by anything in his life, couldn't help being just a little bit aware of his own insignificance when he looked at her. Behind her, back within the shelter of the ladders, he could see what was very clearly a glimmering golden nest. Lex knew that griffins were said to make their nests out of gold, but he couldn't think where Zoey had managed to find so much of it out here in space.

Even more lovely than the nest itself were the three agate eggs inside it. They were all striped in different shades of white and silver. It was a mark of just how affected by the sight Lex was that he did not even think about stealing them.

'You're every bit as beautiful as Gramps said you were,' Lex said softly, bowing lowly to her. 'Zoey, I've come to ask for one of your feathers.'

He straightened from the bow, but remained where he was whilst the griffin watched him. He couldn't go any closer to her – she might see it as an invasion of her space and feel threatened. He had to wait for her to come to him. After twenty slightly tense seconds the griffin slowly moved towards him, the large paws of her back legs making deep tracks in the space frost that covered the planks. The unbelievable thrill of it raced through Lex like electricity as she padded softly over and stopped in front of him. She was so large that Lex's head only just reached past the top of her chest.

This surpassed even the royal crown! He was close enough to *touch* her! He was close enough to see the dusty space frost that lightly covered her feathers and fur; close enough to see the movement of her chest as she breathed and close enough to sense the restrained strength of her majestic, powerful body.

She lowered her head a little so that her long neck was within Lex's reach. Her half-closed eyes glimmered liquid gold in the light from the three suns below them. Lex took a deep breath for the sake of the moment. Here it was – he was about to win the Game, beating Lady Luck and the Judge himself, winning for Jezra and making an immortal name for himself in the Chronicles yet to come.

He reached his hand up and laid it on the griffin's neck. He had not expected the feathers to be so soft. His hand ran lightly down to grip the single black feather at her shoulder and prepare to pull it out. He was very aware of the cold, the suns below them, the stars around them and the utter silence of space . . .

Then there was a *shing* that sliced through the silence, whistled past Lex's outstretched arm and buried itself deep into the griffin's chest. She gave an awful cry of anguish and reached up one clawed foot to try to remove the huge sword from her chest before she collapsed to the ground, making the wooden platform tremble. Lex looked up and saw Schmidt staring down at them with a look of horror on his face. And to the right and slightly below the lawyer he saw the prophet.

Lex dropped down beside the dying griffin, almost unable to believe what he'd just seen. Killing a griffin was . . . well, it was almost like killing a *God*. The griffins were *worshipped* on the Globe.

'Oh, Zoey,' Lex muttered, running his hands helplessly over her bloodstained feathers. 'I'm so sorry – I don't know how to help you.'

Lex knew nothing about medicine. He didn't know whether he should try to remove the sword or whether he should simply leave it there. He didn't know whether there was anything at all he could do to help the griffin or ease her pain. But in another moment she was dead. From above, Schmidt shouted a warning but it came too late for Lex to dodge the blow entirely, so the prophet's stick clipped the side of his head, knocking him back on the wooden planks of the platform whilst the prophet stepped past him and calmly plucked the black feather from the dead griffin.

His head still ringing, Lex shot out an arm as the prophet walked past him, tripping him up so that they sprawled on the planks together, the feather still clutched in the prophet's hand. Lex tried to wrestle it away but, although blind, deaf and dumb, the prophet was much larger and stronger than him.

'Lex!' Schmidt shouted from above. 'Let him go! For Gods' sake, just let him have the feather!'

In another moment, Lex realised why Schmidt had been trying to make him stop, as they both rolled right off the edge of the platform, freefalling terrifyingly. They crashed through several wooden ladders before they landed on another, larger platform. Realising that the feather was in his hand, Lex pushed the prophet away, jumped up and ran to the edge of the platform where a metal ladder led up to a series of wooden ones. He put his foot on the first rung and shot up it like a monkey.

But before he could climb up to the wooden ladders, he became aware of a low groaning sound as the planks beneath his feet began to tremble. Within moments the noise had increased in volume so intensely that it seemed to pierce Lex's eardrums. It went through him with all the force of a physical thing, knocking him down onto his knees, his hands clapped tightly over his ears.

As the planks continued to tremble beneath him, he

thought for one wild moment that the Space Ladders themselves must be collapsing. But then something moved into his line of vision and he realised that the noise he'd heard had not been the Space Ladders collapsing – it had been the groan of orbiting planets. Everyone knew that the Globe was the centre of the universe. The suns passed above and beneath it and the other planets in the galaxy orbited around it. Their nearest neighbour was Plenrii – a water planet for the dead. The Globe was the only living planet in the galaxy and the others that orbited it were all said to be underworlds. There were so many other planets out there because there were always more and more people who were dying and the Gods had to keep creating more planets to provide space for them all.

The prophet, Lex and Schmidt were all motionless on the ladders as the underworld came into view like a gigantic blue marble going directly past them on its cold, solitary elliptical orbit of the Globe. Lex could hardly believe his eyes. As far as he knew, this was the first time in the history of the Globe that any living human had ever set eyes on an underworld.

The deafening roar of the orbiting planet caused no problem for the deaf prophet. He took his chance to grip the ladder below and start climbing up towards Lex, who lowered his hands with the idea of climbing to the next platform, but he realised at once that there was no way he could hold onto the ladder and leave his ears unprotected. Nor could he climb the ladder without using his hands, for the way they were shaking and trembling he would have fallen off within seconds. Still on his knees, Lex stared around the small platform, desperately wondering what to do, for the prophet was sure to be upon him at any moment. He staggered up and walked unsteadily to the edge of the shaking platform, intending to kick at the prophet when his head appeared over the top. But his head never did appear. Just moments later there was such a savage jolt that Lex fell over on the boards, narrowly avoiding toppling over the edge. The prophet was not so lucky. He lost his grip on the shuddering ladder, his hands slipped from the rung. Desperately, he flailed to regain his hold but it was too late. In another moment he was freefalling out into the vast, black coldness of space.

Lex couldn't help but stare – both mesmerised and horrified by the sight of the black figure tumbling over and over, unable to utter so much as a whisper of fear. Twenty minutes went by before Lex and Schmidt were able to remove their hands from their ears and by that time the prophet was long out of view.

CHAPTER EIGHTEEN

THE LANDS BENEATH

Lex slowly climbed the ladder back up to the griffin's platform where Schmidt stood waiting. They both looked sadly down at the griffin in silence. It seemed a terrible waste just for the sake of a game and Lex found it hard to summon up any regret for the fact that the prophet had just fallen to his death. Served him right.

'These Games are appalling,' Schmidt said, breaking the silence at last. 'I just don't see the point of them. They're anachronistic and should be stopped or, at the very least, modernised so that they aren't so dangerous. Look at what's happened on this one alone! Theba died in the first round, the prophet died in the third, Zachary is no longer even in human form thanks to you and now this griffin has perished as well. It's disgraceful.'

Lex agreed entirely that it was a shame about the griffin even if he didn't care in the least about the other three. He shrugged and said, 'The Games would be pointless if they weren't dangerous. They wouldn't be exciting any more.'

'I don't understand that attitude at all!' Schmidt said huffily.

Lex gently stroked the feather he still held in his hand. When he took it up to the Judge he'd be proclaimed the winner. But victory, somehow, now seemed to have gone a little flat. His eyes went to the three silver eggs still tucked away in the golden nest and, after a moment's thought, he took a step towards them.

Then he stopped. There was a rush of cold air, a bright flash of white light, angry blue eyes and a tree made entirely out of crystal, from its huge trunk to the very last twig, leaf and bunch of berries clustered along its branches. There was blood at the base, for someone had cut themselves on the flowers . . . but it was only there for a moment before it was gone. Lex shook his head in bewilderment.

'What is it?' Schmidt asked.

'It's Lucius,' Lex said. He didn't know why he'd said that but he knew it was true. Something had happened to his brother, he could sense it. Perhaps it was a twin thing but he was suddenly absolutely certain that Lucius was in trouble. Before he could think any more about it, Lady Luck appeared on the planks beside them. She looked angry and hurt and Lex guessed that she had somehow found out about his betrayal.

'I can explain—' he began, but she cut him off.

'Explain, Lex? Can you really? After all I've done for you too. But it's backfired on you. For once, I don't think you'll like being lucky.'

'What do you mean?' Lex asked, a horrible feeling of dread creeping up inside him.

'The enchanter you stole that ship from – he arrived whilst you've been down here. Jezra told him that Lucius and the prophet were playing the Game but that you'd sat this round out and were hiding somewhere, so the enchanter searched the ship for you.'

Lex felt the colour drain from his face. 'He found Lucius, didn't he?' he croaked.

'I realised it wasn't you when he started begging for his life. I felt sure you would never beg like that.'

'Is he still alive?'

'The enchanter used magic to send him away. So you see how very lucky you really are, Lex. If you hadn't double-crossed me the way you did then the enchanter would have punished *you* instead of your brother.'

'Where did he send him?' Lex asked. 'I'll go and get him back.'

Lucius might have been a wet, whiny wimp but he was the only family Lex had left. And – against his will – he couldn't help but admit to himself that whatever trouble Lucius was in now was entirely Lex's fault. His old benefactress, the Goddess of Luck, gazed coldly at Lex for a moment before leaning forwards to hiss, 'The Lands Beneath.'

Lex heard the sharp intake of breath from Schmidt beside him. 'The Lands *Beneath*?' he yelped. 'But that's absurd! Humans aren't allowed down there with the Gods!'

'I know,' Lady Luck smirked. 'They'll be very angry with him when they find him.'

'But he didn't do anything wrong!' Schmidt exclaimed. 'He's not the one who stole the ship. He didn't even want to be involved in the Game to begin with! My Lady, I implore you,' Lex heard the crick as Schmidt bent down on one knee. 'The injustice of the situation is—'

'Is something Lex and his brother will just have to live with, I'm afraid,' the Goddess sniffed. 'I know you only ever worry about yourself, Lex. That's one of the reasons I liked you. But if losing your brother will bring you some small measure of discomfort then I'm glad.'

And with that she left Lex and Schmidt standing in silence.

This is a dream, Lex thought to himself. *I'm just dreaming, that's all*.

Lex was going to die young on an exciting adventure. But Lucius was going to live to a ripe old age, doddering around his little farm, gumming his food and reminiscing about the good old days.

There had been a conversation shortly after the priest had confirmed that Alistair Trent was indeed cursed with the soulless wake. It was still in the early days so Alistair's memory had not been too badly affected by that point. He had taken Lex aside one day and spoken to him – quietly, calmly and with just the smallest sad hint of regret.

'This is going to get ugly, Lex,' he'd said. 'Things are all going to change and I just want to . . . apologise now for the pain I'm going to cause you when I don't know who

299

you are any more. Try not to hate me for it. I'm sorry to put this on you two boys but . . . you're strong, Lex, so I know you'll be okay but you've got to promise to look after your brother. Lucius is a good boy. He's gentler than you, perhaps, and more open-hearted. But he doesn't have your inner strength and determination. I know you're not going to stay here on the farm for ever and I wouldn't want you to. But Lucius will need to lean on you soon and I want you to be there for him for as long as you can.'

Of course, Alistair Trent had been quite wrong in what he'd said to Lex that day, for Lucius had risen to the occasion when their grandfather's condition worsened whereas Lex had chosen to run away instead. It had seemed easier to live with cowardliness at the time. Alistair's illness had brought out the best in Lucius and the worst in Lex. After running away, Lex had realised that he wasn't the person his grandfather had believed him to be. He wasn't even the person he'd believed himself to be. But there was no point in moping over it. You couldn't change who you were or undo past mistakes. Better to embrace greed and selfishness and have done with it than to go on desperately pretending to be brave.

'Do you understand now, Lex?' Schmidt asked, breaking in on his thoughts. 'Do you understand that when you break the rules people get hurt, even if it's not always you? What you did might have cost your brother his *life*. If Lady Luck won't help Lucius, you'll have to ask Jezra—'

'Jezra won't do anything,' Lex said. 'Neither will any of the other Gods.'

'What? Why not?'

'Jezra made sure the enchanter believed Lucius to be me by telling him I was hiding on the ship somewhere. He *wants* him sent to the Lands Beneath. The other Gods will never interfere in human matters. Lady Luck might come round eventually or she might not but either way it will be too late for Lucius.'

Schmidt thought about it for a moment before throwing up his hands in defeat. 'You're right,' he said flatly. 'They'll never help. You won't ever see Lucius again. Still, at least you got your feather. You'll win the Game. And that's why we're here, isn't it?'

'Yes, it is,' Lex said, carefully folding the large feather into his pocket. 'Well, thanks for the lecture. I'm going to go talk to the enchanter now. Perhaps . . . if I explain what happened he might be prepared to switch us—'

'No! No, Lex, he won't. He'll just send the pair of you down there. Trust me, he doesn't know the meaning of the word mercy. He won't take pity on you.'

Lex picked up on the tone and looked at him. 'You know this enchanter, don't you?'

'Yes, I know him,' Schmidt said flatly. 'I was his servant for two years, so believe me, Lex, when I say you won't be able to get anything from him. You must stay completely away from him and make sure he never finds out that you escaped.'

'What do you mean you were his servant?' Lex asked, staring at him.

Schmidt sighed. 'Something happened and I had to

leave my home when I was a young man. The only way to do that was on board an enchanter's ship, so I made a deal with him. I agreed to be his lawyer for a year.'

Lex had known from the little things Schmidt had already let slip earlier on in their travels that he must have had some contact with magical peoples. But he'd never dreamt that he had actually once worked for an *enchanter*. He could be disbarred for that, even now.

'I'm afraid that, where you always seem to get good luck, I'm often cursed with the opposite. In fact, sometimes I think I must be Lady Luck's favourite victim. I recognised the enchanter on the docks the morning you stole his ship.'

'Why didn't Bessa recognise you?' Lex asked.

'She wasn't his crone when I was with him.' Schmidt hesitated a moment before going on. 'After my year of service was up, the enchanter refused to let me leave. He kept saying I had to stay just one more month. By the time two years had gone by I realised he was never going to allow me to go.'

'But the things you must have *seen*!' Lex breathed. 'Living and working with an enchanter!'

'The things I saw would make your hair curl!' Schmidt said sharply. 'I was barely treated better than his crone. Besides, I became a lawyer to help people, not to swindle, cheat and ruin them and that's what the enchanter was having me do. The law can be twisted so easily but it's supposed to be something *noble* not just another way of destroying people. It sickened me and I knew I had to get out so I managed to convince his crone to help me escape. She'd grown fond of me whilst I'd been living with them, for I showed her more kindness and consideration than her master ever did. So she helped me to run away when we stopped at the Bandy Towns one night. She gave me some magical help that made it easier for me to disappear and after lying low for a while I was able to change my name and start again. But the enchanter banished his crone as punishment for helping me.'

'How do you know he banished her?' Lex asked curiously.

'I met her a couple of weeks ago,' Schmidt said shortly.

Lex looked at him, puzzled for a moment before he remembered. 'Matilda?' he grinned. 'You really do have bad luck, don't you?'

'That's why she needed to keep the crown,' Schmidt said. 'With an object like that she'll be taken back into the care of an enchanter again, for any one of them would love to get their hands on a royal crown. Crones don't feel complete without enchanters.'

'Why did you have to leave your home in the first place?' Lex asked, quite unable to stop himself from asking the question.

Schmidt hesitated and for a moment Lex thought he wouldn't tell him. Then, with a sigh, the lawyer admitted flatly, 'My real name is Marvin Briggs.'

There was complete and utter silence as Lex stared at Schmidt, his mouth hanging open, wondering if he could be dreaming. '*Marvin Briggs?*' he whispered. 'You almost destroyed a whole *province!*'

The name of Marvin Briggs was respected by every scoundrel, rogue and good-for-nothing in the Lands Above. The name had even become part of popular culture. To 'pull a Marvin Briggs' was to create an unmitigated disaster.

'Oh, don't be so stupid!' Schmidt snapped. 'Can you see me doing something like that? It wasn't me. I was set up. Besides, it was a city, not a province.'

Everyone knew the story. Briggs had been a young, opportunistic lawyer in the Leylands who had flooded the black market with Judges' wigs. Now, Judges' wigs were in some ways similar to enchanters' hats except, instead of storing magic, they stored authority. There was something about a Judge's wig that made anyone who wore it instantly authoritative, so that other people flinched if the wearer so much as raised their voice and almost fell over themselves in their hurry to obey any commands the wig-wearer gave them. As more and more criminal leaders got their hands on Judges' wigs, the Leylands went through a serious crime crisis and the city almost collapsed altogether. Order was re-imposed only just in the nick of time. Marvin Briggs was exposed by another lawyer but evaded arrest and disappeared. He was never heard of again and no one had the slightest clue what had happened to him.

'So what happened?' Lex said. 'If you didn't do it, why did you end up taking the blame for it?'

'It was you!' Schmidt snarled, looking uncharacteristically vicious for a moment before checking himself. 'Or it might as well have been. Someone just like you, Lex, except a few years older. His name was Oliver Simp.'

Lex recognised the name from the story and, after a moment, he placed it. 'The lawyer who turned you in?'

'Yes,' Schmidt said, grinding his teeth. 'We started at the firm at the same time. Oliver was hardworking, industrious, charming . . . Everyone liked him. *I* liked him. And then, one day, I discovered what he'd been up to with the wigs. So I gave him the chance to turn himself in. He said he hadn't known how dangerous the wigs were, that he'd only wanted to make a bit of extra money to pay off his student loans and that everything had just got out of hand somehow. I believed him and said I would help him with any charges that were brought against him. He promised to go straight to the police and thanked me for being such a good friend. The next thing I knew I had police banging on my door shouting for my arrest because *Oliver* had reported *me* as the perpetrator! I would never have believed it of him, never, for he was so *convincing*! A flawless performer, just like you, Lex! That's how I was able to recognise you for what you were as soon as you walked in the door back in the Wither City. I tried to explain what had really happened, that it was all a mistake, but Oliver had been clever about it – planting evidence to incriminate me and destroying anything that could incriminate him; making sure every tiny little detail was correct. And then giving the performance of his life

when I accused him, and acting every bit the hurt, mortified friend who simply couldn't believe that I would try
to shift the blame onto him. People had been injured
because of the wigs and all this money had been lost . . .
I was looking at ten years or more. So I fled and took
the first means of escape I came across with the enchanter.'

'What happened to Oliver?'

Schmid shrugged. 'He got away with it, of course. Last
I heard he'd retired to the Bandy Towns with a huge
fortune.'

'Marvin Briggs,' Lex muttered to himself with an
incredulous shake of his head. It certainly explained why
Schmidt had loathed him so much if he had once been
the victim of a conman himself. 'All right, I know you
don't have the imagination to make up a story like that.
If you say this enchanter can't be reasoned with then I
believe you. I'll just have to go down to the Lands Beneath
and get Lucius out myself.'

Schmidt stared at him. 'You're not serious? Lex,' he
said in as gentle a tone as he could manage, 'it would
take thousands of years to climb all the way down the
Space Ladders so, even if you were able to get food and
water out here, you still wouldn't have enough years to
reach the Lands Beneath.'

'I'm not going to climb the ladders,' Lex said. 'I'm
going to use the enchanter's hat. It's in my bag. I brought
it just in case.'

'Don't be a fool,' Schmidt said softly, cursing himself
for the harsh words he'd spoken earlier. 'Lex, what's

happened to Lucius is tragic and I'm afraid it is your fault and you're going to have to live with that. But there's certainly nothing you can do to fix it; it's too late for that. Heroics will only get you killed as well—'

'*Heroics!*' Lex sneered. 'These aren't heroics, old man! You don't stop being selfish just like that. I told you before – I *want* to die young. It wasn't just something I made up to shock or impress you; I really *meant* it. Lucius is the only one I have left. He doesn't want to die young but I do so I've got nothing to lose by going after him. Besides, I've always wondered what the Lands Beneath look like. I can't let Lucius have all the glory by being the only human to see the home of the Gods. I'm highly competitive. You should know that by now.'

He swung his bag off his back and crouched down beside it on the floor, rifling through it in search of the hat.

'But it won't solve anything!' Schmidt said desperately. 'The enchanter will know you've used his hat and if you ever made it back to the Lands Above he'll be waiting for you. This is why you don't mess around with enchanters, Lex! There are *reasons* for playing by the rules!'

Lex hesitated, the hat now in his hands. 'Well, then,' he said with a slow smile, 'I'll go down and get Lucius now and I'll deal with the enchanter when I get back. All right?'

He stood up and put the hat on his head.

'Human minds aren't built for magic,' Schmidt tried once again. 'Lex, I've told you, you're just as likely to kill yourself with that hat as you are to accomplish anything with it.'

'Look,' Lex said impatiently, 'I'm not arguing with you about it any more. My brother's down there and I'm going down to get him. Or at least I'm going to try. If all I accomplish by putting on this hat is to blow my own head off, well . . . then at least there'll be one less rotter in the world, right?'

'If you really mean to go, take me with you.'

Lex stared at him, shocked into silence for a moment. 'I'm not making up a picnic of it, Monty,' he managed at last. 'I can't think of a single reason why you'd want to—'

'Employer's liability,' Schmidt said promptly.

'Eh?'

'You're a minor and technically still my employee. If I let you go down there and you get yourself killed, I'll be held liable for your death as your employer and sent to prison. Just because we're not in a law office doesn't mean my duty of care towards you is discharged.'

'So fire me.'

'I don't have the authority to fire you on my own. The other partners would have to approve it.'

'Then I resign.'

'It's the same thing!' Schmidt exclaimed in frustration. 'Your resignation has to be accepted by all the partners before it's effective. You never know – I might be of some help to you, so just take me – assuming you're able to get there without killing yourself with magic first.'

'Fine,' Lex said with a shrug, very aware of how much time had been wasted and unwilling to waste any more. He closed his eyes and spread his hands, the silence of space pressing in on them for a moment whilst Lex concentrated on getting them both to the place of the Gods. Then he drew a deep breath and said loudly and clearly, 'The Lands Beneath.'

The stories about the Lands Beneath were all wildly different and had changed constantly since the Great Divide. But most people agreed that there was treasure down there. And monsters. Some people claimed to have seen the Lands Beneath in nightmares but when these accounts were compared they all seemed to be completely lacking in common features.

Despite his worry over Lucius, and fear at his own unbelievable stupidity in trespassing into the home of the Gods, Lex couldn't help but feel a sense of excitement at the prospect of getting to see exactly what the Lands Beneath looked like, and mentally prepared himself to be ready for anything. After speaking the words 'Lands Beneath' on the Space Ladders there was a brief, slightly worrying moment of insubstantiality before Schmidt and Lex found themselves standing in the snow in . . . in the most beautiful place that Lex had ever seen in his life! It was a forest of crystal, set beneath a silver, star-spangled sky. And the colours! Lex didn't even know the names of some of them! Sparkling, glittering, twinkling loveliness . . .

He automatically reached out – to touch, to grab, to close his hands around the beauty that he saw . . . but then his nose suddenly started to bleed. Schmidt said something in a sharp, anxious kind of voice and reached out towards him but Lex pushed him away impatiently.

'I don't need your help!' he snapped.

And then the cornucopia of colours started to spin, reminding him of the kaleidoscope he'd had when he'd been small. He lost his balance on the lurching ground as a deafening silence rang in his ears, blocking out all the sound . . .

About twenty seconds later, Schmidt was still bending over Lex trying to work out if he was dead or not when one of Lex's eyes opened and he squinted at the lawyer in the silver light.

'Am I dead?' Lex asked.

'Not yet,' Schmidt grunted.

'Oh good.' Lex closed his eye and tried to breathe normally, uncomfortably aware of how fast his heart was beating and how cold the snow was beneath him. But after a moment, he couldn't help a soft, rather breathless laugh.

Schmidt stared at him in blank incomprehension. 'What in this whole situation,' he said, 'could possibly be even *remotely* amusing?'

'I got here,' Lex said. 'I'm in the Lands Beneath.' He opened his eyes and grinned at the lawyer. 'I won't believe you if you tell me you're not even the least little bit excited to be here.'

Schmidt sighed and offered his hand to help Lex to his feet. 'I don't think you need have any worries about dying young,' he said. 'It's a miracle you've survived this long as it is.'

'I'm lucky,' Lex replied, dusting the snow off his clothes.

Apart from a slight feeling of nausea, he now felt fine although he was beginning to rather dislike the hat. He considered taking it off now that he was here but decided against it. Although the enchanter could sense him when he wore it, he was most unlikely to attempt to pursue Lex to the home of the Gods. Even an enchanter would fear to do that. So in the meantime, he might as well keep the thing on although even Lex realised by now that if he used it again anytime soon it probably wasn't going to improve his situation an awful lot. But if nothing else, at least it made him look taller.

'This place is *stunning*!' he said, looking round himself properly.

A hundred different colours dappled about them where they stood on the forest floor – for all the trees were made entirely out of crystal. The trunks and branches were white but the leaves were a mixture of bright colours. In fact, no leaf seemed to be the exact same shade. They ranged from emerald green to saffron yellow to peacock blue. The effect was enchanting beyond anything Lex had ever seen before.

The place was utterly silent. There didn't appear to be anything or anybody around. Lucius certainly wasn't there, nor was there any sign that he ever had been. The crystal forest did not move or sway in the breeze – even the smallest leaf was absolutely still. It was cool without a sun but it was not uncomfortably cold, partly because there was not even a breath of wind. The air itself was still and beautifully, wonderfully fresh as if no one had ever breathed it before. It was as if they were polluting it just by being there.

Lex and Schmidt could make out a clearing through the trees so they started to walk and came out of the forest within moments. Lex stared around at the new scenery, sure that his eyes must be almost popping out of his head at what he was seeing. He was used to forests, for there were lots of them in the Lands Above, even if they weren't made of crystal. So whilst he hadn't exactly felt at home in there, he had at least not felt as if he were on a different planet altogether. But the forest really had been nothing more than a small glade put there for recreational or aesthetic purposes and they weren't actually in the countryside at all. They were at the edge of a huge city, the likes of which Lex had never dreamt of.

Towering before them were huge glass skyscrapers that must have been well over a hundred storeys. Considering the fact that neither Lex nor Schmidt had ever seen a building higher than five or six storeys before, this was an awe-inspiring, terrifying sight to them. There was a white monorail running quietly between the tall buildings but other than that there was no sound or movement at all. Gazing up at it all, Lex couldn't help but feel discouraged. 'It'll be a nightmare finding Lucius in that lot,' he said hopelessly. 'Especially now that Lady Luck has abandoned me.'

'She hardly abandoned you,' Schmidt pointed out. 'You double crossed her.'

'Well, it's the same thing,' Lex snapped irritably.

He stalked across a snow-swept path leading away from the crystal forest and towards the city. Schmidt hurried after him and, falling into step beside him, said, 'What's your plan?'

Lex glanced at him. 'Why do you always assume I have a plan? I'm just going into the city to see if I can find some Gods.'

'Is that it?'

'That's all I got,' he said with a shrug.

As Lex had suspected, finding the Gods did not prove to be problematic. Most of the Gods were not omniscient, but they were sharp-eyed, and forbidden trespassers in their realm were not likely to go unnoticed for very long. Lex and Schmidt had only just started to walk down one of the skyscraper-lined streets when two startled-looking Gods appeared in front of them in human form. Lex recognised them from their statues. One was Deryn, God of Music and the other was Saydi, Goddess of Beauty and owner of Lex's favourite sun.

'No, no, *no*!' Deryn exclaimed in a distinctly whiny tone as Lex and Schmidt automatically bowed. 'You're *ruining* the Race!'

'What Race?' Lex asked, straightening up from his bow.

'*This* one,' Saydi said, waving her arm to encompass

the city and glaring at them. 'It's *ongoing*! It's the longest one in our history and you humans are *ruining* it. You're *not supposed to be down here*!'

Lex glanced at the transparent buildings and gasped as he realised, for the first time, that there were *people* moving about in them and, like the buildings themselves, they were made entirely of glass.

'Are they alive?' Lex asked, still staring at them.

'They're half alive,' Saydi snapped, then she paused and stared at Lex. 'You look just like the other one,' she said. 'Except you're wearing different clothes. And you're not bleeding so much.'

'You've seen my brother?' Lex said eagerly. 'My brother, Lucius? Is he okay? He got down here by mistake. We've just come to get him and then we'll gladly be on our way.'

'No, no, no; we simply cannot have humans down here; it just *won't do*! You must be made examples of,' Deryn said irritably.

'What's the point in separating the Lands Above and Beneath if humans are going to contaminate both? You're too unpredictable – you ruin the Races,' Saydi complained. 'It's like trying to play chess with chessmen who won't follow the rules – it undermines the point of even playing at all.'

'Well . . . what is a Race?' Lex asked, giving the glass city a puzzled look. If this was a sort of Game then where were the castles and dragons and other mortal perils?

'It's a Race of Progression,' Deryn said. 'It's taken our

men hundreds of years to get this far. They started out living in caves but just last year they built their first spaceship and started exploring the orbiting underworlds. You humans will never reach such a level because you squabble with each other all the time and it hinders your progress. If one of our glass men comes into contact with you they could be infected with unstable emotions and the entire Race would be in jeopardy then. They wouldn't do what we told them to any more. They'd start thinking for *themselves*. Come along. We'll put you in with the other one.'

And Lex and Schmidt found themselves plucked from the ground by the Gods and deposited some way from the city before a huge, hulking monster of a crystal tree that stood all alone. This was what Lex had seen when he'd had that funny moment out on the Space Ladders. The alarming amount of scarlet blood splattered around the base of the tree was in sharp contrast to the snow, and Lex's heart seemed to lodge in his throat at the sight of it.

A crystal ladder fixed to a branch near the top joined up with the lowest Space Ladder and led on past the twilight sky into dark space above them. The Lands Above couldn't be seen beyond the great mass of Space Ladders but they knew it was up there. Unlike the crystal trees they'd seen in the forest with multi-coloured leaves, the leaves of this tree were all golden – pale and beautiful like they'd been painted with sunshine. There were other snow-covered cities in the distance and Lex guessed that other Gods were playing their own Progression Races in these although there was a still, unbroken silence all around them. In the distance was a sparkling crystal mountain where the Gods lived when they weren't playing Races with the glass men in the glass cities.

Tearing his eyes away from the incredible sights on the horizon, Lex turned back to the tree. The trunk itself was at least twenty feet in diameter and curled up in the middle of this was Lucius, head bent over a bloody ferret that was clutched to his chest and seemed to have gone rigid with fear. In another moment, Lex and Schmidt had been put in the crystal tree with him.

'Lucius, are you all right?' Lex asked, striding over to him, trying to work out where the blood on his arms and on the ferret was coming from.

Lucius jumped at the sound of his brother's voice. After a moment of stunned surprise he scrambled to his feet, clutching the ferret with one hand and flinging his other arm around Lex's neck in a suffocating hug.

'Oh, Lex. I hoped the enchanter wouldn't find you too. I'm sorry he got you but I'm so glad to see you!'

For once Lex allowed himself to be hugged – even hugging Lucius back for a moment before pushing him away and running a sharp eye down him.

'Who's bleeding? You or Zachary?'

'It's me.' Lucius awkwardly held out his arms. 'When I arrived here I fell on the crystal flowers at the bottom of the tree out there.'

Lex glanced out of their tree prison and saw that the blood outside was indeed staining the remains of the broken crystal flowers responsible for the deep cuts on Lucius's arms. Lex rolled his eyes. It was just like Lucius to fall straight over into the deepest patch of jagged crystal he could find as soon as he arrived.

'I just put my hands out automatically when I fell,' Lucius said, looking at his worst arm miserably and turning even paler at the sight of the blood dripping from it.

'Don't hold it out like that,' Lex said impatiently. 'You need to stop the bleeding. Here, use the weasel.'

Lex took the unresisting ferret out of Lucius's hand and pressed him over the deep cuts on his brother's arm.

'Hold him there,' he ordered. 'For God's sake, Lucius, do you want to bleed to death?'

Lex, Lucius and Schmidt all jumped as Deryn knocked on the glass trunk of their prison. 'Hey! Humans!' Although the trunk of the tree was thick, they could all hear the God's voice as clearly as if he were standing right beside them. 'We can't leave you here like this,' Deryn went on. 'We don't know whether to turn you all into glass people and let you stay down here or whether to kill you and send you back to the Lands Above as a warning to the others not to come. Any preferences?'

They all stared at him in horror. 'There isn't a third choice by any chance, is there?' Lex asked. 'Like, maybe, you sending us back to the Lands Above alive? All in one piece?'

'No,' the God said coldly. 'You've got two choices. Pick one or we'll pick for you.'

When the three humans just continued to stare at him

stupidly, Deryn turned away with a sigh and started having a muttered conversation with Saydi.

Lex turned to Schmidt. 'I'm going to have to use the hat.'

'If you do, you won't survive,' Schmidt said sharply. 'Give it to me. I'll do it. You've already used it once today.'

'That's very noble of you, Mr Schmidt,' Lex said, smiling. 'But I don't think it will work. You're old and frail, after all, so the hat would be more dangerous to you than to me. And I doubt you'd be able to do any magic with it anyway.'

'Give it to Lucius then,' Schmidt said. 'He hasn't used it at all yet.'

'What are you talking about?' Lucius asked.

Lex glanced at Lucius but he could tell at once that it was no good. His twin was even paler than usual and had obviously lost a fair amount of blood. He probably wouldn't be able to get them all out even if given the chance. It was going to have to be Lex or no one at all.

It really wasn't at all fair, he thought, as his eyes lingered resentfully on Lucius cowering with fear and clinging to the ferret as if it were a lifeline. Why should Lex have to die so that Lucius might live? What kind of life was he going to lead anyway? Pottering about on some farm, never doing anything more exciting than riding a tractor? Lex was the one who enjoyed life more – he was the one who relished it, made the best of it, stuffed as many experiences into it as he possibly could . . .

Then the thought occurred to Lex that it might not be

so dangerous to transport *one* person out of the Lands Beneath rather than *three* . . . He shook himself in alarm. What *was* he considering? Hadn't he come down here in the first place to *rescue* Lucius? It was a gamble and he would just have to take it for there was no other obvious way out. Perhaps it might be okay. After all – Lex was a lucky person even without her Ladyship. So perhaps the hat wouldn't kill him.

'It's got to be me,' he said, trying to sound grandly self-sacrificing in case any of this made the cut for the final round when it was broadcast to the stadiums. He spread his arms wide and said nobly, 'I shall save us all or die trying.'

Lex closed his eyes and concentrated in preparation but then hesitated again – cold fear pulsing through him . . .

Do it, he said to himself. *Just do it. There's no other way out of this* . . .

But before he could do so, a female voice was speaking in his ear, 'You surprise me, Lex. I would have thought you'd have jumped at the chance to be made into a glass person.'

Lex opened his eyes and looked at the Goddess of Luck standing before him in the tree.

'Are these yours?' Deryn demanded, waving his hand at the prisoners.

'This one is,' Lady Luck said, tapping Lex lightly on the head.

'Well, what are they doing down *here*?'

'It was an accident. Please be quiet,' her Ladyship said, waving the other God into silence. 'Well, how about it, Lex? Are you sure you want to pass up this chance to be made into a glass person?'

Lex stared at her. 'My Lady, why in the world would I want to be turned into glass?'

'Isn't it obvious, darling? These glass men they make down here – they don't grow *old*. They can't catch illnesses or disease. They don't die. They just go on and on, progressing all the time. They're out there, even now, exploring the underworlds in their magnificent glass spaceship. Wouldn't you like to do that, Lex?'

'Well, I can't say that exploring the underworlds in a glass spaceship doesn't appeal to me,' Lex admitted. 'But those glass men have no emotions so life's wasted on them. They're just chess pieces – the only reason they're exploring is because the Gods told them to. It's just . . . pointless. A farce. I don't want to live twice as long if it means I can only be half alive.'

'Well, you're right, of course. This is a silly sort of Game. I don't even really see the point of it myself. It's like being constantly amused with a doll's house. But you realise that if you were turned into a glass person you would never risk getting the soulless wake?'

Lex shrugged impatiently. 'I'll take the risk gladly. There are so many things left that I still want to *do*,' he went on, aware that a slightly whiny tone had crept into his voice. 'I haven't seen enough or experienced enough. I want to see and do everything before I die.'

'Are you asking me for help, Lex?' the Goddess asked, raising an eyebrow. 'After the way you double crossed me?'

'I'm sorry for that,' Lex replied – finding that, for once, he did actually mean the apology. 'I promise – I solemnly swear – that if you take me back I will never betray you ever again for as long as I live. I give you my word.'

The Goddess regarded him, her head a little on one side, making a show of considering what he'd said. 'The problem, Lex, is that I don't trust your word. Not one bit. I know who you are, remember. You're a liar and a fraud and a cheat. You'd say anything to save your skin. So why should I believe you?'

'Because we fit together,' Lex said at once – feeling a little desperate, for it seemed to him that he was losing her. 'I don't trust you either, my Lady. But when all your other followers left you because you were too fickle and unreliable, did those traits bother me? Not at all! I joined your church and prevented it from being closed down. I saved it for you single-handedly. You owe me a second chance for that.'

'Oh, I do, do I?' the Goddess said.

'Yes, you do. I demand it!'

Schmidt and Lucius were staring at him with shocked expressions on their faces and, for a moment, Lex even wondered whether the Goddess might be about to slap him. But then she smiled – a dazzling, brilliant smile, and he breathed a sigh of relief.

'You're my favourite, Lex,' she said. 'Future Games just

wouldn't be the same without you. You know, when I was cross with you before, I never intended to stay angry for ever. And I simply never *dreamed* that you'd actually come down here like this. Dear boy, you might have got yourself *killed* . . . ' Lady Luck fluttered her hands anxiously at the thought. 'Oh, well. Never mind. No harm done,' she said, turning to look pointedly at Deryn and Saydi who were both still standing outside the tree, sulking.

'Sorry to have interrupted your little game, darlings,' she said cheerfully. 'I'll just take these humans out of your hands and then you can go back to your little chessmen.'

'Just see that it never happens again,' the Goddess of Beauty said with a huffy sniff.

'I can put you back on the Space Ladders,' Lady Luck said, ignoring the other Goddess and turning back to Lex. 'Then you're on your own, but it'll be an easy enough thing from there.'

And with one last conciliatory smile at the two disgruntled Gods outside the tree, the Lady picked up the three humans and put them back on the Space Ladders.

CHAPTER NINETEEN

THE LUCKIEST PERSON IN THE WORLD

They were put back in the same place that Lex and Schmidt had left, just above where the dead griffin lay, not too far from the top. Lex expected Lucius to start cringing in terror at actually being on the Space Ladders but he seemed to have used up his fear for the day whilst in the Lands Beneath. As they still had some way to climb, Lex rummaged about in his bag for the first-aid box he'd brought and handed the ferret to Schmidt whilst he bandaged his twin's arms.

'Thanks,' Lucius said softly.

'No problem,' Lex replied. He glanced over at the ferret hanging hopelessly in Schmidt's hands and felt an uncomfortable pang of guilt. 'Look, Lucius, I'll change Zachary back tomorrow, okay? The hat isn't safe for humans and I've already used it once today so—'

'Lex! The hat!' Schmidt said in sudden alarm.

Whilst they'd been in the Lands Beneath there'd been no danger from the enchanter, but now that they were back on the Space Ladders, there was the very real danger that he would be coming after them. And by this time, it was probably safe to say that he would be very, very pissed off indeed. Lex hastily took a deep breath and held it for twenty seconds until the hat fell off.

But it was too late. The enchanter appeared on the platform above them and anger seemed to be emanating from him in palpable waves of wrath. There was no mercy or hesitation in his cold blue eyes and Lex could tell just by looking at him that the enchanter wasn't even going to shout or gloat or taunt first – he just wanted Lex dead.

Without thinking about it, Lex jumped onto the platform below and slithered down several ladders to get to where the dead griffin lay. He had some vague idea that he might be able to get to the sword that was still buried in Zoey's chest and use it to defend himself. If not then at least he had drawn the enchanter away from the others.

He quickly ran to the griffin's side and pulled the glittering sword from her body, but it was so heavy that it was all he could do to hold the thing. When he turned around, the enchanter was standing on the platform behind him, although Lex hadn't heard him come down the ladders.

'Lex Trent,' the enchanter said coldly. 'I thought you would be taller. Older. Capable of holding a sword.'

The sword was so heavy it was making Lex's arms

tremble. It was quite clear to both of them that he wouldn't be able to do any damage with it. So with a shrug, Lex let the sword fall to the ground with a clatter. You couldn't beat an enchanter with a sword anyway. The magician linked his long fingers around his staff and said, 'How would you like to die?'

'I get a choice?' Lex asked in as bright a voice as he could manage. 'Look, I'm sorry about the ship. We didn't make any mess. I'd . . . I'd be happy to pay you a—'

'No one steals from an enchanter! I can promise you that you will suffer dearly for what you've done.' He took a step closer to Lex, towering over him in a distinctly threatening manner. 'Now, what death do you fear the most?'

Although he automatically put up his hands to shield himself, Lex was unable to prevent the magician from placing long fingers alongside his temples. Then there was a brief, but unpleasant, slideshow of images that ran through the air above their heads as the enchanter rifled through the unwanted memories in Lex's head.

Lex tried as hard as he could never to think of his grandfather as he'd been in the last few years of his life, for that old man hadn't really been Alistair Trent. Alistair had loved his grandsons and he would never have shouted at them or lashed out at them. He would not have attacked Lex late one night, thinking him to be an intruder in their home; he would not have almost drowned them both one day when he became agitated in the bath, and he would not have refused to eat dinner with his grandsons one evening because he was waiting for his son to come home with Lex and Lucius . . .

'Adam is coming for dinner soon with his wife and their sons,' Alistair protested agitatedly when Lucius tried to persuade him to sit at the table. 'I don't know who you are but you've got to go. My family will be here soon.'

'Adam is dead!' Lex exclaimed as he pushed food round his plate with his fork. 'A waterwitch sank their boat, Gramps, remember?'

'Dead? Adam's not dead, he's coming for dinner. He's . . . ' Alistair trailed off for a moment before suddenly gripping Lex's arm hard, making him drop his fork as he twisted him around to face him. 'What about the boys?' he asked desperately, shaking Lex a little in his fear. 'Are the boys all right? My grandsons, Lex and Lucius, do you know where they are?'

Lex could do nothing but stare at him. There was a very special kind of misery in having someone you loved look at you without any hint of recognition whatsoever.

'We're right here, Gramps,' Lucius said, trying to prise his fingers from Lex's arm. 'Please just sit down at the table and eat your dinner.'

Lex had never been able to decide which was worse: those moments or the very few occasions when he spoke in a different voice – hesitant and stumbling over his words as if unsure of how to use them. When Alistair had mistaken Lex for an intruder one night, he'd managed to hit him several times with an old wooden bat before

Lucius and Zachary, roused by the noise, had managed to drag him away.

'What did you do to him?' Zachary asked as Lex picked himself up off the floor.

'I did nothing,' Lex replied, not even having the heart to snarl as he spoke.

As Zachary persuaded Alistair to get back into bed, Lucius tried to help his brother but Lex pushed him away and went to the bathroom on his own. He had managed to duck most of the blows so that there was nothing more serious than some bruising on his ribs and a small cut above one eye, but it was the shock of the experience itself that hurt more. Lex knew that fifteen year olds shouldn't cry but, thinking everyone else was back in bed, he sat down on the edge of the bathtub, covered his face with his fingers and tried not to make any noise. He would pack a bag and leave. Now. Tonight. He couldn't stay here another day longer.

He jumped when someone spoke his name hesitantly from the doorway. When he lifted his head and saw his grandfather standing there he fell off the bath, an unpleasant and totally alien tremor of fear shooting through him at sight of the man who had raised him. But this time there was concern in Alistair's eyes rather than aggression.

'Lex,' he said again. His mouth worked silently for a moment and from where he lay, sprawled on the floor, Lex could see the frustration on his grandfather's face as he valiantly tried to piece the words together. 'Are . . . you . . . okay?' he managed at last.

For some reason that one sentence hurt Lex almost as much as the physical blows had done. Alistair Trent was still in there somewhere – they just couldn't get to him.

'Yes, Gramps,' he said, getting up from the floor. 'I'm fine. Let's get you back to bed . . . '

'Stop it!' Lex cried, pushing at the enchanter as hard as he could. '*Stop it!*'

Those memories were making him feel sick. It wasn't the fact that Alistair Trent had died – for everyone had to die sometime – it was the time it had taken and all the bitterness that had had to come first.

'The soulless wake?' the enchanter asked, removing his fingers at last. 'An interesting choice.'

Lex glared at the enchanter, hating him. Over his shoulder he could see Lucius wringing his hands on the platform above and Schmidt rummaging through Lex's bag beside him.

'You don't have the power to curse someone with the soulless wake,' Lex said to the enchanter, desperately hoping that that were true.

'Watch me,' the enchanter said softly. 'Just watch. I told you you'd suffer for crossing me.'

The words: '*I beg you*' rose up in Lex's throat, but he couldn't say them. A mixture of shame and fear stopped him from speaking them aloud. Lex Trent *beg*? He'd see himself dead first! The defiant thought made him raise his chin just a little. It was easier to be proud and defiant when he knew full well that begging the enchanter for his life would have no effect whatsoever. The worst was going to happen and there was nothing he could do to stop it. And that knowledge sent a sudden icy calm through him so that when he looked the enchanter right in the eye and said a couple of choice expletives that would have got him into a huge amount of trouble if his grandfather had heard him, his voice didn't even shake.

The enchanter simply smiled coldly as he raised his staff and prepared to punish the thief who'd stolen his boat and made a fool out of him.

Whilst Lucius had stood wringing his hands uselessly on the platform above, Schmidt had stuck his hand into Lex's bag in the wild hope that his fingers would come into contact with something, anything, that might be helpful. Things had been thrown out all over the place, including at one point a whole flock of doves that had fluttered off nervously into the maze of ladders.

But then, at last, the lawyer's hand came out of the bag clutching a small, fat bottle. Schmidt could hardly believe his eyes and the thought shot through his brain that Lex Trent really must be the luckiest person on the Globe.

As the enchanter pointed his blue staff towards Lex, who couldn't stop himself from backing away even though he had nowhere to go, Schmidt drew back his arm, took aim and threw the little bottle down at the enchanter where it shattered against his back. The enchanter glanced over his shoulder, looking mildly annoyed, but when he saw the broken bottle on the floor all the colour drained from his face and he looked up sharply, recognising Schmidt at once despite the many years that had passed since they'd last met.

'*Briggs!*' he hissed in one venomous whisper.

That word was all he had time for, however, before the little bottle on the ground suddenly became whole again and, although the enchanter raised his staff in an effort to protect himself, he was suddenly and violently sucked into the bottle, staff and all, shrinking into what appeared to be a small, stitched enchanter doll. Lex blinked and bent down to pick up the bottle.

'Lex, are you okay?' Lucius called from above, his voice echoing in the new-found silence. 'Are you all right? Did he hurt you? Lex, are you—'

Lex tore his eyes away from the bottle impatiently. 'Lucius, do I look like I'm hurt in any way?'

'No, but—'

'I'm fine.'

He turned his attention back to the bottle, examining it whilst Schmidt and Lucius slowly made their way down the ladders towards him. The little enchanter inside was no more than a few inches tall. His white beard was made out of cotton wool and his coat and hat even had little white stars stitched onto them. It was rather a good like-ness although he was, perhaps, a little overstuffed so that his arms and legs stuck out from his body at rather odd angles.

'What did you do?' Lex asked when the others stepped onto the platform beside him.

Schmidt took the bottle from him and examined the doll inside with a distinct look of satisfaction. 'This,' he said, holding up the bottle, 'is living proof that you really are the luckiest person in the world, Mr Trent. It's a faery bottle – technically for catching faeries to turn them into dolls for children but it works on any magical person, even if they're bigger than the bottle. You just have to break the glass on them and they get sucked in. They're very rare,' Schmidt said, glancing at Lex. 'The enchanters destroyed most of them because they're just as dangerous to them as they are to faeries. But this enchanter obviously decided to keep one for his own use and I found it at the bottom of your bag.'

'Well, I suppose I should thank you for saving my life,' Lex said.

'I suppose you should.'

There was a little silence. 'Thank you,' Lex said.

'You're most welcome.'

'I bet it made you feel good after having to serve him like a slave for two years.'

'It does give me something of a warm glow,' Schmidt agreed, putting the bottle in his pocket.

'Do you think this means I can keep the ship?' Lex asked.

Schmidt rolled his eyes at him and started to climb the nearest ladder back to the Lands Above. Lucius made to do the same but Lex stopped him. 'I realise this doesn't make much difference now,' he said. 'But if I had to do it all over again, I wouldn't leave. It seemed easier to be selfish at the time but . . . now I wish I'd stayed and had those last months with him. You were much braver than I was. I'm sorry I left you to do it by yourself.'

'I understand why you left,' Lucius replied. 'It doesn't matter now. Look, will you come back to the farm with me? Just for a little while?'

'Sure,' Lex replied. 'For a while. Schmidt certainly seems eager to get home,' he remarked, looking up to where the lawyer was now clinging from a twisting rope ladder some way above them.

'Well, I'm just glad it's over and we all survived,' Lucius said. 'Now we can go home and just try and forget this ever happened.'

He moved over to the nearest ladder and put his foot on the bottom rung but when he glanced back over his shoulder he realised Lex hadn't followed him. His eyes widened in fascinated horror as he saw what his brother was doing. 'Er . . . do you think you should really be doing that?' he called.

'Their mother was killed because of the Game,' Lex replied, picking up another griffin egg and placing it carefully in his bag. 'They'll die out here on their own.'

'Yes but, Lex, you don't know anything about looking after—'

'I'll learn,' Lex replied, placing the last of the eggs in his bag and standing up. 'Keep this under your hat, though, okay? I don't think Schmidt would like it very much.'

When they climbed up the last ladder onto the Lands Above once more, Jezra and Lady Luck were waiting at the perimeter for them. Jezra was holding a trophy and a medal and wearing a smug smile but this was wiped off his face when Lucius climbed out from the ladders after Lex and Schmidt. He stared from one to the other, trying to work out which was which but they really did look identical now and in the end he was forced to address them both, 'Which one of you is Lex?'

Lex raised his hand. 'I am, Lord Jezra. Sorry but as she's very graciously indicated that she'd be willing to have me back, I've decided to return to Lady Luck so I'm winning this Game for her now, not for you.'

'But why?' Jezra asked, looking baffled.

'You told the enchanter Lucius was me and got him sent to the Lands Beneath,' Lex said, raising an eyebrow. 'Lady Luck saved all our lives.'

Jezra gave an impatient shake of his blond head. 'But I did that to save *you*,' he protested. 'Would you rather I'd sent the enchanter after you instead?'

'Yes.'

'Well, tough! I wanted you to win the Game. Lucius is of no use to me.'

'But he's of use to *me*,' Lex said. 'Occasionally.'

'I clearly underestimated you,' Jezra said coldly. 'I thought winning the Game was the most important thing in the world to you and yet you jeopardised it all because of your useless, gutless twin.'

'Yes, but I still won,' Lex said calmly. 'Where's the Judge gone anyway?'

'Back to the Lands Beneath,' Lady Luck said. 'I'm afraid

333

he's more suited to those simpler, more logical glass Races. He's quite good at them, apparently, but he doesn't understand humans, you see. And when his prophet was killed he didn't think there was much point in sticking around. He always was a sore loser.'

'So do I get my trophy now or what?' Lex asked, greedily eyeing the large golden cup in Jezra's hands.

'Yes, come on, Jezra,' the Goddess said, clicking her tongue impatiently. 'Hand me the trophies so I can present them to my winner.'

Jezra scowled blackly and thrust the trophy and medallion moodily towards the Goddess.

'Give me your crystal ball,' she said to Lex.

He dug it out of his pocket and handed it to her. As she held it in her hand it seemed to get bigger so that eventually she had to put it down on the ground and it became as tall as she was. Lex saw the image of a stadium inside it. He thought he could practically smell the popcorn and the hotdogs as the roar of hundreds of spectators came through to him. They were watching the footage from the final round. Not only had Lex Trent obtained the griffin's feather, but he had also been down to the forbidden Lands Beneath and lived to tell the tale before defeating an enchanter on the Space Ladders! The crowd was going wild – they had never, in the whole history of the Games, seen anything like this before.

Of course, the footage did not make it clear that it was Lex's fault Lucius had been sent down there in the first place. Nor did it make it obvious that Schmidt was the one who had thrown the faery bottle at the enchanter and not Lex. All in all, the edited footage made him look even more dashingly daring and courageous than he really was. Lex Trent was the greatest player anyone had ever seen. He had won every round. He had defeated a medusa and a minotaur *simultaneously*; he had escaped from mad kings and draglings by the skin of his teeth; he had thwarted a wicked witch; he had climbed the Space Ladders; been down to the Lands Beneath and won the Game almost effortlessly. Lex's ego swelled even further at the sight of the picture being painted of him. But – at the end of the day – wasn't it all true? Had he not, indeed, done all of those things and more? What an extraordinary person he was!

Then the footage caught up to where they all were in real life – passing straight over the quarrel between Lady Luck and Jezra to the part where the Goddess of Fortune was standing ready to present the trophy to Lex. She nodded at him and he took the by-now-rather-squashed griffin feather out of his pocket and handed it to her. The gold medallion she held had a big, bold **1**st engraved on it and shone impressively in the light from the sun. It was on a golden chain and as Lex bent his head for the Goddess to put it around his neck, the applause of the crowd ringing in his ears, he took a mental snapshot of the moment so that he could take it out and look at it for that special sense of smugness whenever he wanted to in the years to come. As the medal was placed around his neck and the trophy pressed into his hands, the Binding Bracelets on Lex and Schmidt's wrists both fell off at the same time, signalling the fact that the Game had at last come to an end.

That evening, when the three humans and the ferret were settled on the bridge, eating dinner as the magical ship flew over the waves, Schmidt looked up and said to Lex, 'You realise that if I ever see you in the Wither City again after this, I'll have to have you arrested?'

Lex raised an eyebrow at him. 'Does that mean you're not going to keep chasing me?'

Schmidt made a hopeless little gesture. 'It's more than my life is worth to try and chase you. I really don't want to know what kind of things you're going to get yourself involved in next. Anyway I'm tired. I want to go home.'

'Well, I'm turning over a new leaf anyway,' Lex replied. 'I'm not going to steal, lie or cheat any more. Once we've dropped you at the Wither City, I'm going back to the farm for a while with Lucius.'

This was true . . . in a sense. He *was* going back to the farm with Lucius. But he did not intend to stay there long. There was still the Shadowman to consider, and the fact that some copycat thief thought they could steal Lex's notoriety. He had played the Game as Lex Trent but now it would be good to get back to the Shadowman (or some new, improved, superior version of him) for a little while before it was too late. Before – perish the thought – he forgot how to do it.

'No more Games then?' Schmidt asked, watching Lex intently.

'Nope,' Lex lied easily. 'I've got my trophy. Now I'm going to try and do something *constructive* with my clever mind. Perhaps I'll become a lawyer after all in one of the other provinces. From now on, Mr Schmidt, I'm on the straight and narrow.'

THREE MONTHS LATER

The crowd magically seemed to part for the hooded figure as it weaved its way through the bustling central square, stopping at the steps leading up to the huge stone tablet at the centre. At the top, some disgruntled schoolkids were resignedly copying down the names on all four sides of the tablet. By the time the hooded figure located the name he was looking for, the teachers had all rather hurriedly ushered the kids back down the steps, leaving the newcomer alone at the top.

There were many names on the stone tablet, some of them now weathered with age. But there was one near the bottom that was clearly new – neatly printed in fat, engraved letters: **King Lex Trent I**. The hooded figure traced the letters wonderingly with his finger.

'Seems a bit stupid when you were only a king for about ten seconds before turning into a fish,' a voice said from behind him.

Lex turned from the tablet and lowered his hood. 'Ah.

Mr Schmidt. Good afternoon, sir. Yes, it was only about ten seconds but ten royal seconds is like ten years in normal time, you know. How did you guess it was me?'

'Please, Lex. That sign you're wearing on your back has you written all over it,' Schmidt said, moving to stand beside him at the monument. 'I knew you'd be back to see this at some point. Just couldn't resist it, could you? Did you know, Lex, that since the Game ended there have been reports of a new cat burglar – someone calling himself the Wizard who has been striking in different cities all over the Globe?'

'Really, sir?'

'Yes. At the scene of every crime he leaves behind a tiny pointed enchanter's hat.'

Whilst back on the farm, Lex had cautiously explored a little bit more of the enchanter's ship and, upon opening the door of a cupboard, had been practically swept away by the avalanche of little hats that came pouring out on top of him. They were each about the size of his thumb, pointy and blue with little stars stitched onto them. They were, in fact, just like a full-size enchanter's hat except for the fact that they didn't have as much magic. Actually, they only had a tiny bit of magic in them – just enough to make a little flame burst from the tip if you said *Abracadabra*. Lex had no idea what on earth they had originally been for – lighting the enchanter's pipes, he supposed – but they were perfect for what he had in mind and were what had given him the idea for the Wizard in the first place. The little hats were magical and so could

339

not be replicated. And there seemed to be an endless supply of them on board the ship, for although Lex emptied the cupboard that morning, when he opened the door again in the afternoon he was once again knocked over by a great wave of hats pouring out at him.

'Never heard of this Wizard,' Lex said brazenly. 'But from what you've said he sounds much better than the Shadowman ever was.'

'I'm sure I told you, Lex, that if you ever came back to the Wither City I would have to have you arrested,' Schmidt said, clearly not at all taken in.

'Yes, but if you had me arrested I could tell everyone the truth about who you really are, Mr Briggs.'

'You'd certainly be free to try,' Schmidt agreed. 'But you've no proof and, as you once pointed out to me, it's said that Lex Trent will say anything to talk his way out of trouble.'

'You're right. They wouldn't believe me,' Lex said with a shrug. 'Especially since the only one who could back up my story is currently a small, stitched doll living in a bottle and you happen to be the one in possession of that.'

'Actually I gave the doll to Mr Lucas's granddaughter,' Schmidt said. 'She's only two so mostly she just sucks it. The beard has all come off now. And the hat is a bit chewed.' He shrugged.

'Well, that's that then,' Lex said. 'There's nothing to stop you arresting me right here on these steps.'

'Yes but, as you know, considering my age and frailty

I'm sure you'd be able to run away from me if you really wanted to.'

Lex was pleased, but hardly surprised. After all, Mr Schmidt was not a stupid man and he had clearly decided that getting in Lex's way was far more trouble than it was worth.

'How's Lucius?' the lawyer added.

'He's back on the farm with Zachary, so he's happy. Zachary is human again, so he's happy too. Although I don't think I'll ever be his favourite person now after all that ferret business but still,' Lex shrugged, 'you can't win 'em all.'

'No. Will you be here long? I thought you were going in for the quiet life now?'

'Well, I was,' Lex agreed. 'But Lady Luck came to me the other day and said she wanted me to play for her in another Game so what could I say? After all, she is a Goddess and I don't want to be turned into a wooden chessman. Besides, the farm got a bit crowded once the griffins hatched.'

There was a brief silence before Schmidt said, 'I beg your pardon?'

'They're young and playful,' Lex said with a shrug. 'And they have limitless energy. And I'm pleased to say they took an instant dislike to Zachary. I think they could still smell the ferret on him.'

'You took the eggs,' Schmidt breathed, sounding faintly horrified.

'Yes, I took the eggs,' Lex grinned. 'And now I have

three griffins who all think I'm their mother. They're back on the enchanted ship, waiting for me. I'm sure they'll guard it much more effectively than Bessa ever did. They're not full grown yet but their beaks and claws are pretty sharp, judging by what they did to Zachary. I named one of them Monty, by the way.'

'I'm touched,' Schmidt managed.

'He's the grumpy one. Lucius is scared of him more than the others.'

'Lucius was disappointed when you left, I imagine?' Schmidt asked, deciding to change the subject before it could get too out of hand.

'Yes, but he knew I wouldn't be able to stick it at the farm for long. Dungarees and tractors just aren't me. They never were. I'm going to check in on him sometimes though. You know – for birthdays and things.'

'When does this new Game start?'

'Next Week. You don't want to come do you?'

Schmidt gave a bark of laughter. 'I know this will probably be hard for you to understand, Lex, but that Game is honestly not something I ever want to repeat.'

'Yes, that's what Lucius said,' Lex said looking puzzled. 'I don't understand it myself.'

He held up his wrist to show the two familiar Binding Bracelets. 'That's why I'm wearing these signs,' he said as he gestured at the signs Schmidt had commented on earlier. There was one on his back and one on his chest, both displaying the same message in thick, black letters: PLEASE DON'T TOUCH ME – I'M A LEPER. 'I've got to be careful not to touch anyone until I find a companion. Any ideas?'

'As a matter of fact, yes,' Schmidt said with a smile. 'The Wither City has been buzzing with stories about you over the last few months. You did a lot of new things. There's probably about a hundred people who now check in daily with the Guild of Chroniclers to try and offer their services to you in the hopes that you might go exploring or get called for another Game after the success of the last one. I understand that the previous Head of the Guild retired on the membersip fees they received from people joining in the hope of getting to go on a Game with you.'

A broad grin of pure delight spread across Lex's face at the lawyer's words. 'Well, what can I say? My main goal in life has always been to make other people happy or to enable them to retire. That's the kind of selfless guy I am. I think I'll take a little stroll over to the Guild of Chroniclers. You'll be sorry you didn't come though,' Lex said, pulling his hood back up over his head. 'This time we're playing against Thaddeus, the enchanters' God and Kala, Goddess of the Stars. It'll be a blast. Well, so long, Mr Schmidt. I would shake your hand but . . . you know,' Lex gestured at the bracelets on his wrist, 'it would be much more hassle than it's worth for the sake of a courtesy.'

He waved and turned away from the monument to weave his way down the steps. When he reached the bottom and started to make his way across the square to the large white building that housed the Chroniclers' Guild, people on all sides quickly – almost magically – seemed to part for him as soon as they read the signs stuck to his clothes. It's usually a pretty safe bet that no one wants to become a leper and have their hands and feet drop off.

Lex smiled to himself as he opened the large wooden doors and stepped inside, in search of the Chronicler who would make his name famous – or even *more* famous – across the provinces. At that moment it very much looked like his grandfather's wish would soon be fulfilled and that *The Chronicles of Lex Trent* would indeed one day line library bookshelves, teaching a whole new generation of children that if you really wanted to win you absolutely had to be prepared to cheat.